Pr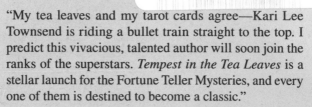
*Tempest in*

"My tea leaves and my tarot cards agree—Kari Lee Townsend is riding a bullet train straight to the top. I predict this vivacious, talented author will soon join the ranks of the superstars. *Tempest in the Tea Leaves* is a stellar launch for the Fortune Teller Mysteries, and every one of them is destined to become a classic."

—Maggie Shayne, *New York Times* bestselling
author of *Twilight Prophecy*

"Kari Lee Townsend has a hit with her delightful new series about a fortune teller who finally leaves home to pursue her dreams and finds herself solving a murder. A little romance, a big white cat, and a Victorian house make for a fun read. The true meaning of what Sunny sees always reveals itself—and in this case, a killer."

—Joyce Lavene, coauthor of *A Touch of Gold*

"You don't need a crystal ball to predict a bright future for Townsend's Fortune Teller mystery series!"

—Dorothy Howell, author of *Clutches and Curses*

"Smart, funny, and gutsy fortune teller Sunny Meadows is a delightful new star on the psychic horizon."

—Cynthia Riggs, author of the
Martha's Vineyard Mysteries

WITHDRAWN

# Tempest
## *in the*
# Tea Leaves

## Kari Lee Townsend

**BERKLEY PRIME CRIME, NEW YORK**

THE BERKLEY PUBLISHING GROUP
Published by the Penguin Group
Penguin Group (USA) Inc.
375 Hudson Street, New York, New York 10014, USA

Penguin Group (Canada), 90 Eglinton Avenue East, Suite 700, Toronto, Ontario M4P 2Y3, Canada
(a division of Pearson Penguin Canada Inc.)
Penguin Books Ltd., 80 Strand, London WC2R 0RL, England
Penguin Group Ireland, 25 St. Stephen's Green, Dublin 2, Ireland (a division of Penguin Books Ltd.)
Penguin Group (Australia), 250 Camberwell Road, Camberwell, Victoria 3124, Australia
(a division of Pearson Australia Group Pty. Ltd.)
Penguin Books India Pvt. Ltd., 11 Community Centre, Panchsheel Park, New Delhi—110 017, India
Penguin Group (NZ), 67 Apollo Drive, Rosedale, Auckland 0632, New Zealand
(a division of Pearson New Zealand Ltd.)
Penguin Books (South Africa) (Pty.) Ltd., 24 Sturdee Avenue, Rosebank, Johannesburg 2196,
South Africa

Penguin Books Ltd., Registered Offices: 80 Strand, London WC2R 0RL, England

TEMPEST IN THE TEA LEAVES

A Berkley Prime Crime Book / published by arrangement with the author

PRINTING HISTORY
Berkley Prime Crime mass-market edition / August 2011

ISBN: 978-0-425-24275-9

BERKLEY® PRIME CRIME
Berkley Prime Crime Books are published by The Berkley Publishing Group,
a division of Penguin Group (USA) Inc.,
375 Hudson Street, New York, New York 10014.
BERKLEY® PRIME CRIME and the PRIME CRIME logo are trademarks of Penguin Group
(USA) Inc.

PRINTED IN THE UNITED STATES OF AMERICA

10   9   8   7   6   5   4   3   2   1

*This book is dedicated to my parents, Chet and Marion Harmon. To my father for giving me courage, honor, and integrity. You've been my rock, lending me strength and always being there when I needed you. To my mother for encouraging me to follow my dreams and making me believe I could do anything. You've been my mentor, giving me advice and lending an ear whenever I needed one. I love and adore you both.*

# ACKNOWLEDGMENTS

First and foremost I want to thank my husband, Brian, for loving me unconditionally and supporting me every step of the way. I am grateful to have you in my life and know you are behind me in everything I do. I also want to thank my children: Brandon, Josh, Matt, and Emily. As always, you give me great inspiration and lots of laughs. I have to say I am one lucky lady!

Second, I want to thank my partner in crime and agent extraordinaire, Christine Witthohn of Book Cents Literary Agency. You never cease to amaze me with the lengths you will go to in making sure I am a success. Remember, you can never retire until I do, because I seriously can't do any of this without you.

Next, I want to thank my fabulous editor, Faith Black, for taking a chance on me and believing in my work. You have a fantastic eye and an uncanny ability to bring out the best in a book. We make a great team. I love working with you and look forward to working on the rest of this series together.

I also want to thank my special peeps, the original

# Acknowledgments

BC Babes: Barbie Jo Mahoney, Danielle LaBue, and Liz Lipperman. You really do keep me going and make this whole process worthwhile. And last but never least, a special thanks to my extended family: the Townsends, the Russos, and the Harmons. The best support team anyone could ever ask for.

# 1

❖❅❖❅❖❅❖

"Sylvia Eleanor Meadows, get back in this penthouse immediately!" my father, Donald Meadows—the almighty doctor and king of his domain—thundered as though I were still nine. He stood on the busy street in Manhattan and stabbed a finger toward the enormous building behind him, his gray-streaked, perfectly coiffed brown hair not moving an inch.

"It's Sunny now, Dad, and has been for almost a decade." I pulled my long sweater coat closed over my SAVE THE PLANET T-shirt in a useless attempt to hide the hole in the thigh of my jeans. My parents' perusal of my person and the disapproval reflected in their eyes revealed they'd seen it all. I suddenly felt the same sense of failure and inadequacy I always felt whenever I was around them.

Just one of the many reasons I was leaving the city.

"You'll always be Sylvia to me." He squared his shoulders in his precisely tailored Armani suit, and I knew he'd never budge on that one. As my parents' only child, they'd both been hurt when I'd changed my name, but I couldn't help it. I hated the name Sylvia, and I was nothing like them. I sometimes wondered if I was adopted.

"I'm not going inside, Dad." I threw my single tattered plaid suitcase that had once been my grandmother's into my brand-new car: a used, slightly rusted but well-loved white VW bug. The orange, yellow, and pink flowers on the sides suited me perfectly. "I've told you dozens of times already that I'm moving. You need to accept it." I added a large box filled with my fortune-telling supplies right next to the single suitcase in the backseat.

"Don't be silly, darling. You can't go anywhere in that, that . . . thing. Why, I don't think it could even make it across town, especially in this weather." My mother, Vivian Meadows—the ruthless lawyer and queen of high society—took me by the arm. She dusted the light snowflakes off her expensive suit and smoothed her golden blond, chicly styled hair. "Come inside, and let's have brunch. It's freezing out here. We'll have Eduardo make us a nice espresso."

"I hate coffee, Mom. Have my whole life." I sighed. No matter what I said, they still weren't hearing me, and that was half the problem. "My heater works fine in the car, and I took a course in auto engine repair, remember? I'll be okay, and I plan to grab a hot chocolate at the D and D on my way out of town." I reached in and turned the engine on to warm up my bug. She sputtered to life with a few groans and one loud backfire, which startled a few pedestrians and earned me several frowns.

Story of my life.

No one around here understood me, and I sure as heck didn't fit in. Getting my hair cut at cosmetology schools instead of expensive salons and shopping for my clothes in thrift stores apparently wasn't cool enough for these people. At twenty-nine, it was long past time I moved on and started living *my* life—not the one my parents had chosen for me.

"I wasn't kidding when I said I will cut you off if you go," my father stated with no emotion.

"I don't need your money. I have my trust fund," I retorted, lifting my chin and meeting his eyes square on.

"Which won't last forever, dear," Mom added, her smile pleasant enough, but her eyes calculating as her brain undoubtedly searched for a way to stop me.

"That's why I'm going to open my own business," I pointed out in a serious, firm voice.

My father's laughter boomed out of his broad chest, hanging in thick puffs of cold air between us. "You call that a business?"

"I'll call you when I get there," I said through my clenched teeth, refusing to let him bait me. I looked them each in the eye, one last time. "Good-bye, Mom and Dad. Take care of yourselves." I slid into my car and pulled away from the curb without a backward glance, feeling free for the first time ever.

I'd prove them wrong if it was the last thing I ever did, and then we'd see who would have the last laugh. What could possibly happen to me that was worse than what I'd had to endure thus far?

Divinity was a small town in upstate New York. Far enough away from the city to give me peace of mind, yet still a part of the state I loved. The four seasons had always appealed to me, and I couldn't imagine living in an area that didn't have them all. Each season brought its own unique qualities, adding variety to the life we lived, and I'd learned to appreciate every little aspect.

Even ice and snow.

My sputtering little bug chugged its way down Main Street, my tires sliding through the late afternoon slush as I pulled into Rosemary's Realty and cut the engine. I took a deep breath of clean air and felt exhilarated. This was it. The day I picked up the keys to my new house. I had already closed months ago, but I had Rosemary hold the keys. Organization was not one of my strong suits.

I grabbed the batch of homegrown tea leaves I'd made especially for Rosemary as a thank-you and hurried into the realty office. Five minutes later, I had keys in hand, ready to walk out the door and start my new life.

"Are you sure you're ready for this?" Rosemary asked, slipping her tiny spectacles off her nose and letting them hang around her neck from the delicate chain they were attached to.

"What do you mean?"

She shook her platinum blond bees' nest of hair. "You seem like a sweet girl, and well, I'd hate for anything bad to happen to you on account of that old place being haunted and all."

I patted her hand. "Oh, don't you worry about me. I don't scare easily." I winked.

"If you say so." She sniffed the can of tea leaves and closed her eyes for a moment as though in heaven. "Thank you, sweetie. And good luck to you." Her smile looked more like a grimace, and I could have sworn I heard her mumble, "You're gonna need it," as I walked out the door.

A few minutes later, I drove back down Main Street, turned onto Shadow Lane, and pulled my bug into the driveway of an ancient Victorian house with a massive wraparound porch. When I'd first seen this old, beautiful painted lady that held so much charm, I knew I had to have her.

Lady Victoria.

No one in town wanted to own a haunted house full of old antiques, so I got her for a steal, and "Vicky" became mine. From the moment I first stepped foot in the door, I felt at peace. Like she approved and had been waiting for me. Like she knew I would understand what it was like to be different. Unwanted. Boy, did I ever.

I smiled fondly as I stared up at my new home in desperate need of a fresh coat, making a mental note to add painting the house to my spring project list. Along with trimming the overgrown trees and bushes surrounding the lot. They might be bare of needles and leaves now, loaded down mostly with ice and snow, but it was plain to see come spring, they would bloom and suffocate the poor neglected house.

"You've been alone and neglected for far too long, old girl," I said as I slid the key in the lock and opened the door.

A gust of wind swirled around and rushed in after me as though Vicky were taking a deep breath. The door slammed closed behind me, and I jumped, then laughed. All the rumors must be playing tricks on me.

I wandered through the parlor and looked over the formal living room with pleasure. No TV, which was perfect, and a floor-to-ceiling bookshelf filled with old treasures I couldn't wait to get my hands on. One of the benefits of buying this house was that it came fully furnished with Victorian pieces. All except for one room off to the side. I peeked in the door and stared in wonder.

My sanctuary.

The room was small but cozy and filled with great light. This room had been left empty. Like a sign that I was meant to decorate and use this room for my readings. Not one to question signs from the cosmos, I made another mental note to spend all week giving my sanctuary a makeover.

Shivering, I realized how cold it was in the house. The thermostat read fifty-five degrees. It was a wonder the pipes hadn't burst. I hurried to the kitchen and checked the phone, but nothing had been turned on yet even though I'd made arrangements well in advance. I pulled a pad of paper and pen out of my tassel-fringed knapsack and made an actual note to follow up on that, but I refused to let anything get me down. I chalked it up to the wonderful pleasures of owning my first home and taking care of her myself—no staff in sight.

In the meantime, I found a stack of wood that looked

like it had been there for centuries. I'd had the house inspected, so I was pretty confident if I started a fire in the fireplace, I wouldn't burn the house down. The one activity I had wanted to participate in as a child—that my mother had actually agreed to—was Girl Scouts, where I learned to build a fire with sticks.

Wonder of all wonders, it paid off.

I bit my bottom lip and pride swelled within me. A roaring fire came to life as evening settled over Vicky and me. Quickly getting to work, I made myself familiar with the house and all its nooks and crannies while there was still enough light. Locating several candles, I brought them to the living room and lit them, then called the gas and power company again from my cell phone. They assured me they would get right on it.

In the meantime I unpacked my single suitcase in the master bedroom, changed the sheets, and slid into warm flannel pajamas. Adding groceries to my list, I made a cup of cocoa from the stash I had brought with me and carried it to the living room to enjoy my first night of independence, freedom, and solitude.

So why couldn't I shake the feeling I wasn't alone?

The next morning I blinked my eyes open to a dark and gloomy day. Snow fell in heavy flakes outside my bedroom window, and the house was freezing again. The fire must have burned out overnight, and obviously the furnace still wasn't on. Burrowing deeper beneath my down blankets, a shiver raced up my spine with the same feeling I'd had the night before.

Someone was watching me.

Turning toward my bedroom door, I sucked in a breath and yanked the covers over my head with a little shriek. My heart pounded and my pulse raced. I slowed my breathing and forced myself to relax. There was no reason to be afraid. It wasn't like a monster was out there, I told myself, and slowly lowered the covers.

"Hello," I said in a careful voice, staring at the large cat who sat a mere foot away from my head.

He studied me with the blackest eyes I'd ever seen, and his fur was nearly glowing it was so white. He didn't hiss, didn't meow, didn't purr, didn't so much as blink. He simply stared as though he were making up his mind about me.

I wasn't afraid, but I had to admit, it was a bit unnerving. "Where on earth did you come from?" I mused aloud. When I'd toured the house over a month ago with Rosemary, he hadn't been here. There had been no evidence a pet or person or anyone had stepped foot in this place in a very long time.

Rosemary had said she'd kept the house locked up tight until yesterday when she'd handed over the keys to me. I couldn't help wonder how he had gotten inside and who had been taking care of him all this time. He certainly didn't look hungry. He looked perfectly fit, perfectly groomed, and perfectly beautiful . . . in a creepy sort of way.

I flipped back the covers and sat up, but the cat didn't even flinch. Add perfectly calm and in control to his list of eerie qualities. I shook my head in wonder. "Okay, then, there's only one thing to do. Call Rosemary and

8

see who you belong to. Because there's no way you could have survived all this time out here on your own."

I hopped out of bed, tossed on my thick terry-cloth robe, and padded in fuzzy slippers all the way downstairs. At the bottom, I stopped short. The cat sat on the hardwood floor, looking at me. "Wait a minute, you were just upstairs. How'd you beat me down here?"

Again with the quiet, piercing stare. At least this time, his ear twitched.

"Aha, I saw that." I pointed at him. "You really are alive and not some stuffed animal or, worse, a figment of my imagination. I'm on to you. You're not so tough there, buster."

He blinked, like he was getting tired of our game, and turned around to walk regally to the living room and take up residence on the sofa as though he owned the place. Guess that meant he'd decided I was harmless as well.

I chewed my bottom lip, tapping my slipper on the cold wooden planks as I studied him. Something about this feline called to me. Something that said he was different and all alone in this world, but I still couldn't fathom how that could be. It might actually be nice to have someone around to keep me company, I decided. Only he wasn't mine. What if he really did belong to someone else?

I shivered, feeling the morning chill, and went over to stoke a fire in the fireplace. Glancing at the cat, I did a double take. I could have sworn he arched a brow at me.

"Oh, please, a little confidence here," I said, and once the fire was roaring to my satisfaction, I gave the cat a satisfied smirk.

He turned his head in the other direction, the little stinker.

I went into the kitchen, picked up the phone, and was greeted with a dial tone. Yes, it was working! I called the real estate agent's office, and Rosemary answered on the first ring.

"Oh, Rosemary, thank God."

"What's the matter, sweetie? I knew it was a bad idea to let you buy that old place."

"I'm fine, Rosemary, there's just something I need to ask you." I peeked around the corner at the cat, and he pierced me with an accusing look. I shrugged as though I had no choice and then ducked back behind the wall where he couldn't see me.

"Fire away," she said.

"Well, I seem to have inherited a cat along with the house." I turned around and jumped out of my skin, letting out a yelp.

He sat on the kitchen floor at my feet, his black eyes narrowed.

"A cat? What cat? And why did you yell? Do you need me to call animal control?"

"No!" I took a deep breath, my hand on my chest, then said, calmer, "No, I'm fine, really. I thought I saw a mouse." A lie.

And there went the cat's eyebrow again.

I frowned as I continued. "I'm wondering if the cat belongs to anyone in town. He's bright white with jet-black eyes, and really big. Not overweight big, but really built for a cat, I guess you could say. Very svelte and sleek. Quite lovely in a spooky, eerie, masculine sort of way."

The cat puffed out his furry chest and started licking his paw. He looked as though he could understand what I said and was pleased. He had quite the personality, I was finding out, and I couldn't help being amused.

"Honey, I've lived here all my life. No one in town owns a cat like that. Must be a stray, though I can't for the life of me figure out how he got inside that old house."

"Still, I'd hate to take him away from some poor soul who might be missing him," I responded. "He's quite a character."

The cat shot me a look I could have sworn was a scathing response to my sarcasm.

Rosemary sighed as though in defeat. "I'll put some flyers around town for you if you want. If no one claims him in a week, I say keep him. You could use an ally in that death trap."

I giggled. "It's not like he's a watchdog."

The cat stopped cleaning himself, gave me a disgusted look, and pranced out of the kitchen with his head held high.

"Either way, he's better than nothing. You never know if all them ghost stories are true."

"I'll keep that in mind. Thanks, Rosemary." I hung up and added cat food, toys, a scratching post, bed, and litter box to my shopping list, secretly praying no one would claim him. Like it or not, we'd somehow bonded, and I didn't plan to give him up without a fight.

Later that day, I left the cat on the couch by a

well-stoked fire with a small bowl of water, and then I headed into town. I tried to ignore the signs posted about the mysterious cat found out at the old Victorian house on Shadow Lane. Rosemary hadn't wasted a moment in respecting my wishes, even though I secretly prayed no one would claim the cat. He felt like a sibling, something I'd never had. For some reason, I already felt closer to him than I did my parents. Sad but true.

I continued on down the street and bought a week's worth of groceries and plenty of cat supplies, meeting a few residents along the way. The last stop I made was at the hardware store. I bought supplies for my sanctuary's makeover and ordered a sign to be hung above my front door, then headed home.

"Home," I whispered, smiling. I liked the sound of that.


After spending all week redecorating my sanctuary and waiting for the phone to ring from someone claiming the cat, Rosemary called and said she'd taken the signs down.

The cat was mine.

I stared at the feline, knowing in my gut I was more his than he was mine, and decided I couldn't keep going around calling him "cat." But what on earth was I going to name him? I paced my living room as he sat watching me from his usual perch on the sofa.

Glancing into the kitchen, it dawned on me that in the entire week of knowing him and trying to care for him, he'd pretty much continued to care for himself. He hadn't touched his food or water, hadn't played with his toys, and hadn't slept in his bed. No one in town had ever heard about or seen him, yet he'd been in the house alone for months before I'd moved in.

It was almost like he was immortal.

I stopped pacing and stared at him. That was it. I grinned. The perfect name.

"I'm going to call you Morty," I said.

Morty looked at me for a full intense moment, and then he meowed for the first time since I'd met him. I swear if I didn't know better, the corners of his lips tipped up a smidgen.

"Morty it is, then. It's you and me, pal, because from here on out, I guess we're in this together." I reached out to scratch behind his ears.

And he let me.

# 2

❂⋯❊⋯❊⋯❂

"Tell me now! Please, I have to know. You have to help me!" A woman with long auburn hair half falling out of its updo barged through my front door at 5 P.M. Monday evening, a gust of wind and snow swirling in on a cloud of crystals behind her. She stood there, staring at me all wild-eyed in her disheveled dove gray suit, looking on the verge of a nervous breakdown. "What do you see?"

A psycho crazy lady, I wanted to say, but I could tell she was seriously upset. Something told me those words would push her right over the edge. I pasted on my most comforting smile and said, "It's okay, calm down." I hurried to close the door, shutting out the frigid evening temperatures. January in upstate New York could be brutal, and this lady hadn't even worn a winter coat. It looked as though she'd simply walked out of her house in a panic, and in the dark, no less. "Why don't you come warm yourself by the fire and tell me how I can help you?"

"Y-Your sign says Sunny's Sanctuary. Is that you? Are you Sunshine Meadows, the fortune-teller?" She stood rigid in the same spot, wringing her hands.

If this was Crazy Lady's idea of calming down, I was a little alarmed to find out what the rest of my customers would be like. "Slow down for both our sakes. Don't make me pull out my Valium." I winked, only half kidding.

Crazy Lady did *not* look amused.

"All righty, then. Yes, I'm Sunshine Meadows, but everyone calls me Sunny." I'd only been here just over a week, yet people already knew my name and what I did for a living. I'd call that a success. "And you are . . . ?" I asked, gently taking her arm and carefully guiding her into the front parlor.

"Oh, sorry. I've had a rather rough week." She held out her hand. "My name is Amanda Robbins, and I'm the town librarian."

We shook hands, and then she sat down in a high-backed chair. She stared into the fire, reflecting on something that obviously troubled her, judging by the frown lines surrounding her mouth. I sat in the matching chair, giving her a moment to gaze into the crackling orange and yellow flames until she calmed down a bit.

Morty wasn't the only thing keeping me here. Something about this mystical town called to me, as though the universe was telling me this was where I belonged. The people here needed me. I peeked at my troubled guest and knew in my gut the universe was right.

"Yoo-hoo, Ms. Robbins, you in there?"

She looked at me and blinked.

"Ah, there you are. Good." I gave her a cheeky grin. "Now, why don't you tell me what has you so upset?"

She took a deep breath. "I can't tell you, but I'll pay you whatever you want. Please, you have to read my fortune and tell me what's going to happen to me." Her chest began to heave again, and there went those fidgety hands.

So much for calm. "Okay. Keep in mind the more relaxed you are, the clearer my vision will be." She nodded once and took a shaky breath as I stood up. I was determined to put her at ease however I could. "Come with me."

"Y-You do your readings in this house?" She looked around a little warily as though just now realizing where we were. "Don't you find it . . . you know . . . creepy?"

"Of course I do my readings here. I live here." I took in the same walls that had freaked her out. "I don't find this old house creepy at all. I find it comforting." The pipes groaned, the walls creaked, and I couldn't help but chuckle. "No worries," I said to Ms. Robbins. "The house has more bark than bite, I'm finding out."

The librarian yelped, lifting her feet off the floor. "What was that?"

"Don't mind him, that's Morty." I picked the pristine white cat up off the floor and deposited him on the couch. "He was here when I moved in, all alone with no collar. I guess he's decided to let me stay." I gave him a stroke and then sat back down.

"I've never seen a cat so white with eyes so black

before." She shivered as Morty kept his cold, dark stare focused on her.

"I know, he's kind of intimidating, but he has a way of growing on you."

She shivered. "I don't know about that."

"He won't bother you." I shot Morty a look that said, *Be good*. He twitched his lips, making no promises. Shaking my head with a half smile, I met the librarian's eyes as I said, "Follow me. You'll be fine, I promise."

She followed me without saying a word into the room I'd set aside specifically for my fortune-teller business. Parting the strands of crystal beads, we entered my sanctuary.

"Oh my. It's rather charming . . . and unexpected." Ms. Robbins's lips parted slightly as she scanned the small, cozy room, her flowery perfume mixing with the scent of my aromatherapy oils.

I'd painted the walls a soft, pale blue meant to relax the seeker while the seer—that would be me—reads his or her fortune. New age music poured quietly out of the speakers, a tropical fish tank bubbled away in one corner, a fireplace popped and crackled in the other, and various green plants and herbs were scattered about. Constellations covered the ceiling in a dazzling imitation of the universe, and when I dimmed the lights, they glowed—my favorite part. And last but not least, my fortune-teller paraphernalia sat on shelves in the other corner.

"Please sit down," I said, pointing to the old-fashioned tea table in the center of the room. When she sat, I plopped down across from her and reached out. "Put your hands in mine."

She swallowed loudly. "O-Okay."

"Good," I said in encouragement. "Now close your eyes and breathe deep, letting your body relax from the top of your head down to your toes."

When she did as I told her, I closed my own eyes and breathed slow and deep until I went into a meditative trancelike state. About ten minutes into the process, I felt the librarian relax, and just like that, I knew which psychic tool would work best on her. It always happened that way for me.

"Tea leaves." I squeezed her hands and let go.

"Excuse me?" Her eyelids fluttered open.

"Certain psychic tools work better on certain people. You, my dear, are a tea leaf sort of girl." I nodded once with conviction, then got up and went over to my supply shelf.

"Are you sure?"

"I'm positive."

"Because I need you to be accurate."

"Trust me. I've always had a gift of seeing into the future. I've simply found certain tools enhance my visions. I've never been wrong before." I bypassed my crystal ball, tarot cards, pendulum, and astrology and palm reading charts and finally found my special batch of homegrown tea leaves.

"My readings always come true. I admit I sometimes have trouble interpreting them. That's something I'm working on. But in the end, the true meaning eventually reveals itself." I returned to the table and set my supplies down. Right next to the lovely ancient china tea set I'd found in Vicky's kitchen.

"Ready to get started?" I asked.

"More than you'll ever know." She exhaled heavily, and I couldn't help wonder what could possibly be so bad.

"Fabulous!" I tried to inject some positive energy into her gloomy mood. "First I need you to brew the tea."

"All right." She glanced around. "Where are the tea bags?"

"Oh, I never use tea bags." I shook my head. "The bigger the tea leaf, the better the shape. I have my own special batch I put together right here." I pushed the canister in front of her. "Place the loose tea leaves in this small white cup while I boil the water."

She did as I told her and when the whistle on my teakettle blew and steam billowed into the air, I brought the kettle over to the table and set it on a hot plate. "Now pour the water into the cup and stir the tea with a spoon as it brews."

Again she followed my instructions, and I watched carefully. I'd learned over the years that a skilled seer could interpret signs right from the start of the brewing process. For example, if any tea leaves spilled, it was a good sign.

Unfortunately, everything stayed inside the cup.

A sudden feeling of doom saturated me. Not good. I stifled the urge to groan and continued the ritual. She set her spoon on the saucer. "Whoops, I didn't see you already had a spoon there. Sorry for dirtying a second one."

I breathed a sigh of relief. "Congratulations."

"About what?"

"You're having twins."

She gasped. "How's that possible?"

"Two spoons on the same saucer." I squinted into the cup and then realized I'd spoken too soon. "Whoops, hang on a sec. It's not twins I see, but"—I paused and swallowed a gasp—"twin tumors." I bit my lip. So much for good news. "I'm so sorry."

She pursed her lips and lifted her chin a notch. "I'm fine, and I trust you'll keep this confidential. The doctor is the only one who knows, and miracles happen every day. Let's continue, shall we?"

"I won't say anything," I said, hating this part of my job. I cleared my throat. "Okay, then. Drink the unstrained tea and think about exactly what it is you wish to know. When you only have a teaspoon of liquid left, stop."

She sipped the tea. "Wow, this is surprisingly delicious."

"Thanks"—*I think*—"but focus. Concentrate on nothing else except what you want to know."

I continued to watch, her brow furrowing as she drained most of the cup. "Now what?"

"Hold the cup in your left hand and swish three times in a counterclockwise motion. Then tip the cup upside down on the saucer, allowing the excess liquid to drain. Hand me the cup when you are finished."

The woman did as I requested. I held her cup carefully in my hands, with the handle pointing toward the librarian, and read the pattern of the tea leaves.

21

Starting at the handle, I worked my way around the cup in a counterclockwise motion from the rim to the bottom. Leaves to the left of the handle represent the past and to the right of the handle represent the future. Leaves at the top of the cup near the rim represent the immediate future while those at the bottom represent the distant future.

I puckered my brow. There were no leaves at the bottom of the cup, but a feeling in my gut told me it didn't have anything to do with her tumors.

"What's wrong?" Ms. Robbins asked.

"I'm not sure." I felt that feeling of doom spread to my every cell. "Let me concentrate and keep looking."

"Sure," she said, but from the corner of my eye I could see she was back to wringing her hands again.

Tea leaves provide two sets of patterns. The images that appear in the white space are positive and good, while the images that appear in the tea leaves are negative and bad. I cleared my head, staying focused, and concentrated hard on the shapes before me, so my clairvoyant mind could interpret them correctly.

A single large clump of tea leaves across from the handle indicated there was trouble ahead and someone else was causing it. There was a distinct long white stalk representing a white man. I took that to mean a man was the one causing the trouble.

"What?" she fairly shrieked. "I can't take it anymore, just tell me."

"You asked for it," I muttered. "Brace yourself now. I see trouble ahead. Trouble involving a man." I squinted harder. "And I see a deer, which means a dispute or quarrel, probably with this man. I also see a flag, which means danger from wounds inflicted by this enemy."

"Yes, he's wounded me. He broke my heart, but I wouldn't call him an enemy. He needs time to come around. He would never hurt me."

I took one more look into the cup and gasped. "Oh my God, a kettle." I had never seen this image before in all my years of reading people's futures.

"A kettle? What on earth does that mean? That he's going to make me tea, too?"

My vision blurred into tunnel vision, and I stared into the future, looking out of someone else's eyes. I could feel the anger, feel the hatred . . . feel the panic. Suddenly I was standing in a room full of books, staring down at a woman who was lying on her back, a broken cup on the carpet beside her and blood along the side of her head. I sucked in a sharp breath and jerked, snapping myself back to the present.

"Good Lord, is it really that bad?"

"It's worse." I met the librarian's gaze dead-on. "He's not going to make you tea."

"Then what's he going to do?"

"He's going to kill you."


"Detective Stone, ma'am. Captain said you wanted to speak with me?" the big, dark, brooding hulk of a man said from my doorway at 7 P.M. He had a slightly crooked nose and a long, jagged scar along his square jawline.

I stood there like an imbecile for a minute, trying to find my tongue. He was huge, and intimidating, and I should have been scared to death—but I wasn't. I wouldn't call him handsome, but there was something so captivating about him, so mesmerizing. And he smelled amazing. A hint of aftershave, a smidgen of starch, and a dollop of coffee. He had a vulnerability about him that he was trying too hard to hide, simmering just beneath the surface. Like with the librarian, I knew in my gut he needed me. I wasn't quite sure how, but I was intrigued enough to want to find out.

"Oh, right," I finally said, and stepped back. "Please, come in."

His eyes flashed and he gave me a quick, but thorough, once-over. He stepped across the threshold, scanning every inch of the room before focusing back on me. "Is there somewhere we can sit?"

"Right this way, Chief."

"It's Detective."

"I know, I just meant—"

"If you don't mind," he cut me off, "I'm kind of in a hurry." His blank, unreadable face stared at me pointedly.

"Oh-kay, never mind." Mr. Grumpy Pants wasn't *that* intriguing. I led him to the same spot in front of the fireplace where I had first talked to the librarian. Morty's hackles raised, and he let out a hiss. "Be polite, Morty. Don't you know if you can't say anything nice, then don't say anything at all?" Morty stood, thrust his nose in the air, and pranced out of the room. "Sorry about that."

"Interesting pet you've got there."

"Oh, he's not mine. This is his house."

"Lady, no one's lived here for years."

"Well, he certainly has. I'm beginning to see he

doesn't warm up to just anyone. Can I get you something to drink, Detective?"

"No thank you, ma'am." He reached into the inside pocket of his sports coat and pulled out a pen and paper.

"Please, call me Sunny," I said. "Ma'am reminds me of my mother."

He arched an ink black brow the same shade as his thick hair. "Sunny? Unusual name."

"Thank you." Ever the optimist, I took his comment as a compliment, though it probably wasn't meant as one. "It's Sunshine Meadows to be exact." His brow crept higher. "My parents named me Sylvia, but I changed it as soon as I was of age. I don't know, Sylvia sounded way too stuffy. I always thought Sunshine suited me better, don't you think?"

"Tinker Bell suits you better if you ask me," he mumbled, flipping open his notebook.

"Tinker Bell?"

"You know." He gestured toward my overall appearance with his pen. "Cute blond pixie cut, green eyes, petite frame . . ."

This time I quirked a brow at him and stifled a smile. Maybe he had potential after all. I bit the side of my lip.

"Never mind." His voice was curt. "Why did you call me here, Miss Meadows?" His eyes met mine. "Or is it Mrs.?"

A little zing zipped through me. "Oh no, it's definitely Miss. Not that I'm against being Mrs. or anything. But I'm not one." I could feel my pale cheeks flush pink, my freckles undoubtedly bright red. "Call me Sunny," I snapped, irritated with myself.

He stared at me for a full minute, scribbled something in his notebook, and then spoke. "So, Miss Meadows, how can I help you?"

"Right." I felt like a fool and had no idea why he rattled me so much. "Sorry." I sobered, remembering why I'd called the police in the first place. "I wanted to speak to a detective because this matter is of grave importance."

"What matter?"

"I witnessed a murder," I finally blurted.

He surged to his feet. "Are you crazy? Why didn't you call 911?" He pulled out his cell.

I jumped to my feet and grabbed his arm, feeling a tingle travel through my fingertips and warmth hum through my veins. I yanked my hand away and clenched my fist, my eyes locking with his shocked ones.

He cleared his throat. "You didn't answer my question. Why didn't you call 911?" he repeated, shifting his stance.

"Because the murder hasn't happened yet," I finished.

He sat back down, his eyes guarded and full of wariness now as he rubbed his forehead. "How the hell did you see a murder if it hasn't happened yet?"

"Tea leaves," I answered quietly, afraid to meet his eyes and see the same look everyone back home always gave me. Total disbelief and speculation that I had more than one screw loose. I peeked up at him. Oh yeah, he had "the look."

"Are you kidding me?" He scowled. "You mean to tell me you saw this so-called murder in one of your readings?"

"That is correct," was all I could get out. This was

why I had waited an hour after the librarian had left before calling the police. I'd warned the librarian, gave her some calming tea leaves to drink later, then sent her on her way. Yet something told me it wasn't enough. I needed to do more, even though I knew this would be the response I would get.

He rubbed his whiskered jaw, looking like he didn't have a clue what to do with me. Well, he wouldn't be the first, that was for sure. "I'd heard you were some fortune-teller from the Big Apple, but come on," he finally said. "You don't really believe in all that hocus-pocus, do you?"

I jerked my shoulders back. "As a matter of fact, I do. I'm psychic, Detective. Tools like tea leaves simply help me interpret my visions more clearly."

"Then why don't you clear a few things up for me. When is this murder supposed to take place, and who is supposed to commit the heinous act?"

"I don't know," I said sheepishly.

"Well, that's crystal clear, now isn't it?" The detective stood, closing the book on this case . . . on me.

I rushed forward and blocked his path to the door. "Look, I might not know when it's going to happen, but I do know it's a man who commits the murder. If you don't do something quickly, that poor little librarian is going to die."

"I saw Ms. Robbins this morning, and she was fine."

"Um, hello, hence the words 'it hasn't happened yet.' " I looked at my watch. "Clock is ticking, Detective."

He sighed, grumbling, "Fine. I'll check on the librarian, but that's as far as I'm prepared to go. I don't like playing games, Miss Meadows."

"I'm not playing games. I'm telling you the truth." I opened the door for him. "Thank you, Detective. You won't be sorry."

He turned and strode out the door into the frosty night, mumbling, "I'm already sorry, Tink," and then he was gone.


Twenty minutes later, I heard sirens wailing and screeching in the distance. My heart started pounding, and all I could do was pray it wasn't the librarian. Or if it was, then maybe they'd gotten to her in time and caught the bad guy before he could hurt her. Either way, justice must be done.

The siren was so loud now, it sounded like it was right outside. I went to peer out the window but jumped back when someone pounded on my door.

"Who is it?"

"Detective Stone, Miss Meadows. Open up."

I scrunched up my face. What on earth was the detective doing back at my house? Exhausted and weary, I wanted this day to be over. I opened the door wide to a pair of handcuffs dangling from his fingertips.

"W-What exactly do you plan to do with those?" My voice hitched.

"Nothing if you come along peacefully." His eyes studied me as he finished with, "I'm taking you in."

Shock ripped through me like ice water. Taking me in? In where . . . jail? This was not how I'd expected the first day of my new job to go, and my future was most definitely not looking bright.

I pushed my fear aside and allowed my outrage to consume me. "Taking me in for what? I haven't done anything wrong."

He simply stared me in the eye with that stern, unreadable expression of his. "Just doing my job," he answered, his deep voice devoid of any emotion. "Sunshine Meadows, you're wanted for questioning about the murder of Amanda Robbins."

# 3

*How could I have ever been attracted to that Neander-thal?* I thought, dusting off my clothes. The nerve of him actually hauling me into jail like I was some dangerous criminal. Me . . . Tinker Bell, for God's sake. Honestly, what did he think I could possibly do to someone? Pixie-dust them to death?

"You're free to go, Miss Meadows." Detective Stone parted his sports coat, placing his hands on his jeans-clad hips as he leaned forward an inch, exposing his weapon. "Don't leave town. You're still a suspect in this murder. Until I catch the killer, you won't be able to blink with-out me knowing about it. Do I make myself clear?"

"As my clean-freak mother's windows," I ground out between clenched teeth. "Are we done here? I would think almost two hours of questioning would be more than sufficient."

He stepped back. "I'll be watching you."

"Enjoy the view," I snapped, turning around and storming out of Divinity's cold and dreary police station, leaving the detective in my dust.

"It's dark outside. Need a lift?" he called out from behind me.

"Not from you," I hollered, and kept charging down the snow-covered sidewalk.

Detective Stone might not have enough evidence to detain me, but that didn't mean he wouldn't keep looking for a way to pin this murder on me. I had to clear my name and find the real killer. My business would fail for sure if people thought I gave fortunes of doom and gloom. Or worse, if they thought I was a murderer. No way would I return home to hear my parents say I told you so. Also, I felt somewhat responsible for Amanda Robbins's murder. I should have called the police immediately instead of waiting for an hour.

Guilt was an ugly beast.

Slowing my pace, I strolled along Main Street. The moon was out and as full as it could get. I should have known. Quacks came out in droves during a full moon and did all sorts of crazy things. I watched fluffy white snowflakes dance in the amber glow of the old-fashioned brass street lanterns. It felt like I stood in the middle of a snow globe. Quaint Victorian houses, fine restaurants, and elegant storefronts lined the streets, still decked out in their leftover holiday decorations even though they'd already rung in a brand-new year. Like they were afraid to let go of the past.

It was only 10 P.M., yet there wasn't a soul in sight.

Back in the city, things were just getting started. I had to admit, I liked the slower, quieter pace of small-town living, but my system hadn't quite adjusted yet. I was wide-awake and admittedly could use a drink after the ordeal I'd been through. Stopping at the sign for my street, I looked up at the corner bar and decided to go in.

Opening the heavy door, I slid inside Smokey Jo's Tavern. Everyone stopped . . . and stared. So this was where all the people were. The place was packed, and apparently news of the librarian's murder and my questioning had already spread. People whispered and gossiped, undoubtedly speculating about what might have happened.

I made a beeline for the bar and slapped my money down on the rich mahogany surface. "You Jo?"

The blond-haired, blue-eyed hottie behind the bar winked. "You must be new to town, love." His chuckle came from deep within his impressive chest barely hidden under his painted-on-shamrock T-shirt that left little to the imagination. "The name's Sean O'Malley, lass. That"—he jerked his head to the side—"is Jo."

A tall, robust, burgundy-haired woman with smokey gray eyes and a sinfully red cocktail dress swayed over behind the bar and handed the blond hunk a set of keys. "Sean, would you be a darling and bring out another case of wine?"

"Anything for you, Jo." With one more flash of his dimples in my direction, the man disappeared in the back.

The woman turned her attention on me, her smile warm and friendly. I liked her instantly. "Watch out for

33

that one. He's the biggest flirt this side of the river and just as big of a heartbreaker." She stuck out her hand. "Joanne Burnham, but everyone calls me Jo."

I shook her hand. "Sunshine Meadows, but you can call me Sunny."

"I like to play a game whenever I meet a new customer. You see, as a bar owner, I'm a student of human nature and have a knack for sizing up people from looking at them. Do you mind?"

"Not at all. Go for it."

She studied me. "Let me guess. You don't look like the high-society wine type we usually get passing through from the city or the sophisticated, chic, martini-Cosmo type the other half is." She tipped her head to the side. "Yet you smell of money. Probably born into it, although you thumb your nose at it with your simple haircut, makeup-free face, and peace sign T-shirt. I'm guessing you rebel in your choice of drink as well, probably horrifying your parents." She grinned. "Beer?"

I laughed. "Normally, yes, but tonight I'll take a shot of whiskey." My smile dimmed. "Make it a double. I'm in the mood to get a little tipsy."

She arched a winged, auburn brow. "Rough day, honey?" She poured the light golden brown liquid and slid it across the bar in an expert fashion until it stopped right in front of me.

"You could say that." I downed the shot, and tears sprang to my eyes. The fiery liquid burned a path straight to my gut, warming the chill from my bones and numbing the shock I still felt over being a suspect in a murder case. I motioned for another. "Don't worry," I said, responding to her hesitant look. "I'm not driving. I walked. You're good, by the way. You should be a shrink."

"I sort of am, if you think about it." She handed me a napkin along with a refill. "Comes with the territory."

"I hear that. People always want me to solve their problems, fix everything. I might see what's going to happen to them, but there's nothing I can do to change it." I shook my head, saddened once more over what had happened.

"I heard about Amanda Robbins. Nice lady, but an odd duck. A bit of a spaz, if you ask me. Still, she didn't deserve to die." Jo looked around the bar. "Everyone's pretty set right now if you want to unload."

"Oh, that's okay." I dropped my chin. "I couldn't, really."

"Really, sweetie." She peeked down to meet my eyes. "You could." Her smile was so sincere I couldn't seem to help myself. The entire story spilled out of me, and I had to wonder if this woman had a little magic of her own. It felt great to have someone to talk to. Something I needed desperately right now.

Nearly an hour later and after yet another double, I had officially reached tipsy status as I finished with, "That stubborn detective has made me his prime suspect. Can you believe it?"

"Anyone can see you're not the murdering type, sugar. Mitch is the biggest cynic around. He acts all tough and serious because of his ex-girlfriend." Jo leaned in close, and her eyes sparkled as though she loved a good juicy piece of gossip.

"He used to live in the city, too, you know. Moved here a year ago to be a small-town cop. Said he'd had enough of city life and all the crazies that resided there. She really did a number on him, if you know what I mean." Jo ran her fingertip down her jawline, and an image of the detective's scar flashed in my mind's eye. Had his ex-girlfriend really done that to his face? "He refuses to date anyone now, much to the dismay of all the women in town."

Well, that explained a lot about why Grumpy Pants was so serious and, well, grumpy. A part of me softened toward him, and I felt an overwhelming desire to help even though he wanted nothing more than to ruin me. I wrinkled my forehead, tracing circles around the top of my glass. "So . . . what exactly did this woman do to him?"

The bell above the door jingled, and Jo turned the heat in her stare up several notches, her smile nearly blinding now as she saluted the new patron. "Hey, Mitch. The usual?"

I glanced over my shoulder, and my stomach flipped. As much as I wanted to help him, I equally wanted to throttle him. And right now he was the last person I wanted to see. "What are you doing here?" I turned around and stared straight ahead.

Detective Stone sat on the stool right beside me, of course, and took a chug from his longneck before answering. "Can't a man enjoy a beer after a hard day's work?"

"Aren't you still working?"

"Divinity's finest is *always* working." Jo shook her head. "Isn't that right, Mitchell?"

36

"Something like that." Mitch took another swig of his beer, then nailed me with those penetrating eyes of his. "But my 'official' shift ended after I finished with you."

Jo went about making herself look busy by wiping off the top of the spotless bar.

"Hey, Jo, bring the lady a refill, would ya?" Mitch's eyes narrowed as he sized me up.

"Sure thing." Jo poured me another double whiskey.

"Getting me drunk won't make me slip up and tell you anything, Detective. As I've said a million times already, there's nothing more to tell. I had a vision, it came true, and now the poor woman is dead while the real murderer is running around free as a bird." I downed this double whiskey a little easier now, as my body was already buzzing and numb from the others. I wasn't much of a drinker, I didn't have nearly enough food in my system, and I weighed little more than the "real" Tinker Bell. I set the glass back on the bar and wobbled a bit.

Four double whiskeys in one hour . . . *not* a good idea.

"Easy now, lass." Sean winked. "I'd say that whiskey's gone straight to your wee little head," he added, while restocking the bar beside Jo. "I'd be happy to help you home. Just say the word."

"I'd say you're right, Mr. O'Malley." I giggled. "And I might have to take you up on that lovely offer."

Mitch reached out and caught me before I tumbled to the floor, his eyes traveling between the hunky bar back and myself with a disapproving look, then finally settling on me. "You're a bit of a lightweight, I take it."

"Ya think?" I giggled near hysteria now, going all floppy in his arms and letting him take all my weight. I barely had the energy to blink. I had come to Divinity right after New Year's to start my life over, and now my life was a total mess.

"I think you need to go home and sleep it off." He shot Sean a hard look. "I'll drive." The detective met my eyes once more. "And I don't want any arguments from you. You're not walking home like this." He sat me back on my stool.

I started to protest, but good ole "Mitchell" ignored me, paying our tab and helping me to my feet. "Let's go, Tink."

"Fine, Captain Hook, cuz you sure aren't Peter Pan," I slurred. "Nothing carefree or fun about you, uptight scallywag."

He ignored me, half carrying me to his squad car for the second time that day.

"Really, daaah-ling, we have to stop meeting like this." I snorted, my common sense gone with my sobriety.

He shook his head, drove me home in silence, and then fished my keys out of my purse. Unlocking the door with one hand, he carried me inside since my legs no longer seemed to work. I had to admit there was something very appealing about Detective Stone. He was big, strong, and ruggedly handsome, making a woman feel protected and safe, but he was also distant, aloof, and off-limits. Oh, who was I kidding? That was half the attraction. I felt suddenly sleepy.

"Where's the killer kitty?"

"Who, Morty? He's harmless." I yawned. "He disappears at night, you big scaredy-cat."

"You weren't the one he was hissing at and staring down with those freaky eyes."

The detective scanned the entryway, honing in on the same couch we had sat on earlier, then deposited me on my back. He tossed an ancient afghan over my body, and the shutters on the outside of the house shook as though it was storming out. But other than soft snowflakes, the night was still and quiet. The detective glanced around with a puzzled look on his face, and I began to wonder if the house really was haunted.

The house quieted.

A V formed on the detective's forehead.

I giggled.

"Stay put. I mean it," he said, shaking his finger. I wanted to protest, but instead I closed my eyes, no longer able to keep them open. He tucked the edges of the blanket around me, making me smile just a little, then he mumbled, "The streets aren't safe, Tink."

I could hear him lock the door on his way out, and for the first time since this whole awful ordeal had happened, I felt hope. *The streets aren't safe, Tink*. He didn't actually think I was the murderer. He might not believe I was really psychic, but he also didn't believe I was capable of killing another human being, no matter what he said.

Maybe it was about time I proved him right.

Hours later, just before dawn, I slipped out of my house. With flashlight in hand and plenty of warm, dark clothing, I tiptoed behind bushes, weaving in and out of people's backyards until I reached the librarian's house. It hadn't been hard finding her address since her name was still listed in the phone book. Police tape surrounded the premises, forbidding others to cross the yellow line. But I had no choice. I had to clear my name, and they'd never let me snoop around during the light of day.

Although now that my alcohol-induced buzz had worn off, my brain was rethinking my rash decision.

I chewed the inside of my cheek, peeking around once more. No one was up. I wasn't going to break or enter anything, so what was the harm, really? Creeping forward before I could change my mind, I walked around the entire house. I didn't see any signs that someone had broken a window or forced their way in. Either the librarian had left her doors unlocked at night, which seemed out of character for Crazy Lady, or there was only one other explanation.

Amanda Robbins had known the person who killed her.

Well, that didn't narrow the suspects down much. This was a small town. I was pretty sure everyone knew everyone else. But who would she welcome into her home after dark? My tea leaves had clearly shown a man was the killer, not to mention the eyes I had witnessed the murder through had most definitely belonged to a man. A bitter, angry man, to be exact.

Shivering, I finished walking around the house, preparing to make my escape before the sun rose completely. I happened to glance down and saw footprints other than mine. Footprints that had to be at least a half day old. It had snowed last night, so they were partially filled in but not completely. Hmmm. They were right outside the master bedroom window . . . but they did *not* belong to a man.

I knelt down and studied the prints. Small. That didn't make any sense. The killer couldn't be a woman; I was sure of it. Another thought hit me square in the gut. There was a witness out there that no one knew anything about.

I straightened and turned to leave.

"Going somewhere, Tink?" Detective Stone stood before me, arms crossed and definitely back on duty. Steam rose in misty puffs around him with every word he spoke.

"For a walk?" I said uncertainly, matching him puff for puff. I could have kicked myself for my hesitation. "I'm an early riser," I added with more conviction. *So* not the truth. I was much more of a night owl and a late sleeper, but somehow that didn't sound like it would help my case right now. Given my current situation, I thought it best to plead the Fifth.

"You always walk on other people's properties?"

"Okay, so I admit curiosity. Never mind that. Did you notice in your investigation that there are footprints by the bedroom window?" I pointed smugly to the ground beside me.

He slid a pair of aviator-style sunglasses on as the sun cleared the horizon, the frigid morning air ruffling his thick hair. "There's not much I don't notice, Miss Meadows."

I threw my hands up. "Then you must realize there might be a witness out there walking around who can clear this whole unfortunate mess up."

"Or the killer is a woman, not a man like your so-called reading revealed." His head tipped down, and I could tell he was sizing up my boots. Then he looked

over the top of his rims so I could see his intensely serious dark eyes. "A woman with the same size feet as you,
I'd wager."

"Normally that would intimidate me, but I heard you
last night. You were worried about me because you know
the real killer is still on the loose. You don't really think
I'm capable of killing anyone, Detective." I crossed my
arms over my own chest and lifted my chin a notch. "I'm
on to you."

"You heard nothing," he said with a blank expression,
pushing his glasses up all the way. His cheek twitched
once, just a little, but I saw it. "Move along, Miss Meadows. This is private property and a crime scene." He
turned around and headed for the street. "Don't you have
a business to run?"

"You and I both know that no one is going to come to
me for a reading until this case is solved." I hurried after
him. "I'm helping you out." I waved my hands about.
"Sticking to you like glue and all that, so you can keep
your eye on me."

He grunted. "Not gonna happen, Tink. Go pester
someone else, and let me do my job." He kept walking
down Main Street, several yards ahead of me, then
glanced over his shoulder and stopped.

"What? Last I checked this street was public domain."
I fluttered my lashes at him. "You can't stop me from
walking on it."

He rolled his eyes and then resumed walking, picking
up the pace. I had to practically run to keep up with him.
He stopped at the coroner's office, pausing outside the
door. I quickly slowed to a power walk, waved at him,

and kept moving as though I did this every morning. Once he hurried inside, however, I did a quick turnaround and slipped in after him.

I stood back in the shadows as he jogged down a stairwell, then I carefully followed him to a morgue-type room below. He entered the coroner's office labeled Kip Johnson, with the door slightly ajar. I tiptoed to the edge and peeked inside, seeing the detective standing by a middle-aged man with brown hair parted on the side and small, round spectacles perched on the end of his nose. They both stared down at the sheet-covered body of Amanda Robbins. I huddled close, my ear near the crack.

"You're telling me she had a reaction to nuts, Kip?"

"Yes, but that's not what killed her," said a sharp, piercing voice that reminded me of Maxwell Smart. "She was poisoned," the voice finished decisively. "The time of death appears to be around six thirty P.M."

"What about the blood on her temple?" Detective Stone asked, his voice much deeper and smoother. I forced myself to concentrate on what they were saying.

"Probably fell after her heart stopped," Kip speculated. "It doesn't take much digoxin to stop a person's heart. Pretty lethal stuff if used in the wrong dose, and I found plenty of it in her system." A pause filled the room. "Plenty in her teacup as well."

I sucked in a sharp breath. Someone put poison in the tea I'd given the librarian?

The door whipped open, and I tumbled inside the office, bouncing off the detective's wide sculpted chest. Coroner Kip stared bug-eyed above his bifocals, his mouth agape.

"Oh my, I, um . . . Oh, hell, I got nothin'." I stared at them both sheepishly.

"I'd say you've got plenty," Detective Stone said, his eyes accusing. "Plenty of clues that point in your direction, Miss Meadows. Right size foot, right kind of tea leaves. What you don't have is an alibi from the time the librarian left your house at six P.M. until I arrived at seven P.M. With a time of death at six thirty, you would have had plenty of time to commit the murder."

"I also don't have a motive, Detective, and you don't have hard evidence." I tried to poke him in the chest, but he caught my hand. Jeepers, he was quick . . . and jumpy. Once again I wondered what his ex-girlfriend had done to him. "You can't prove that digoxin came from me." I stood to my full height, which barely hit his shoulder.

"It's only a matter of time before you slip up, Tink." He let go of my hand. "And when you do, I'll be waiting. There has to be something more you're not telling me."

Oh, there was. Like the fact that my father was a world-renowned doctor who had access to digoxin. Now more than ever I needed to find the real killer before Detective Stone locked me up and threw away the key for good.

# 4

A knock on my door later that afternoon had me hoping and praying for another customer. Maybe someone hadn't listened to the rumors and had decided to give me a shot. If people didn't give me a chance, I was doomed to fail for sure. And the last of my trust fund money was dwindling fast. If that happened, I'd be forced to go homeless or go home. I wasn't sure which option would be more unpleasant. I took a deep breath and opened the door with a smile.

My smile vanished like a puff of incense smoke, and I gasped. "Mom? Dad?"

Vivian and Donald Meadows stood on my doorstep, in the flesh, within touching distance. Something they'd promised would never happen, and I'd prayed they were right. Glancing around to make sure no one was looking, I quickly ushered them inside and closed the door behind them.

"What are you doing here?" I asked.

"Nice to see you, too, darling." My mother air-kissed my cheek as always.

"Sylvia." My father nodded and then patted my shoulder.

"I hope you're not here to convince me to come home with you," I said. "Because that's not going to happen. This is my home now."

"Oh, we're not leaving anytime soon, dear," Mom clarified. "Of course, we're not staying in this dreadful place, either. Why, it's simply spooky is what it is. I don't know how you sleep at all." She tsked. "Oh my God, what is that thing?" Mom raised her fingertips to her lips, careful not to touch her cashmere gloves against the perfectly lined mauve lipstick. "An albino rat?"

Morty turned up his nose and wandered upstairs, not giving my mother the time of day. "That *thing* is Morty, and he's not a rat. He's a cat." I'd have given anything to turn my back on my parents and follow his lead right about then.

"You hate cats."

"No, Mom, you do."

She shuddered. "All the more reason not to stay here. Your father and I both cleared our schedules and will be staying at that charming inn on the edge of town. We're here to support you one hundred percent, darling. After all, family is family, you know."

"So you've always said. You can't choose your family; you have to make the best of what you've got. That works both ways, Mom. Does that mean you've finally accepted me for who I am?" I purposely looked at my sanctuary and then back at them. "For *what* I am?"

"We've accepted you need help, Sylvia," Dad chimed in, nodding once. "And that is precisely what we are prepared to do. Help you out of this little mess you've gotten yourself into before you tarnish all our names."

I should have known it was too good to be true. They were worried about their own name. Okay, so maybe they didn't want to see their only child go to jail, but one thing was certain. If I let them help me, there'd be consequences. They'd insist I go home with them. I'd rot before I'd let that happen. "Hey, wait a minute. I know news travels fast, but come on. How'd you find out about the murder so soon?"

"Murder?" my mother shrieked, losing her composure, which never happened. "No one said anything about murder. Donald, we have to do something."

"Don't worry, Viv. We're not leaving until this case is closed. Things are much more serious than I thought. Do you see why we should never have let her leave?" Dad paced my foyer. He only paced when he was really worried. "He said you were in trouble, and he needed to ask us some questions. Nothing about murder."

God, when would I learn to keep my big mouth closed? For someone who could read the future, I hadn't seen that one coming at all. Wait a minute. . . . *He?* "Um . . . who needs to ask you some questions?" Suspicion clawed at my insides. I swear to God if a certain someone had brought this misery to my doorstep, I'd—

"Mr. and Mrs. Meadows, so glad you could make it."

The devil himself waltzed through my front door without even knocking. "The name's Detective Stone."

Only one thought ran through my mind over and over: here was a murder I'd gladly do the time for.

"I'd ask you to come in, Detective, but gee, you already did." I closed the door behind the real rat in the house. Where was Morty when I needed him?

"Sylvia, mind your manners, dear," my mother said. "I raised you better than that." I knew she was frowning on the inside even if her Botoxed wrinkle-free face didn't show it.

"Sorry, Mom, it's been a long day," I mumbled, feeling like a child. Every time I was around them, they had that effect on me. Might as well roll with the mood I was in. I stuck out my tongue at the detective behind her back, and his lips twitched. If he laughed at me, I'd smack him good. "I was about to take a lunch break when you guys, er, surprised me. Anyone hungry?"

"We already ate," my dad said, following my lead to the kitchen.

"Tea, then?" I entered Vicky's massive kitchen with her well-worn hardwood floors, antique harvest table, and chipped china.

This room had been frequented regularly over the years. I could see why. The table sat right by the large windows that allowed the glorious rays of afternoon sunshine to pour in and warm the area, making the room come alive. The decor in this room, like the rest of the house, was older than my great-grandmother's hope chest. So full of charm and history. I loved it all.

A musty whiff of mildew and mothballs drifted past

my nose. I smiled warmly. Morty was here, somewhere, no doubt hiding. And watching . . . always watching.

"I'll take coffee if you have some," Dad said to me, then turned to the detective. "Not a big fan of tea, although Sylvia's is reported to be outstanding." He went to sit at the head of the table, and the chair slid from beneath him all on its own. He fell down hard, and my mother rushed to help him up.

"Oh, dear me, this place is a death trap." Mom dusted off the back of Dad's coat.

"Gotta watch these old houses and all the creatures within." Detective Stone glanced around warily, and I knew he was looking for Morty. "They can be temperamental." He chose his seat carefully on the side of the table. "I'll take tea. I'm pretty observant." He stared me down. "Maybe I can guess what's in it."

"Sorry, Detective." I smirked, sitting at the head of the table with ease and relishing the looks on their faces. Most people would be freaked out, but I wasn't most people. I didn't spook easily. "Can't give away my award-winning secret recipe, now can I?" I said to the detective.

"Depends on the *secret* part." He swirled his tea around as he talked. "What you put in it could land you in jail." He smelled it and took a couple sips.

"She's not going anywhere." My mother sat up straight, her eyes taking on a calculating gleam, her tone becoming no-nonsense.

"Says who?" Detective Stone met my mother's gaze, studying her closer, no doubt reassessing her.

"Says her lawyer," she said matter-of-factly. "Pass the cream and sugar, please."

*Um, yeah, not going to happen.* "Wait a minute, Mom. You're not my lawyer. I don't need a lawyer because I'm innocent."

"Innocent of what, exactly?" My father slid the cream and sugar in front of my mother and faced the detective head-on. "What exactly has my daughter done this time?"

"Dad!"

"I take it she has a history of getting into trouble?" The detective set his nearly empty tea down and wrote in his notebook.

"Not trouble per se." Mom waved her hands about. "Just predicaments with her little hobby."

"Mom!"

"Hobby?" Detective Stone asked, writing more of God-knew-what in that damn notebook of his.

"You know, her little fortune-teller act," Mom clarified.

"So you don't believe she's psychic, either?" The detective looked at both my parents with renewed interest.

"Good Lord, no," Dad answered. "She's seen some things that have come true in a roundabout way, I suppose, but we simply chalk it up to coincidence. Being a man of science, it's hard for me to be a 'true believer,' as she calls them." He looked at me and winced. "Sorry, honey. The truth hurts, but you need to hear it for your own good, so you will stop wasting your life and do something real." He took a sip of his coffee, then cursed.

"Careful, dear," Mom said, dabbing the corners of her mouth, her eyes darting about the kitchen. "There's something odd about this house and everything in it."

"That burned my lip." Dad rubbed his mouth. "I don't remember the coffee being that hot. It's almost as if the cup heated itself."

I ground my teeth hard, as if I were grinding fennel seeds in the mortar while making my tea. "My fortune-telling is not an act, Mother. Or a hobby. It happens to be what I do. Who I am. Like it or not, Dad, I'm not normal like you guys."

The detective grunted. "I could have told you that." He never looked up, still writing in his book . . . until his pen broke and spurted ink all over the front of his white dress shirt. "What the hell?" He jumped back and grabbed a napkin, scrubbing the darkening stain.

"Serves you right. And you might want to blot, not rub, the threads right off," I pointed out, enjoying every minute of my afternoon tea.

"Thanks." Detective Stone narrowed his eyes.

"Anytime." I batted my lashes at him. "On a more serious note, just because I have visions doesn't make me a freak. It makes me special. You should be glad I can see into someone's future. And if you had listened to me, Detective, Amanda Robbins might still be alive."

"Oh, dear Lord, this whole mess doesn't have something to do with one of your visions, does it?" Mom asked.

"She had a 'vision' of the librarian getting murdered by a man, and then it came true," Detective Stone explained. "Or so she claims." He shot a look at me and then turned to my dad. "Mr. Meadows, is there any way your daughter could have gotten hold of some of your digoxin?"

"Absolutely not. I don't have digoxin lying around. No doctor does. It's a controlled substance. Pharmaceutical reps aren't allowed to sample it. The only way to get some would be to have a doctor write a prescription, and I can assure you, I didn't write any for her. Since I know Sylvia doesn't socialize with a doctor-type crowd, I'm confident there's no way she could have gotten hold of digoxin. Why do you ask?"

"The tea leaves she gave the librarian were laced with digoxin."

My mother spit her tea out all over my table, and a soft noise echoed from the other side of the room, sounding suspiciously like a chuckle. Mom puckered up her face. "Honestly, if I didn't know better, I'd swear that bizarre cat of yours is close by and laughing at me."

"Mother, please." I wiped up the mess. "You don't seriously believe I murdered that poor woman, do you?"

"No more than I believe cats can laugh, but someone obviously wants us to think you did. You need a lawyer whether you like it or not. Putting our differences aside, you know I'm the best there is."

"That settles it. We're not going anywhere until this case is solved." Dad nodded.

"Oh, yes you are." I stood. "You've got an inn to check in to, and I can defend myself. I'm twenty-nine years old. I can make my own decisions."

"Fine, but we're still not leaving, dear. You'll change your mind, I'm sure of it. Come along, Donald." Mom got up and led the way to the door. "We'll be right here in town waiting when you do, Sylvia."

"Good day, Detective." Dad slapped his hat on his

head. "You know where to find us if you have any more questions. You have our full cooperation. Our daughter might be a little different, but she's not a murderer. You have my word on that, and a Meadows never breaks his word."

With that, they were gone.

I sighed, rubbing my throbbing temples, and a deep meow rumbled softly, sounding more like a groan.

Detective Stone twisted completely around, his hand hovering just above his weapon. "I, uh, gotta run, Tink, but make no mistake . . . I'm nowhere near done with you. I've got a case to solve. I won't let up on you until I get some answers." He bumped into the table, knocked over his teacup, and the last little bit of liquid spilled into his saucer. He righted the cup and set it down on the table. "Thanks for the tea."

"You're welcome, Detective. Just know I won't go down without a fight."

"I'm counting on it." He nodded once, with a gleam in his eye that said he loved a challenge, and then he closed the door on his way out.

I huffed out a breath, then couldn't help but giggle a bit. "Where are you, you stinker? You are one mischievous old cat." Vicky might have character, but I had a suspicious feeling I'd just discovered who was doing the haunting.

I was answered with a full-blown loud meow.

"I know," I agreed. "They make me angry, too, but if you don't stop spooking people, word will get out and no one will come to me for a reading."

The meowing quieted to a soft purr.

"Apology accepted." I started cleaning up the mess in the kitchen. "Now quit being elusive and come out of hiding to keep me company."

I looked around, trying to catch a glimpse of Morty, when my wandering eyes landed on the detective's teacup. It was sitting there, calling to me. Biting my bottom lip, I picked up the cup still warm from his hand and pointed the stem to the seat where he had sat. Did I dare? I probably wouldn't get much of a reading, but he had come to me for some answers. I couldn't help wonder what question had been burning in his mind the most?

Morty magically appeared from nowhere and circled my feet, rubbing up against my legs. I took it as a sign.

Talking myself into doing something I would never normally do—invading someone's privacy—I rationalized this wasn't just anyone. This was Detective Stone, and he made no apologies about invading mine. He deserved everything he got.

Sitting down, I closed my eyes and breathed deep, relaxing my mind and body. Maybe, just maybe, I would see something. Anything to help me understand the man I was up against. Opening my eyes, I peered into the cup and studied the pattern of tea leaves he'd inadvertently made.

The first thing that jumped out at me was a mask. The good detective was hiding something. Big surprise there. The next thing I saw was a distinct heart, representing love and pleasure. He'd fallen hard for someone, and I couldn't help but think about his ex-girlfriend. Right below it was a pair of scissors. The relationship had ended in quarrels and separations. The strongest feeling

I got that overrode everything the cup revealed was that of intense passion.

So much passion.

My head snapped back and once again everything around me blurred, leaving only the scene being played out before me in the center of my tunnel vision. I stared through the eyes of a woman being held so tenderly in the detective's strong arms. I could feel his warm embrace, experience every sensation coursing through her body.

His head dipped toward her, the look in his eyes unmistakable. Lust, passion . . . love. Then his lips pressed firmly against hers, moving sensually, as pure, raw electricity passed between them. That same electricity roared through my body now, firing up every nerve ending, every cell, every blood vessel. I couldn't breathe, couldn't move, could barely stand from the sheer pleasure of it all.

They broke apart, and I nearly fell off my chair. Gripping the teacup harder, I felt as breathless as the woman whose eyes I had just stared through. My heart ached, and the same helpless, hopeless feeling she felt, I felt. I couldn't hear what they said, but they argued, and he stormed out. Dejected and devastated, she turned toward the mirror, and I gasped.

The relationship hadn't happened in the past. I'd read the wrong side of the cup. Not the one that represented the past but the one that predicted the future. This woman was setting herself up for the biggest heartache of her life.

The woman was me.

\* \* \*

No way in hell would I allow myself to get involved with Detective Stone. I was smarter than that. I nodded with conviction. He was stubborn and annoying and determined to put me in jail. Besides, it took two to start a relationship, and it was easy to see I was clearly not the detective's type.

My body quaked, remembering the detective's kiss, even if it hadn't happened yet. If just the memory of it did amazing things to me, I shivered to think how the real deal would affect me. I swallowed hard, regretting going so long without the company of a man. Stupid traitorous body. I took a deep breath, determined to get a firm grip on my hormones and my good sense.

Someone knocked on my front door, and I dropped the detective's teacup, shattering it into a gazillion pieces and cutting my finger. "Ow!" I yelped, wrapping a napkin around my index finger. Glancing around, I noticed Morty had vanished once more. "Coming," I yelled, jogging to the door. Who could possibly be here now?

I opened the door and Mitch stood there, tall and strong, filling my doorway. I sucked in a breath. "Wh-what do you want?" I shrieked.

He drew his brows together. "You having a spell or something?"

"Something like that," I choked out.

"Should I call a doctor?" He stepped back a bit.

"I'll be fine in a minute." I fanned my face.

"Good, because I need you."

"Okay, not fine." I stumbled back, my heart racing harder.

He cursed under his breath, grabbed my arm to steady me, and walked me into my kitchen. He sat me down in a chair at the table and poured me a glass of water. "Here, drink this." He looked around, his eyes settling on the shattered teacup. "Well, that's a mess."

"Exactly. It would be a huge mess, that's why it's so not gonna happen."

"Okay." He tipped his head to the side and stared at me as though I really was having some sort of spell.

I gulped down the water, took a moment to clear the fog from my brain, and then repeated, "You need me?"

He jerked a shoulder. "Yeah, that's what I said. I need you to come with me to the police station."

"Okay, that is *not* what you said. To the station gives an entirely different meaning to that sentence."

"Huh?" He ran a hand through his thick hair. "Never mind. We don't have time for you to have a breakdown. Grab your coat."

"Gee, my knight in shining armor." I scoffed, grabbed my coat, and barely had time to lock up Vicky before he shoveled me into his squad car for the third time.

"This is really beginning to get on my nerves, Detective."

"You and me both, Tink, but there's not a damn thing I can do about it."

"*Now* who's the one who's not making any sense?" I crossed my arms and waited for an explanation from the tight-lipped conversationalist.

"We're here," he said, pulling his squad car into the police station.

"Why are we here again? I already answered all of your questions, and so have my parents. What more could you possibly want from me?" Shoot, I shouldn't have asked that. I chewed my lip, terrified of what he would say, and even more so of what I would do.

"I don't want anything from you," he answered, looking at me funny. "You okay? You're acting weirder than normal, and you look a little pale."

"Fine. Confused is all."

"Look, Captain Walker called me right after I left your house, saying he wanted to speak to me. He asked me to bring you. I don't know anything else, either. Believe me, I'm as confused as you." He looked me over. "Well, maybe not just as confused."

"You're hilarious. Has anyone ever told you that?"

His lips moved, and I could tell he was fighting back a grin. "I have my moments." He climbed out of the car and opened my door before I had a chance.

I refused to dwell on any of his positive qualities. My vision might have revealed incredible passion and chemistry between us, but it had also predicted heartache. Something I'd had more than my share of and didn't want to experience ever again.

"You'd better lay off the tea. You look like crap," he said.

"Thank you." I felt remarkably better.

He'd reminded me of how wrong we were for each other, and that was all I needed. I planned to get this meeting over with, then stay out of his way while I did a little sleuthing of my own, as far away from Detective Stone as I could get. If he wasn't near me, then there was no way my vision could possibly come true. The fact that all of my visions had *always* come true niggled at the back of my brain, but I simply had to believe there was a first time for everything. And a little help on my part couldn't hurt.

"You're welcome, I guess." He reached for the door to the police station.

"I got it." I grabbed it before he could and pulled it open. "Don't do me any favors . . . really." I wrinkled my nose at him and ushered him inside. "After you, Spanky."

"You're one strange woman, Tink." He led the way inside with long purposeful steps.

"I've been called worse." I hurried to catch up.

# 5

A tall, wiry man with a bald head and a neatly trimmed goatee opened the door to a room and stepped out into the hall. "Ah, just the man I wanted to see. Right on time as always, Detective Stone."

Mitch shook the man's hand firmly. "Captain Walker." He turned to me. "Sunshine Meadows, meet my captain, Grady Walker."

"So nice to meet you, sir," I said with a smile, and shook the man's hand.

"The pleasure's all mine, ma'am." He bowed slightly and then swept his hand toward his office. "Come on in and take a load off. We've got some business to discuss."

My eyes briefly met the detective's, and I could tell he really didn't have any more of a clue than I did as to what this "business" was all about. I followed Mitch inside, then sat in an overstuffed chair across from the captain, who closed the blinds so the rest of the station couldn't see us, then perched on the corner of his desk. Mitch walked over to the window and remained standing.

Finally, he turned around and faced his captain. "What's this all about, sir?"

Captain Walker stared hard at Mitch. "You're not going to like this, but you don't have a choice."

Mitch stiffened. "What's that supposed to mean?"

"That means, this isn't my decision. This is coming from the top. Mayor Cromwell is up for reelection. He wants this murder case solved quickly, and Chief Spencer is backing him up all the way. I was told in no uncertain terms that whatever it takes to get the job done, we will do."

"And what exactly does he think it's going to take?" Mitch asked, narrowing his eyes.

Captain Walker looked from Mitch to me and back to Mitch again. "You two working together."

"Whaaat?" I shrieked, surging to my feet. The plan had been to stay away from Detective Stone, not work side by side with him.

"No way am I taking on a partner, Grady." Mitch began to pace.

"I might be your friend, Mitch, but right now I'm speaking as your captain." He scrubbed a palm over the top of his gleaming head. "My hands are tied on this one."

"Well, untie them. She's a suspect. You can't be serious."

"Dead serious. Right now she's the only lead we have. She knows more than any of us about what might have happened. The last thing we want is a cold case, Mitch, you know that."

"*She* is standing right here, boys, and *she* doesn't like this any more than Detective Grumpy Pants does," I snapped.

Captain Walker glanced in my direction with his hands on his hips. "Detective Grumpy Pants?"

"I, um, uh . . . well, he is," I grumbled, feeling my cheeks heat. "And it's not just his pants that are grumpy; it's every ounce of him." I waved my hands about.

Captain Walker chuckled. "I likc hcr."

"Good." Mitch glared at me. "You can have her. I won't do it, Captain."

Captain Walker's chuckling stopped as his face grew hard and serious. "Then you won't have a job, Detective. Am I clear?"

A muscle in Mitch's jaw bulged. "Fine. But don't be surprised if she's more of a hindrance than a help."

"Uh, hello, still standing right here, and it's not fine. I have a business to run, remember?" I glared right back at the detective. "You're the one hindering me. I don't have time to run around playing cops and robbers."

"Thought you didn't have any customers and wanted to stick to me like glue." Mitch lifted an eyebrow in my direction. "You changed your tune in a hurry. Wonder why that is."

"Oh, stop analyzing my every move, you big oaf. Ever think I just don't like you?"

"Good, because that makes two of us, you quack." He put his hands on his hips and towered over me. "I'm the only one qualified to solve this case."

"Ha! Seems to me that you're the one who doesn't

have a clue." I matched his stance and shoved my face up in his. "You need me more than you think. You're just too proud to admit it."

"Glad you agree, Miss Meadows," Captain Walker said.

"Wait, I didn't say—"

"You don't have a choice, either, ma'am." Captain Walker gave me a stern look. "You're still a suspect. I suggest you cooperate fully with our department. You of all people should want to solve this case."

I did, just on my own, not with Detective Stone. "Fine, partners it is."

"Oh, hell no. Not partners. Never forget I'm in charge. You're just my assistant." Detective Stone headed for the door. "Come on, Tink, we've got a case to solve."

"Whatever," I said, having no choice but to tag along behind the man in charge. "And quit calling me Tink."

"You should talk. Grumpy Pants? That's so childish."

"Oh, that's rich coming from a man who gave me a fairy-tale nickname. You started it."

"This ought to be good," the captain's words trailed us out the door, "if you don't kill each other first."


Look out, Divinity, because murder number two was just around the corner. Who needed digoxin? I was so ready to kill my new "partner" with my bare hands and not give a hoot.

"I'll ask the questions, got it?" Detective Stone shot me yet another warning look, and I just fluttered my lashes at him as we left the car at the curb.

I didn't want to be there any more than he did, but he

didn't have to make the situation unbearable. He made a guttural sound in the back of his throat and clenched and unclenched his fists several times before focusing on the door of the librarian's neighbor. After taking a few deep breaths, he rapped three times with the back of his knuckles.

"Who is it?" asked a shaky voice from the other side of the door.

"It's Detective Stone, ma'am. We'd like to ask you a few questions."

A pause filled the space, followed by, "We . . . ?"

"My—"

"*Partner*, Sunshine Meadows," I interjected as the door opened a crack. I held out my hand, not daring to glance at the detective, who I knew *must* be fuming, but I didn't care what he said. His captain had made me his partner—temporary or unofficial, it didn't matter.

He would have to deal with it.

The tiny woman with caramel-colored skin, a wobbly smile, and big red-rimmed eyes looked us over carefully and then opened the door fully and shook my hand. "Come in, please."

"Thank you," the detective said, nodding once, then stepping all businesslike past me into the room.

I shook my head, giving her a look that said, *Men! Enough said*. I reached into my enormous, over-the-shoulder tote bag and fished out a tissue. "You're very kind, Miss Hanes. I know how hard this must be after losing someone so close to you."

She pressed her lips together, dabbed at her eyes, her lips wobbling a bit. "Thank you, Detective Meadows, for understanding. And please, call me Carolyn." She shot a disapproving look at Detective Stone as she closed the door and joined us in her living room.

"She's not a detective," he said, clearing his throat and not quite meeting her eyes as he pulled at the collar of his shirt. "It's warm in here." He frowned at the crackling flames in the fireplace.

She let out a little hmph and ignored him. "What shall I call you, then?" She sat down on the couch and patted the seat beside her.

"Just Sunny." I joined her on the checkered sofa next to the tall bookshelf. A whiff of spiced apple drifted to my nose from the candle burning on the end table nearby.

"Well, aren't you ever. The name suits you."

"Thanks." Warmth oozed over my insides, bringing a smile to my lips. "I try."

A snort came from the detective's vicinity, but he didn't say anything. Just took the matching chair catty-corner to us. The warmth I'd felt a moment ago cooled to match the temperature outside. Moments like these were all I needed to remind me why my vision had to be off. We were so wrong for each other. The insensitive oaf pulled out a pad of paper and a pen and opened his mouth to speak.

"Would you care for some tea?" Miss Hanes asked.

"No, thank you," the detective said.

"Yes, that would be lovely," I said simultaneously.

Our eyes locked, and I gave him a nasty look. I knew he hated tea; however, Miss Hanes was obviously as reclusive as the librarian had been. They were neighbors and reported to be best friends. It was apparent she was lonely and craving human contact. Either he wasn't very observant, or he had no patience. I was betting on the latter.

The detective closed his notebook, rubbed the bridge of his nose, and sat back with a polite smile for Miss Hanes. "Sure thing, ma'am. That would be, what was it again . . . oh yeah, lovely."

She beamed and hustled off to the kitchen to brew the tea.

"Now that wasn't so hard, was it?" I whispered.

His smile faded. "We don't have time for tea."

"I suggest you make time, or you won't be getting any answers out of her, just plenty more tears." I brushed an imaginary piece of lint off my pants, but even through my peripheral vision, I saw his face pale at the word "tears."

"Fine, we'll play it your way, but like I said . . . I'll ask the questions. We clear?"

"There's nothing like a spot of tea to lift one's spirits, don't you agree?" Miss Hanes said, carrying in a large tray and setting it on the coffee table in front of us.

"Absolutely." I reached for my cup and took a sip. "It's delicious." I leaned forward. "Would be even lovelier with a dash of whiskey. Coffee isn't the only thing that the strong stuff is good for. If you have any handy, that is." I winked, not letting on that I'd already seen the bottle on the counter through the open kitchen door when we first came in.

Her eyes brightened. "A woman after my own heart. I'll get the bottle." She jumped up, moving faster than I had thought possible.

"Are you crazy?" the detective hissed when she was out of earshot.

"*You* might be on duty, but I'm not a detective, remember?" I smirked. "And after that whiskey, I'll bet her spirits will definitely be lifted . . . and her tongue a little looser."

"You're also not a drinker. Remember that, Tink."

"You're such a worrywart." I waved him off. "I know what I'm doing, Spanky."

"Somehow I doubt that." He tossed up his hands and sat back with a slight shake of his head.

Miss Hanes beamed as she waltzed through the door, looking as though she'd downed a shot already. "Care for a pick-me-up, Detective?"

"I'm good. The, uh, tea hit the spot." He rubbed his stomach.

Miss Hanes shrugged and then poured a generous dollop in her own tea as well as mine. As she turned around to place the bottle of whiskey on the table behind her, I dumped half my tea into the nearest potted plant, then took a tentative sip. My eyes nearly crossed as she sat down beside me. Wowzer, that certainly was a generous "dollop." Poor plant would either giddyup and grow, or it would join its roots six feet under by sundown.

I set my cup down. "Speaking of tea, I didn't know Ms. Robbins well, but I do remember she seemed to like a good cup of the fine brew."

Miss Hanes's face lost a bit of color, but there were no tears. "Amanda loved tea. It had a wonderful calming effect on her."

Detective Stone perked up, set his barely touched cup down, and pulled his notebook back out. "Was something troubling Ms. Robbins?"

"A lot of things were troubling her. This year's library budget, the staff she had to let go, her love life . . . She was a very private, complicated woman, but she was my friend." Miss Hanes downed the rest of her tea without so much as a grimace.

"Was there anything specific she mentioned recently?" Detective Stone asked.

"Well, she did say she felt like someone was stalking her at night. She would hear sounds right outside her bedroom window, but there was never anyone there whenever she looked."

"Aha!" I shouted, and the poor woman fell right off the couch. "Sorry, I didn't mean to startle you." I helped her up and patted her hand, then looked at Mitch. "The footsteps outside her window. Someone *was* there that night. I told you."

"But the footsteps belonged to a woman," Mitch clarified. "Not some guy she was seeing and having issues with."

"Wait a minute. I remember something," Miss Hanes interjected. "The morning Amanda died someone came to visit her. I didn't see who it was, but they argued. I could hear them, and the voice definitely belonged to a woman."

"Did—" Mitch started to ask.

"Oh my gosh, really? What did they say?" I sat on the edge of my seat, ignoring Mitch's blazing eyes.

"Well, I couldn't make out all the words, but I did hear the woman tell Amanda to stay away or she would be sorry."

"Are you—" Mitch tried again.

"Did you hear that, Mitch?" I sputtered, grabbing his arm and shaking it.

He looked down at my hand clutching the sleeve of his sports coat. "It's Detective Stone, and yes, I heard Miss Hanes. Now, if—"

"I can't believe it," I went on, releasing the now-wrinkled fabric. "A real clue." I stood and began to pace. "So maybe those footprints weren't from a witness. Maybe this woman was involved in the murder, because I still believe the murderer is a man. I mean—"

"Tink," Mitch snapped. "The investigation is ongoing," he said calmly, but his eyes screamed, *Quit revealing all we know!*

"Oh, right. Sorry." I winced.

"That's not all," Miss Hanes added, snagging our attention once more.

"What else—" Mitch started.

"You mean there's more?" I gaped at her and then turned to the detective, excitement forming patterns in my brain like tea leaves across the inside of a cup, helping me decipher the mystery. "There's more, Mitch." I held up a hand before he could correct me. "I mean, Detective Stone."

"Imagine that," he said dryly.

"Well, if you'd stop interrupting, you would have heard the poor woman. Jeesh." I turned to Miss Hanes and rolled my eyes in Mitch's direction. "I'm sorry, what were you saying?"

"Only that Amanda was really upset after the woman left, and shortly after that, she went to the doctor's."

"What for?" Detective Stone asked.

"She didn't say. She called me to ask if I would let the staff know she'd be late to the library, and then she hung up."

Detective Stone closed his notebook, slipped it back inside his sports coat, and then stood up. "Thank you for your time, Miss Hanes." He handed her his card. "If you think of anything else, please don't hesitate to call day or night."

I thanked the woman and hurried after him, thinking I needed to get some cards of my own. "Where are you going?"

"Home," he said after we had stepped outside into the brisk evening air.

"What about the doctor's office?" I zipped the new puffy coat I'd picked up at a thrift shop, feeling like a marshmallow, but I had to admit I was toasty warm. Except for my ears. I'd have to pick up a hat and mittens on my next shopping trip.

"Doc's office is closed." The detective's sports coat hung wide-open, but he didn't look cold in the least. He looked . . . I swallowed hard and tore my gaze away from his dress shirt pulled tight across his sculpted chest and flat abs. Why again weren't we right for each other? I wondered. "We'll visit him first thing in the morning." Mitch broke into my thoughts, sounding irritated. "In the meantime, I've had enough for one day."

Ah yes, there was the reason we weren't a match, because I'd certainly had enough of his crankiness. I pressed my lips together and didn't say a word.

He opened his car door for me and tipped his head to the side, studying me. "No argument?"

"Nope. I do believe I've *given* you enough for one day."
I nodded, playing along as a plan formed in my mind.

"Why does your comment make my head pound even more?"

"Maybe you should have had the whiskey."

He grunted, got in, and drove me home in silence while I sat back and silently schemed. Doctors might not make house calls these days, but that didn't mean I couldn't.

"Papas?" My mother turned up her nose and eyed the restaurant before us with doubt and suspicion. "Is it any good?"

"It's Greek, Mom. I'm sure it's fabulous," I answered.

"At least we know the portions will be big," my father stated, and opened the door for us.

"Who needs big portions?" My mother smoothed her stiff pencil skirt. "I can't afford to gain an inch in this outfit."

"Well, I'm starving," I said, and my mother pursed her lips at my much roomier, elastic-banded skirt with loads of gauzy material flowing down to my ankles. Mother weighed barely over one hundred pounds and wore a size 2. My healthy size 6 probably horrified her. I smiled.

The people of Divinity had moderately filled Papas Restaurant, but there were plenty of available tables left. The restaurants my parents frequented in the city would have been packed already. I scanned the inside, taking in the marble statues of godlike men and women, looking for . . . him.

A small smile of satisfaction tipped up the corners of my lips.

"Here's an empty spot right over here by the window." My father started leading the way, but I placed my hand on his arm.

"Wait, Dad. There's someone I want you to meet." I stopped at a table right by the one we were headed to and plastered on my most friendly smile. "Excuse me, Dr. Wilcox, but my name is Sunshine Meadows. You can call me Sunny. I'm new in town, and I've been meaning to introduce myself, but well, my life has been rather chaotic lately."

He was a decent-looking guy, sandy blond hair parted on the side, clean shaven, with a lean, average build. At the mention of my name, his green eyes widened for a second, but then he blinked and donned a pleasant expression, dabbing his mouth with a napkin.

"Ah, yes, I've heard about you," he said. "You're that fortune-teller from the city who bought the old Victorian down at the end of Shadow Lane, aren't you?"

"That would be me. It's nice to finally meet you." I held out my hand.

"Likewise." He shook my hand, looking at me curiously.

My mother sniffed sharply, implying a dual meaning with that one simple gesture: (1) I had the right to remain silent, and therefore I *should* when referring to my recent "troubles," and (2) I was being rude by not introducing them promptly.

"Forgive my manners, Doctor. These are my parents, Vivian and Donald Meadows. They're visiting for a little while."

"*Doctor* Donald Meadows." Dad shot me a frown and then shook Dr. Wilcox's hand.

Dr. Wilcox got to his feet. "*The* Dr. Meadows, as in world-renowned cardiologist?"

My father puffed up his chest. "One and the same. What is it you specialize in?"

"Oh, I dabble in internal medicine. I run a small family practice in the center of town. Nothing noteworthy like you."

Dad clapped a hand on the other man's shoulder. "Don't sell yourself short, my boy. Any form of medicine is a fine career. Your life has purpose." He tossed me a meaningful look. "Someone could learn a lot from the example you've set."

"Please, won't you all join me? I often dine alone. It would be nice to have company for a change."

"Why, that would be lovely," my mother said. "What do you say, Sylvia?"

Dr. Wilcox wore a confused expression.

"It's Sunny, and I say absolutely." My eyes locked onto the doctor's as I added, "I'm sure we can find something to talk about."

And I had the perfect topic in mind.

# 6

❖✻❖

My mother ordered the Horiatiki salad and red wine. She sipped daintily and nibbled at the tomatoes, olives, and feta cheese while avoiding the hot peppers and red onion with a downward turn of her lips.

My father ordered roasted lamb with potatoes and a Manhattan. He took a swig of his drink and ate the cherry, then precisely cut his lamb into pieces as though he were performing surgery. It was fascinating and creepy at the same time. Once again I wondered how I could possibly have sprung from their loins.

I ordered the moussaka and an iced tea. I chugged my tea, then dug into the layered eggplant and spiced meat with gusto. The creamy béchamel sauce dripped down my lip, and I licked it off, much to my parents' horror.

"So tell me, Dr. Wilcox, where is Mrs. Wilcox?" my mother asked, dabbing at the corners of her lips.

"Oh, there is no Mrs. I'm quite single." He cut his meat the same way my father did, and I almost blurted out, *Gee, I can't imagine why.* I shuddered. It had to be a doctor thing.

My dinner hit the bottom of my stomach with a thud, and I gaped at my mother as her intentions finally sank in. Oh, yeah. She had a calculating gleam in her eye that I'd seen countless times in the past.

"Really," my father boomed right on cue. "Now isn't that a coincidence? Our Sylvia here is single as well."

Dr. Wilcox's eyes widened larger than the saucers beneath my teacups. He looked as horrified as I felt, thank God!

I sighed, a nasty headache forming in my temples, then stilled as a thought came to me. "Having twins is so scary," I finally said, setting my utensils down and rubbing my now aching stomach.

"Excuse me?" My mother's face paled whiter than her porcelain veneers. She dropped her fork as her eyes slowly lowered to my midriff.

"The thought of going through something like that alone is even more terrifying, don't you think?" I wiped my hands on my napkin and looked thoughtfully at the ceiling, still rubbing my stomach. Acid indigestion was only the beginning of my problems.

"Tw-Twins?" my father managed to say seconds before he downed the rest of his Manhattan.

"So, you're pregnant?" Dr. Wilcox asked. "Who's your doctor?"

I waved my hand in the air. "Not me, silly." I held him captive with my eyes. "The librarian. And by twins I meant the twin tumors she had."

"Good heavens, Sylvia, don't do that to me again." My mother fanned her cheeks with her shaking hands. "Do you know the scandal that would have caused?"

My father flagged down the waiter and ordered another drink while wiping the perspiration off his brow. "Scandal? I'd be ruined."

"For God's sake, you two. I'm nearly thirty, and we aren't living in the Dark Ages."

Dr. Wilcox's eyes narrowed a fraction. "How did you know about Ms. Robbins's medical condition? That information is private."

Thankful for the interruption, I focused on the doctor and simply said, "The tea leaves told me."

My father muttered something under his breath, then grabbed the waiter's arm as he walked by. "Make my drink a double."

"Tea leaves?" Dr. Wilcox smirked. "I didn't realize they could talk."

I breathed slowly and deeply, striving for patience. It wasn't the first time I'd heard comments like that. "When I read Ms. Robbins's tea leaves, I saw twins. At first I thought that she was pregnant, but then I realized the twins were twin tumors. My visions are always accurate. They just sometimes take a bit for me to interpret correctly. She was upset and rightfully so. I can't imagine discovering news like that. She seemed so alone. I heard she had no family around here, pretty much spending all her time in the library. I don't know how she had the energy or how no one discovered she was ill."

The smirk left the doctor's face, a sober expression taking its place. "I can't discuss Ms. Robbins's appointment because of doctor-patient confidentiality, Miss Meadows. You should know that, given your father's occupation."

"Exactly, Sylvia." My father shot me a disapproving look. "You know better than that."

All I knew was that I was still a suspect, and I would pretty much do anything to get to the truth and solve this case. I leaned in close to the doctor and plastered the most innocent expression on my face.

"I'm just saying no one should have to go through something like that alone. It's just not right having no one there for you." I shook my head sadly.

The doctor's jaw hardened as his beeper went off. He checked it, then abruptly stood. "I'm sorry for the interruption, but I'm going to have to cut dinner short. It was very nice to meet you all, and I'm sure we'll be seeing each other soon." His eyes cut to mine once more, and then he was gone.

We'd be seeing each other soon, all right; he just didn't realize how soon.


"Come on, Tink, what's taking so long? We need to leave," Detective Stone said as I opened my front door bright and early the next morning. His thick dark hair was still slightly wet, the ends curling up a smidgeon. He wore a light blue dress shirt under a fawn brown sports coat with no tie. The top button of his shirt was undone, revealing a tanned throat, neck, and face. I took in his five o'clock shadow barely covering his jagged scar and settled on his full lips. It wasn't like he was drop-dead gorgeous, so why did he do funny things to my insides?

Those same full lips turned down at the corners. "You having another spell, Tink?"

"Apparently so," I snapped, and raised my eyes to his. "Please shake me when I get like that because I've obviously lost my mind."

"Well, hurry up and find it, would ya? We're late."

"Hang on for two seconds. I can't leave without my phone in case the vet calls." I kept searching through my bag but couldn't for the life of me remember where I had left my cell.

"The vet? Why, is that demon cat of yours sick?" He scanned the inside of my house before he stepped across the threshold.

I paused. "He's not a demon—at least I don't think he is—but he definitely *is* different." The corners of my lips tipped up slightly. "Special," I added, then scowled at Detective Stone. "And don't look so excited over the thought of Morty being sick. He's not sick. I just want to make sure he's up on all his shots and healthy."

"Whatever." The detective glanced at his watch. "Hurry up or the doc's waiting room will be full and he won't have time to talk to us."

I bit my lip, struggling to remember where I'd left my phone. Suddenly a muffled voice started shouting, *Butthead calling, Buuutthead calling.* My eyes bugged and I bolted over to the couch to snatch my phone from between the cushions. The voice grew louder, repeating the phrase over and over until I silenced my phone.

Feeling my cheeks flush hot, I turned around and forced a smile.

He held his phone in his hand, his eyes springing wide. "You set *that* as my ringtone?"

"Accidentally."

"How does someone accidentally set a ringtone?" He looked me over in disdain. "How old are you?"

"Old enough to tell time." I thrust out my chin. "Full waiting room, remember? I thought you were in a hurry." I scrambled past him out the door and climbed in his car, refusing to speak until we arrived at Wilcox Family Practice.

Just as we'd thought, Dr. Wilcox's office was packed. It was standing room only until the door opened and the doctor walked a little old lady out. An old man who I was guessing was her husband stood to join her.

"I'm telling you, Doc, there's something wrong with me. I'm sure I'm dying. And if I'm not actually dying, then I'm for sure in danger of getting murdered. The streets aren't safe. What if that maniac tries to kill me?" The frail little lady wrung her hands together, her hair slightly blue and teased out as though trying to hide its natural thinning, and her reading glasses tilted crooked on her nose.

"Mrs. Sampson"—Dr. Wilcox patted her thin, bony shoulder—"I assure you that you are fit as a fiddle. Your exhaustion simply has to do with age. Try to get some rest. Isn't that what retirement is about?"

"Bah, retirement is for the birds," Mr. Sampson said. "Come on, Maude, I told you there ain't nothin' wrong with you. You're just a hyper-complainer is what you are.

Never happy unless you got some aches and pains to nag about." The old man stood tall, thrusting his relatively stocky build forward. He slapped his chest. "You don't hear me complaining. Spent half my life working in that steel mill. Probably spend another ten years before I'll get to retire. Sorry for wasting your time again, Doc."

"It's all right, Bernard. Just get her home safe." The doctor squeezed his shoulder and then stopped short when he saw Detective Stone and me. "Nurse Doolittle, push my appointments back by a half hour. Something important has come up."

Mrs. Sampson broke free of her husband, showing a surprising burst of strength for such a little thing. "Detective Stone, you must catch this monster." She placed her hands on his cheeks and lowered his head to within an inch of hers as she stared hard at him with wild, crazed eyes. "I'm in danger. I can feel it in my bones, and I've seen it in the stars. Stars don't lie."

Mr. Sampson gently took his wife and peeled her off the detective. "Sorry 'bout that. Them stars is all in her head. She gets dizzy once in a while, thinks she sees things. You know how it is."

"She's fine, Bernard," the doctor interjected. "People often get a little confused as they get older."

He nodded once and then whispered to his wife as he led her out of the office at a fast clip.

"She must be related to you," the detective said to me as he rubbed his jaw, watching the woman leave the office. "Crazy as a cuckoo bird," he muttered under his breath.

"I heard that." I smirked. "You're a regular riot, you know that?"

"Gee, I didn't know 'buttheads' could be funny." His eyes met mine, and he made a face. "Thanks."

"Ooooh!" I stomped my foot, drawing the stares of several patients in the waiting room, but I didn't care. The man was a brute.

"Follow me, Detective," Dr. Wilcox interjected, shooting me a confused look. "Miss Meadows?"

"Captain Walker made me his partner," I explained.

"Assistant," Detective Stone grumbled, all teasing aside, then pushed past me into the doctor's office.

"He's a little touchy about the details." I followed suit.

The doctor joined us, closing the door tightly. He sat in his chair behind his desk, and a serious expression settled over his features. "Ms. Robbins was a remarkable woman. She didn't deserve to die like that."

"I agree." Mitch took a small notebook and pen out of his suit coat. "So where were you the night of the murder?"

The doctor sat up straight and choked. "I beg your pardon?"

"Sorry, Doc. Detective Grumpy Pants hasn't had enough coffee yet."

"I've had plenty of coffee. The doc has small feet and access to digoxin. You do the math."

"Ah, but what motive could I possibly have?" asked the doctor.

"Unrequited love." A calculating gleam entered Mitch's eye as the doctor's face paled. "Small town, Doc."

"Well, then, you'd also know I eat dinner at the same

time every night at Papas Restaurant. They can verify my alibi. And you're right. I did have a thing for Amanda. I would never hurt her, but she made it clear she only wanted to be friends and that would never change. All I wanted to do was be there for her."

"Is that what you said to her when you told her about the tumors?" I asked softly. "So that you'd be there for her and she wouldn't have to go through that alone?"

"Kip didn't release that information to the public in his coroner's report." Mitch stared hard at me. "How did you know about her medical condition?"

"Tea leaves, remember? Or maybe the cuckoo bird told me." I fluttered my lashes at him, and he grunted, rolling his eyes. I turned to the doctor. "That must have been rough when she rejected your attempt to comfort her in her time of need. Especially when she had no one else."

He clenched his jaw and ground out, "Look, I'm not the one you should be talking to. Amanda was a sweet, quiet woman, but that didn't mean she didn't have enemies. Callista Papas hated her for some reason. I never realized how much until the morning of Amanda's death."

The doc stood and began to pace. "Amanda came into the office all concerned about her health once again. She's allergic to nuts and would never eat them knowingly. Yet when she walked through this very door, her face was swelled up like a blowfish. When I asked her about it, she swore she hadn't had nuts that morning, just a banana muffin from Papas. I'd bet my practice if you had a sample of that muffin, you'd find ground walnuts as part of the ingredients."

"Oh my gosh, Mitch, do—"

"Detective."

"Whatever. Do you think Mrs. Papas could be the woman Miss Hanes said Ms. Robbins argued with on the morning of her death?"

His look said, *Shut up now, Tink, you're revealing too much again*, but his words came out polite and respectful and directed toward the doctor. "Thank you for your time, Dr. Wilcox. Here's my card. If you can think of anything else, please give me a call day or night." Mitch stood, grabbed my arm, and dragged me out of the office to the parking lot.

"Easy there, Conan." I dug in my heels and stopped short before his car. "This is the new millennium. Being a barbarian went out centuries ago." I crossed my arms over my chest.

"Yet being a blabbermouth is apparently still in fashion."

I looked sheepish. "Sorry, this whole partner thing is still new to me."

"Assistant."

"That really bugs you, doesn't it? Look, I want to solve this case more than anyone. Just because I'm a woman doesn't mean I'm going to screw you over like your ex."

A blast of icy snow swirled around us, and Mitch's face hardened. "Don't go there, Tink."

"I'm sorry, okay? It's just you have a really big chip on your shoulder that has nothing to do with me. I only want—"

"Drop it and get in." He climbed in his car and slammed the door shut.

"Fine, but—" My phone started playing the theme song to the *Addams Family*. "Morty," I whispered with concern. I'd had a funny feeling when I'd dropped Morty off at the vet this morning, so I'd set that song as my ringtone for their office just in case they called.

"Your cat can dial the phone?" He gaped at me. "What the hell's next?"

"Don't be ridiculous," I scoffed.

"Hey, I wouldn't put anything past that thing. And how come he gets a cool ringtone?"

I rolled my eyes and answered the call from the vet. "Hello, Dr. Parker, is something wrong? I thought I wasn't supposed to pick up Morty until the end of the day. Is he sick?"

"Hi, Sunny, please call me Sherry. I don't want to alarm you, but I really don't know how Morty is. He looked healthy to me, but I never got the chance to examine him. There's no way he could have escaped, but when I went in to the exam room, he was gone as though he'd simply vanished."

A calm settled over me, and I knew in my gut that Morty was fine. He was home, I was sure of it. He didn't want to have a physical, and that was that. End of discussion, and end of vet appointment, apparently. "Thanks, Sherry. I think I know where he is."

"Do you want to reschedule his appointment, then? I could make an exception and come to your house if you think it would be easier on him."

"Morty's not afraid, he's stubborn. Can I get back to you on the whole house call thing?"

"Sure. No problem, just give me a call."

I disconnected and climbed into the detective's car.

"Everything all right?" he asked.

"Everything is fine. Where to, boss?"

"*Now* you call me boss?" He shook his head. "How about lunch?"

"Good, I'm starving."

"I know the perfect place." He fired up the car and pulled away from the curb. "Care for a little Greek?"

I rubbed my hands together. "You read my mind exactly."


Papas was pretty busy when we entered at noon, not a free table in sight. Detective Stone asked to speak to the owner, and we were treated to her own personal table in the back.

Once we'd all ordered, Mrs. Papas said, "Nice to see you again, Miss Meadows. Did you and your parents enjoy your dinner with Dr. Wilcox last night?"

Mitch choked on his hamburger, took a swig of water, and then wiped his mouth with a napkin. "You didn't tell me you had dinner with the doc." He stared at me accusingly.

"I'm sorry, I didn't know we were sharing information. I thought I was just an assistant." I looked up at him all innocent-like and sipped my iced tea.

He studied me for a full minute. "What else are you hiding?"

I tossed up my hands and sat back. "Nothing, okay? It was just dinner, and my dad wanted to meet a fellow doctor, that's all."

"Riiight."

"As much as I enjoy the entertainment, you two, I know this isn't a social call," Mrs. Papas said. "What do you want to know?"

The detective set down his fork and took another drink of water, then he wiped his mouth. "For starters, where were you on the night of Ms. Robbins's murder?"

Mrs. Papas threw back her head and laughed. "Running my restaurant, of course."

"Your husband never takes a turn?" I asked.

The smile left her face. "My husband takes a lot of things, but taking a turn at work is not one of them. I run the restaurant while he keeps the books. I work my fingers to the bone while he goes to the gym . . . or so he says. Do you know what my name stands for?"

I shook my head no.

"Callista means 'most beautiful.' My husband's name, Damon, means 'constant and loyal.' It didn't seem quite so ironic when I married him. Why doesn't he see he has the most beautiful woman already? I never should have married the lying cheater."

"Did you visit Ms. Robbins the morning of her death?" Mitch asked.

"I cater the library's author readings and book talks. I needed to speak to Amanda about the menu."

"Her neighbor heard you two argue," I added.

"Was poisoning her on the menu as well?" the detective added.

"Oh, please." Mrs. Papas thumped her fist down on the table. "That little tramp was having an affair with my husband. I knew her allergy wouldn't kill her. She deserved far more than a slight reaction to some nuts. I was simply warning her to stay away."

"Maybe your husband was about to leave you for the librarian, so you killed her," the detective said point-blank.

Her face hardened. "Nonsense. We have been trying to start a family for years. If my husband leaves me for another woman, he knows I will castrate him myself. He knows I want children, but he has been unable to give them to me, so now I make his life a living hell in return. Maybe I should seek elsewhere for that as well, no?" She leaned forward, looked Mitch over, and licked her lips. "Having children is my passion."

He loosened his collar, eyeing her uncomfortably.

"Why not divorce?" I asked, saving his butt from her unwanted advances. Why, I had no clue. If I were smart, I'd let him squirm.

"We don't believe in it." She blew out a heap of air. "No, we made our choice, and now we have to live with it." She stabbed a finger in our direction. "But that doesn't mean I'm going to make it easy on him."

"What size shoe does your husband wear?" I asked as a thought occurred to me.

"My husband has very small feet. Why?"

"Just wondering." I struggled not to be a blabber-mouth, but my eyes spoke volumes as I stared at Mitch and winked several times.

"Honey, you should have that twitch looked at," Mrs. Papas said to me.

"I know, it's really irritating, but no matter what I do, I can't seem to make it go away." I refused to look at Mitch, but I felt his gaze sizzle in my direction.

"Speaking of the doctor. You should talk to him. The whole town knows he had it bad for Ms. Robbins."

"We already did. He says they were only friends," I said.

"Yeah, but a lot of people heard him argue with her that day when she came in to see him about the nut reaction. He treated her and then asked her to marry him, saying he would take care of her in her time of need— whatever that meant. She turned him down flat, and he threatened her. Said one day she'd be sorry and regret turning him down."

"Can't be the doctor. He has an airtight alibi," Mitch said.

"He might . . . but does his nurse?"

"His nurse? Why her?" I asked, realizing she had access to digoxin as well.

"Word around town is she was jealous over all the attention he gave to Amanda. You look a little hot under the collar, Detective. Maybe it's time you had your temperature checked." Mrs. Papas winked at Mitch.

Mitch kept his emotionless cop face firmly in place and then stood. "Thank you for lunch, Mrs. Papas, here's—"

"My card," I finished, and handed her the business cards I'd had made for Sunny's Sanctuary. It was all I had, but at least it had my contact information on it. "If you hear anything at all, please don't hesitate to call. . . . Oh yeah, day or night." I beamed at Mitch, starting to feel like I was getting the hang of this.

He handed over his card as well. "Ma'am." He saluted the Greek woman and then turned to me. "Let's go, Tink, we're still on the clock, and I've got a whopper of a headache."

"I know just who to go to for some aspirin."

# 7

"What are you doing?" I asked Mitch as he dropped me off at home after lunch.

"Taking care of my headache."

"Ha-ha, very funny. I thought we were going to talk to Nurse Doolittle?"

"*We* aren't doing anything. *You* are staying here while I talk to the nurse."

"But I thought Captain Walker said we were to work together."

"Just because we work together doesn't mean we have to be together 24/7, Tink." He brushed a hand over his face and then stabbed a finger at me. "You give me a hell of a lot more than a pain in my head."

I plopped my hands on my hips. "Ditto, buster. But what exactly am I supposed to do?" My mouth fell open as I glared at him.

"Close your mouth, for one. I can see your tonsils, Tink."

I snapped my jaw shut and ground my molars so hard my ears tingled. But I couldn't stay quiet. "No, seriously, what should I do?"

His lips twitched once, and then he grew stern. "Hell, I don't know. Take up knitting? I really don't care so long as it doesn't involve you screwing up my case. Play around on the Internet, make notes, whatever. . . . Just quit interfering with my leads. You're messing up my system, and I don't like it."

"Well, I don't like you." I poked him in the chest.

"Good. Then we're even." He poked me back, and I gasped. He had some nerve. I wriggled my nose as if conjuring a spell, but he just smirked and then turned around to march out to his car.

Morty dropped from a tree and landed right in front of him on all four paws with hackles raised.

"Jesus, Mary, and Joseph," Mitch bellowed, and stumbled back, reaching for his gun. "I thought that, that . . . thing was at the vet's." He gave Morty a wide berth, weapon drawn and held tight in his hands but pointed down at the snow-covered ground.

Morty blinked at him, stretched, and then flicked his tail, which had Mitch flinching. Then the cat walked inside Vicky's open door with what sounded suspiciously like hissing laughter.

I had never loved him more.

Mitch cursed softly under his breath, sheathed his gun, and then stabbed a finger in my direction. "Stay out of trouble, Tink. That's an order."

* * *

Staying out of trouble didn't mean I had to stay home.

Back in the city I never went to the gym. I was blessed with good genes and happy about my size, thank God, because physical exertion wasn't really my thing. Walking or riding my bike through Central Park I could handle. Climbing on equipment more complex to operate than my father's medical devices or my mother's BlackBerry, not so much.

"You'd better be worth it, Damon Papas," I grumbled to myself as I changed into Tweety Bird sweatpants and a white tank top.

"Bye, Morty, wherever you are. You don't have to hide anymore. I get it, no more vet. Pray I come back in one piece," I hollered, and grabbed an oversized canary yellow hooded sweatshirt instead of my bulky winter coat. Snagging my keys, I headed out the door.

I locked up Vicky and then drove down my street, past Smokey Jo's, and around the corner to Wally's World. Five minutes later I stood inside, second-guessing my decision to call and make an appointment with a personal trainer.

Wally was a massive man. At least six foot eight inches of creamy milk chocolate, not a speck of hair on his big beautiful body, and features more exotic than any I'd ever seen on a man or a woman.

"You must be Sunny. Welcome to my world," he said in a deep, rich voice, and then stretched his lips wide, revealing blazing white teeth. "Ready to get Wally-sized?"

"I, well, um . . . oh my. That depends on what's

involved," I answered in a shaky voice, scanning the inside of the gym.

I knew I probably wouldn't see Mr. Papas since his wife had told us he usually worked out at night, but I thought maybe I would meet some people who might know him. Find out more about him since I had no clue where else he hung out or anything else about him. And I couldn't sit home and do nothing, no matter what Detective Stone had ordered me to do. I wouldn't interfere in any more of his leads. . . . I'd simply find my own.

Wally tipped his head back, and laughter boomed from the depths of his chest out his wide mouth. "I'll be gentle. Promise."

"Don't listen to him, lass. There's nothing gentle about the beast. I'm afraid if he gets ahold of you, he'll break your wee little body." Sean O'Malley winked at me, his blue eyes twinkling and adorable dimples sinking deep. "Besides, Big Bertha just got here, and she insists on only working with her hunka hunka burnin' love." He turned to Wally. "Her words not mine, boss."

"You're not fooling anyone, son. You just want this breath of fresh air for yourself." Wally grinned right back at Sean. "If I weren't short-handed, I'd fire your behind and send you packing."

"I'm too good, and you know it."

"You're too something, all right." Wally eyed me up and down. "Watch your heart around this one. You blink your eyes, and he'll steal it for sure." Wally walked off and gave Bertha a huge bear hug, and then he dragged her unceremoniously into the gym. She didn't kick or scream once. In fact, she looked like she was in heaven.

"Wow," was all I said, peeking up at Sean. "Thank you, I think."

"Ah, no worries. You're in good hands, love."

"That's what I'm worried about." I giggled and pointed my finger at him. "Behave yourself."

"Or what?" Sean leaned close and whispered in my ear, "You'll spank me?"

"Wal—"

He clapped a hand over my mouth and chuckled. "Touché." He crossed his bare arms over his spandex-covered chest and pulled his lips into a devilish grin. "So, tell me. What are you really doing here?"

"Getting into shape . . . *really*."

"I like your shape." He looked me over. "What I can remember of it. Can't see a blasted thing beneath that crazy workout getup."

"That's the point." I adjusted my sweatshirt. "What about you? I thought you were a bartender at Smokey Jo's?"

"That's my night gig. This is my day job. What can I say?" He lifted one finely toned shoulder. "I'm surrounded by all kinds of people at both jobs. Keeps things interesting. I'm just lucky, I guess."

"I agree with Wally, you're something all right." I punched him on that same shoulder.

He snagged my wrist. "You're about to find out exactly what I am as I whip your adorable hind end into shape." His blue eyes took on a mischievous glitter. "A little weights, a lot of cardio, some Zumba."

"Some whata?"

"Just the latest craze in exercising and one of my favorites. Can't wait to show you the Booty."

"I'll bet," I said as I trotted after him into the weight room. I sucked in a breath, flabbergasted at my luck. I had spotted Damon Papas coming out of the locker room and heading for the door, so I dug in my heels and yanked my wrist free from Sean's light grip. "Ow, my side."

Sean stopped, all teasing aside and a concerned look crossing his perfect features. "What's wrong?"

"Cramps."

His eyes grew heavy-lidded, and he stood with his hands on his hips. "You're the one who made this appointment. You wouldn't be wimping out on me, now would ya?"

"Okay, so you caught me. I hate working out, but I really do want to get into better shape. Just not at this moment. I actually do have a pain that won't go away unless I tend to it." I looked quickly toward Damon. I hadn't lied. "Rain check?"

"Yeah, sure, but I'm holding you to that. How about tomorrow?" Sean tapped the tip of my nose with his fingertip.

"It's a date." I kept my eyes locked on Damon, not wanting to miss his exit.

"That's what I'm counting on."

"I didn't mean—"

"Too late. You threw it out there, and I'm holding you to it for blowing off working out today."

"Fine, whatever." I waved my hand absently. "But I really do have to go now."

Sean's eyes followed mine. "Hmph, haven't seen him around here in a while. You know that guy?"

"No, but I'd like to talk to him." I glanced around to make sure no one was eavesdropping and then said in a quiet voice, "I'm hoping he can help shed some light on this case. Clear my name. His wife said he comes here every evening. I was surprised to see him here this early."

"Good luck, lass." Sean shot a disgusted look in Damon's direction. "That might be what he's telling his wife, but I can assure you he hasn't worked out in weeks."

I knew Damon had been having an affair with Amanda Robbins and figured that was probably where he'd been going all these weeks. But now that she was dead, where on earth was he going this time?

Only one way to find out.

I was kind of excited at the thought of tailing someone for the first time. I glanced down at my clothes and bit my lip. I hadn't really thought that far ahead when I'd chosen my outfit.

"Gotta go." I grabbed Sean's hand and drew his attention back to me. "We'll talk in the morning. Tell Jo I'll call her. We'll have a girls' day."

"Will do." He squeezed my hand and then let go. "Take care, now. And don't forget to call me so we can figure out where we want to go tomorrow. Don't worry, love. I'll make it worth your while," he said in his body-melting Irish brogue.

Wow, he was good. I bit back a grin but giggled as I backed away toward the door, holding my side for good measure. Sean chuckled and moved on to his next victim.

After exiting the gym, I ducked behind a bush and watched Damon stand by his truck. A few moments later, he looked around as a car pulled up. Once he was sure no one was in the parking lot of the gym, he jumped into a car I didn't recognize and slouched down as a person who wore a dark hood behind the wheel drove off. I quickly scurried over to my bug and turned the key, praying she'd start. Seconds later she sputtered to life as the other car's rear end disappeared out of sight.

Shifting into gear, I followed at a safe distance. Where on earth was he going and whom was he with? They drove the car to the edge of town and pulled into the driveway of a house down a short dead-end road. They drove straight into the garage and closed the door behind them. I parked down the street, got out, and jogged to the back of the house. I peeked in the downstairs window and stifled a gasp.

A woman. I recognized her from my first day in town when I bought supplies for my sanctuary's makeover. She'd introduced herself and had seemed so sweet. So proper. She was the kindergarten teacher at Divinity Elementary. Unbelievable. First the librarian and now the schoolteacher. Damon was married to a tyrant but obviously had a "good girl" fetish. Callista had said her husband claimed to have been at the gym during the time of the murder. If I were a gambling woman, I'd bet money he'd already moved on to his next fling. Why else would he be talking to the woman? It wasn't like he had children who were in her class.

I couldn't go on mere suspicion. I needed proof.

They headed into the kitchen, so I tried the window, but it was locked tight. Biting my lip, I scanned the back of the house. A massive oak was situated close to the upstairs windows. Maybe if I climbed high enough, I could see or hear something. Even better, maybe the window up there would be unlocked.

I rubbed my hands together and started climbing the tree. Heaving and puffing my way to the top, it dawned on me that I really did need to get in better shape. I looked down and let out a little yelp. The tree hadn't appeared this high from the ground. I found a sturdy branch and scooted my way to the edge. Dusk came early during the month of January in upstate New York, and it was getting hard to see.

I tried the upstairs window and lucked out. It opened. Not fully but enough for me to squeeze through. The screen to this window was missing, so I was able to climb right inside. I landed with a thud and scrambled to my feet.

"What was that?" I heard from right outside the bedroom door, and the knob started to turn.

It was too late to scramble back outside without killing myself, so I closed the window and darted into the closet. As I closed the door, a whiff of starch mixed with mothballs gagged me. I held my breath and peeked through the slats. Seconds later the couple strolled inside in a full embrace.

Good Lord, what had I gotten myself into?

"Don't worry about it, baby," Damon said, kissing the schoolteacher's neck. He was short but well built with dark masculine features and black slicked-back hair. All he needed were some chains around his neck, and he'd make the perfect gigolo.

"It was probably the wind knocking the tree branch

against the glass," he went on. "I told you that you need to have the landscaper trim that back in the spring."

"Are you sure no one knows where you are?" the woman asked.

"Stop worrying, Mary. We're safe, but I don't have long." He pushed her back onto the mattress.

"Because if people find out, my reputation will be ruined," she continued. "That's why you can't use me as your alibi for the night Amanda Robbins died."

"Your reputation? What about my life? My wife will kill me. Things were over a long time ago with Amanda. She wouldn't take no for an answer. Even tried to trap me by getting pregnant, but it wouldn't have worked, anyway. She hadn't counted on my vasectomy. You're the one who really makes me happy, baby."

"Awwww, sweetie," Mary said, and then they kissed passionately, her bun still firmly in place.

Damon pulled back and said while breathing hard, "Wanna watch a naughty movie?"

Mary giggled. "You read my mind."

Ewwww! I looked away and sat back, but that didn't stop my ears from burning. The TV blared out sounds and dialogue so descriptive it left nothing to the imagination, no matter how hard I tried to block the mental image.

My phone chose that moment to ring. Thank God I'd had the sense to put it on vibrate. I checked the caller ID and groaned inwardly. "Hey, Detective, what's up?" I whispered as quietly as I could and cupped my hand over the mouthpiece. Didn't matter. The noise in the other room was so loud, my teakettle could go off, and they wouldn't hear it.

"Why are you whispering?" he asked.

"Bad sore throat. Contagious. Stay away." I peeked through the blinds and slapped a hand over my eyes. "Far, far away."

A peal of giggles and shrieks rang out.

"Where are you?"

"Home. It's the TV. Bad, bad TV."

"Good God, what are you watching?"

"You don't want to know." I pried one eye open and then squeezed it shut again. "Let's just say the rating is off the charts."

There was a pause. "Really?" His voice sounded gruff.

I'd roll my eyes if they were open, but there was no way I was taking a chance of seeing any more of *that*. My retinas would never be the same. "Men, you're all alike," I ground out. "I stumbled across this movie, but trust me, it's not something I ever care to see again. I'm changing the channel now. Was there something you wanted, Detective?"

"No." He grunted. "I don't want anything from you. Why would you think so?"

"That's good, because I have nothing to give you. Nothing at all. Got it?"

"Oh-kay. You been sniffing glue, Tink? Cuz you're acting strange again."

"I'm acting strange? That's rich coming from the man who wants nothing from me . . . yet you're the one who called me," I pointed out, adding a mental *Duh!*

"Oh, that." He sounded all business-like once more. "I called to tell you the nurse isn't talking, not to me, anyway. She has no alibi for the night of the murder. Says she was home, but I can't get a good read on her. She's getting her hair and nails done tomorrow at Pump up the Volume Hair Salon and Spa. I thought maybe you . . . Nah, it's probably a bad idea, especially with you being sick."

"What is it?"

"Well, I thought maybe you could go and see what you can find out. But I don't know if you're ready. It takes a lot of planning to pull off a stakeout or tail someone."

I glanced down at my Tweety Bird outfit and canary sweatshirt. Add in the fact that I was stuck in a closet, and I was forced to concede he had a point.

"To infiltrate a scene and blend in is even harder," he kept talking. "I'm not sure you can handle it, Tink. But if I show up, she won't say anything. Yet if you show up, she'll know something's off. Everyone knows you're not exactly a salon type of woman. See my dilemma?"

"I'm ready, I swear," I snapped as much as one can snap in a whisper voice. "I'm sure this sore throat is a twenty-four-hour thing," I whispered even lower, still bristling over his comment about me not being the salon type. "I'm not a country bumpkin, you know. Besides, I have the perfect cover. I have a date with Sean O'Malley tomorrow, so I'll—"

"Excuse me, come again?" he sputtered.

"You heard me."

"I don't think that's such a good idea. Sean's a good guy, but he's a smooth operator. He'll talk circles around you and before you know it, you'll be the star of your own unrated movie."

"Who says I don't want to be?" I paused, but the detective was speechless for once. "Listen, I can take care of myself there, Spanky. It's just a date."

"Whatever." He coughed. "I really don't care what you do with your personal life. I was thinking of your reputation."

"Good God, you sound like my parents." I shuddered. "Here's the plan. I'll have Jo take me to the salon at the same time Nurse Doolittle will be there. We'll have a girls' day, and I'll get a makeover in preparation for my date. Women do that all the time, and I'll bet my tea leaves that Nurse Doolittle will be talking by the end of our session. Let's pray I won't have to endure a full makeover before she spills the beans."

The couple on the bed stood up and stumbled about in their passion, crashing into the closet door. I flattened myself against the back wall behind a row of dresses, preparing myself for discovery. What on earth would I say if they found me playing Peeping Tom? The door didn't break, thank goodness, but it was loud. Then they fumbled their way into the bathroom and turned on the shower.

"What the hell was that?" Mitch asked.

I let out the breath I'd been holding. "Um, an action film, but no worries. I've had enough TV. Think I'll get some rest."

"Good idea. Report in tomorrow."

"I will." I hung up and quickly slipped out of the closet. I made my way over to the window, opened it as far as I could, and then squeezed outside on the branch, barely closing the window behind me.

Ice had formed on the branches now, and I carefully slid my way toward the center of the tree. I had almost made it when I slipped off the branch. I let out a little screech, my arms flailing about. Oh my God, I was going to die! I covered my face as I tumbled to the ground headfirst. Something jerked me to a stop, and I hung suspended upside down, my heart pounding wildly. The edge of my canary yellow hoodie had snagged on another branch, but who knew how long that would hold.

I whipped out my phone and dialed as fast as I could.

"I thought you were resting," the detective asked as soon as he answered.

"I need your help now!" I said in a perfectly clear, non-sore voice.

"That has to be the fastest recovery in the world. What was it, a twenty-four-second bug?" he asked suspiciously.

"Just get over here now, and don't ring the doorbell or let anyone see you. Go out back by the tree and look up."

"Huh? You really are crazier than a cuckoo bird, aren't you, woman?"

"And you really are a butthead. Just . . . hurry." I gave him the address and disconnected as I started to slip.

Mere minutes later an all-too-familiar smooth, deep voice from below said, "You've taken bird-watching to a whole new level, Tweety."

"I thought it was Tink."

"Not today, apparently, because you sure can't fly. What the hell were you doing?" He stood there with his hands on his hips, scowling up at me.

"I wasn't bird-watching. I was tailing a perp." A ripping noise sounded, and I dropped a few inches, letting out a yelp.

"He's not a perp. He's a suspect. I thought I told you to stay out of trouble. And what on earth are you wearing? Don't you know anything?"

"Who cares about that, just get me down. Can't you see I'm going to fall? The point is Damon has an alibi. They're playing school as we speak."

"The unrated movie, I take it?"

"And the action flick . . . so not pretty. If I wasn't sick before, I am now." Another ripping noise sounded, and I squeaked like a mouse.

Mitch sighed. "What in the world am I going to do with you, Tink?"

"For starters, get me down from here. My head is pounding from the blood rush, and I don't know how much longer my sweatshirt is going to hold."

He stood directly below me and held out his arms. "Don't worry. I've got you."

"And you call me crazy?" I sputtered.

"It's too icy for me to climb up. I'm twice your size, Tink. I'll just catch you when you fall. I won't drop you." I glanced down at him and met his eyes as he added, "Trust me."

Something inside me believed him, and I did exactly that. Squeezed my eyes closed tight and waited for the inevitable. Seconds later, my sweatshirt gave way and I tumbled to the earth below.

He kept his word and didn't drop me, but unfortunately, I flattened him good. He lay sprawled on his back with me flat on top of him, belly to belly. We both fought to catch our breath, but I fared much better than he did.

I could feel his heart beat beneath mine, and the heat of his body warmed me through my tattered hoodie. "Thanks," I finally got out, feeling safe, not wanting to leave the warmth of his arms. I lifted my head and looked into his eyes.

He stared at me for what seemed like forever, looking like he wanted to kiss me and throttle me at the same time. I knew exactly how he felt. "You're welcome, I think. Though this hurt a lot more than it would have ten years ago. I'm going to pay for this tomorrow, I'm sure."

"We should probably go, huh?" I asked.

"Probably," he responded.

"Why aren't you moving?"

"I'm not sure I can."

"Me either."

"Besides, you're on top."

"Oh . . ." Soft snowflakes started to fall from the darkening sky above us and stuck to his thick, sooty eyelashes as he gazed up at me, looking troubled and confused. That made two of us.

I blinked and my lips parted.

He stared and licked his lips.

My head started to lower with a will of its own, and he didn't pull away. I had almost made contact when a car horn sounded from down the street, and we both jumped. I scrambled to my feet, and he frowned, rolling to his feet much slower.

"We need to talk," he said.

"Ya think?" I squeaked.

"Not here."

"Then where?"

"My place." He nailed me with a hard stare. "I'm not going near that demon cat of yours."

I swallowed dryly. "Take the lead, Detective."

He locked eyes on me for a good ten seconds, then said, "Don't worry, Tink. I plan to."

# 8

I followed Mitch home and parked my bug in the driveway of his apartment complex. The building was made of red brick to better withstand the lake effect snow the area gets hammered with all winter long.

"You coming, Tink?" Mitch turned around and looked down at me from his perch on the staircase.

Of course he had to live on the top floor in an apartment with a cast-iron staircase on the outside of the building. Just my luck. I was freezing, and my sneakers were slippery. Not like boots made for snow and ice. I really hadn't been prepared for a sleuthing expedition, but I'd sooner fall on my butt than admit that to Detective Stone.

As though reading my mind, he grabbed my hand and pulled me along behind him, ignoring my slips and stumbles. Finally we reached the top. He unlocked the door and held it open for me to pass through.

"Thanks," I said, stepping inside and surveying his home.

I blinked, totally surprised. I would have thought he'd have the standard bachelor pad, but he didn't. Black leather furniture filled the room, white painted bookshelves lined the walls, and fabulous paintings of New York City were strategically placed around the room. Marble sculptures sat atop tile-and-glass end tables and the coffee table.

Modern, elegant, and classy—who knew?

"I can cook, too." Mitch narrowed his eyes at my expression, closed the door behind him, and hung up his sports coat. He set his gun on the table and rolled up the sleeves of his dress shirt.

"Wow, I just thought . . . wow."

"It's one of those 'you can take the man out of the city, but you can't take the city out of the man' things, I guess." He headed for the kitchen. "There's a fleece throw inside the ottoman if you're cold."

I lifted the top off the ottoman and pulled out the softest, most luxurious fleece blanket with gorgeous tigers scattered all over the fabric in various poses. Powerful and dangerous creatures, yet extremely gentle when they wanted to be.

Kind of reminded me of someone else.

Mitch carried a cup of coffee for himself and cocoa for me into the living room and set them on the coffee table in front of the couch. I gave him a surprised look, but he hoisted a shoulder and said, "Just a guess," making me wonder what that was supposed to mean. He stared at me with his hands on his hips for a moment and then chose the seat beside me on the buttery-smooth leather couch.

The smell of leather, soap, and the outdoors drifted past my nose. Instinctively, I scooted back an inch.

"Why did you bring me here?" I asked, not sure I wanted to know the answer.

He blew out a huge breath and looked me in the eye. "It seems we have no choice except to work together, but neither one of us can do our jobs efficiently if we don't clear the air between us."

"The air looks clear to me," I sputtered.

"Are you kidding me? It's full of tension, and I can't take it anymore." He surged to his feet and began to pace the room, then stopped and faced me, square on. "You're acting weirder than usual, Tink."

My jaw unhinged.

"Don't give me that look." He pointed at me. "I want to know why."

"Trust me, you really don't." I let out a sigh. "Thank you for the cocoa, by the way, but I'm afraid it's not going to be enough to get me through this conversation." I patted the seat beside me. "Sit down. You're putting a crick in my neck."

He eyed me warily and then sat beside me on the couch. I took a sip of creamy chocolate, wishing for some of Carolyn Hanes's whiskey right about now. Then I set my cup down and rubbed my hands together, missing the warmth already. This time, *he* scooted back an inch.

"I'm listening," he said.

He might be listening, but I knew in my gut he wouldn't believe me. He was right, though. We couldn't go on with all this tension between us if we were ever going to solve this case.

"All righty, then. Here goes." I took a deep breath. "That day in my house when you met my parents and drank my tea, I, um, sort of read your tea leaves after you left."

"Wait a minute." He held up his hand in a stop motion. "Not that I buy into any of this, but isn't that, like, an ethics issue? Don't you need my permission or something?" He took a sip of his coffee, looking as though he were contemplating the situation. Knowing him, he was probably trying to see if he had enough grounds to press charges.

"Gee, I don't remember you asking me for my permission when you called my parents and checked me out. Consider this my way of checking you out."

"It's not the same. You invaded my privacy." He glared at me.

"Ha! Trust me, talking to my parents is sooo invading *my* privacy." I glared right back.

"Whatever. This is getting us nowhere. Let's call it a draw." He swiped his hand through the air, and then we both grew silent. After several more tension-filled minutes, he stared down into the depths of his cup, not meeting my eyes as he finally asked in a quiet, curious voice, "So what'd you see, anyway?"

I chewed my lip, feeling ridiculous over what I had to say. Especially given the fact that all we did was argue. "Fine, but remember, you asked. When I read your tea leaves, I thought I was seeing into your past. You know . . . your relationship with your ex-girlfriend."

Mitch's jaw bulged, and he stared me down. I could tell his teeth were clenched, but all he said was, "Go on."

"You were arguing about something. Big surprise there." I couldn't help but get that little jab in.

He smirked, and I fluttered my lashes. I was the one to look away first.

"Then you kissed her. I've never seen—or felt—so much passion." I peeked up at him.

His eyes flashed with an expression of pain and sorrow but only for a second.

"And love," I added.

His eyes narrowed slightly, looking a little disbelieving and confused.

"And finally heartache," I finished.

"The heartache I buy. What I don't get is why that vision disturbed you so much. Why do you care about my love life?"

"Because my vision wasn't of your past like I first thought. I read your future by mistake." My eyes locked onto his and held. "And the woman was me."

His eyelids sprang wide-open, and his mouth parted slightly. He couldn't seem to look away from my lips. "You?" his deep voice rumbled in shock.

"Now do you see why I'm so disturbed and full of tension around you?" I wrapped his blanket more securely around my shoulders, feeling suddenly vulnerable.

I should have known his "true" self would put me at ease soon enough, though. He doubled over, laughing harder than I'd ever seen him. He'd stop, look at me, and then start laughing all over again. This went on for a good ten minutes until I'd had enough.

"If you're done now, I'll be going. I've got a salon to visit tomorrow and a date with a real man." I stood up.

That stopped his laughter. He climbed to his feet as well. "Sean O'Malley is not a real man. He's a boy toy."

"Gee, why should my love life disturb you?"

He held up his hands. "Hey, whatever pixies your dust, Tink."

I folded the detective's blanket, put it back in the ottoman, and headed toward the door without another word. Why did I let the big oaf get to me?

"There is one way to prove your little vision wrong, you know," his deep voiced rumbled from right behind my ear, and I nearly flew out of my skin.

"Yeah, what's that?" I asked, slipping my shoes back on and still not facing him. I didn't dare.

"This," he answered, spun me around, and then swooped down to kiss me hard on the lips.

My eyes widened, then crossed, then slowly fluttered closed. His lips were so firm and warm and tingly. He started to pull back, but I stood on his feet and wrapped my arms around his neck, plastering my body to his. He hesitated a second and then deepened his kiss.

Blazing heat shot through my veins. Chocolate mixed with coffee made the most delicious mocha taste fill my senses. He plunged a hand into my hair, cradling the back of my head, and pulled me even closer with his other arm wrapped tight around me. He'd obliterated the chill from my body until every cell poured out steam.

I was on fire!

Suddenly, he tore his mouth from mine and stared at me in shock and horror. He stepped back and rebuttoned the front of his shirt that I had somehow undone halfway, then cleared his throat. He couldn't quite meet my eyes as he said, "See? My point is proven. I felt nothing."

*Liar!* my mind screamed, and I gaped at him. I inhaled a shaky breath and tugged my torn hoodie down over my tank to cover my bra, which had miraculously undone itself as well. "Me too. Absolutely nothing. See you tomorrow, partner."

"Boss."

"Whatever."

I grabbed my keys, slipped outside, and welcomed the relief of the icy evening air as only one thought matched the pounding in my head:

Much ado about nothing just took on a whole new meaning.


After a sleepless night and a failed (alcohol-laden) attempt to obliterate the touch and taste of one hot, yummy, annoying butthead of a detective, I had a serious case of cotton mouth and a nasty headache.

Nothing, my big ole behind!

All I knew was, damn the detective for making me acutely aware he had a whole lot more than grumpiness in his pants. And damn him for proving my vision right. I didn't need heartache right now, and I certainly couldn't afford the distraction.

He hadn't helped the tension one bit. If anything, he'd made our situation a whole lot worse. This was ridiculous. We were adults. We would simply have to choose to control ourselves and focus on solving this case.

Someone pounded on my door, and I winced, grabbing my head. "Coming," I said in a voice that wasn't very loud but was all I could manage under the circumstances. I peered through the peephole and saw Jo, looking fabulous as always. I opened the door with a wince.

"Hey, you, are you ready to go?" She flipped her burgundy hair back and scanned my body. "Scratch that, you are beyond ready. We need to leave, pronto."

Allowing her to lead me to her car, we got in and she drove past Gretta's Mini-Mart and two blocks down to Pump up the Volume Hair Salon and Spa. We walked inside and the room oozed comfort and class. Overstuffed chairs to sit on, cucumber or lemon water to sip, the latest magazines to read, soothing sounds of nature to relax to, and therapeutic smells to boggle the senses. I had to admit I was beginning to understand the appeal.

Everyone recognized Jo immediately, which didn't surprise me. She had class and style coming out her ears.

Me . . . not so much.

"Tracy," Jo said to the owner. "We're gonna need the whole enchilada for this one."

"No worries, I've got the perfect package."

A while later after having my ultra-pale blond hair low-lighted with golden blond streaks, Tracy placed me under the heating lamp and set the timer. Then she dragged Jo off to have her own burgundy highlights touched up. I picked up a magazine and pretended to read while I listened to the conversations around me.

A few ladies from the Historical Society—the loudest wore an ultra-modern, gaudy, leopard-print scarf I'd not soon forget—were complaining about some bigwig new guy in town who'd been trying to close down the library and open a chain bookstore. They were speculating that maybe he had killed Amanda Robbins because she was his biggest adversary when she was alive.

*Note to self: check out bigwig and avoid store where Scarf Lady shops.*

They paid and left while a group of freshly dyed women who called themselves the Bunco Babes took their place under the dryers. They started chatting on and on about their recent escapades and the latest gossip circulating around town.

Nurse Doolittle walked in and stopped to chat with them. She thanked one of them for helping her carry the doctor's dry cleaning into his house the week before. My mind raced. That meant she must have had a key, and what day had this happened? I leaned closer as the shampoo lady took her in the back to wash her hair.

I jumped at the chance to speak to the other women while Nurse Doolittle was out of earshot. "Hi, I'm Sunny," I said to the one who was sitting closest to me.

"Well, hi there. I'm Lulubelle, but everyone calls me Belle. I've heard about you." She wagged her brows. "I can't wait until you reopen your sanctuary. I don't care what those busybody old church ladies say about you being heathen and all. I don't believe a word of it. Why, you look too cute to be a devil-worshipping murderer."

"Thanks, I think." Good Lord, being psychic did not make me a devil worshipper, and since when had I closed down my fortune-telling business? I'd have to set the record straight, but right now Belle was on a roll, and I didn't want to distract her.

"I'm living on the wild side today. Went from a blonde to a brunette and even cut my bangs. Maybe this will finally make Big Don down at Don's Auto wake up and notice me." Belle was a large woman with equally large hair and cherubic cheeks. "I mean, I can't afford to keep having bodywork done on my car, but I do have another body he can tackle anytime he wants." She winked.

"I'm sure he'll love it," I replied. "I mean, your new look. Speaking of men, I overheard you talking to Tina Doolittle. If Miss Doolittle is a nurse, how come she was picking up the doctor's dry cleaning?" I prodded, hoping to get the conversation back on track.

Belle leaned in close and whispered, though why she bothered, I had no clue. Her whisper was loud enough to wake the people in the next county. "I asked her the same thing. She said she was being nice on account of the bad mood the doc was in after his fight with Amanda Robbins that morning. He swore revenge and then took off, leaving his waiting room full of angry patients. She took his spare key from the office, picked up his dry cleaning, and dropped it off. Only, it don't take that long to drop off a load of clothes. I can't imagine what that woman was doing in there all that time." Her laugh was bawdy and raucous, drawing several eyes in our direction.

I flushed self-consciously and leaned in to meet her halfway, lowering my voice so only she could hear. "Oh my, you mean the doctor is her Big Don?"

"Oh no no no, child. Don't get me wrong. That one would love for Doc Wilcox to do bodywork on her, but he's as blind as Big Don. Always pining after the librarian when he has a perfectly good woman right under his nose." She harrumphed. "That Tina's a fool for running his errands. The things a woman will do to get a man's attention." She shook her head, and her triple chins jiggled.

"Any chance you remember what time she delivered the doc's laundry that night?"

Belle pursed her lips in thought. "Sure do. That was the night I hosted Bunco. She came just before we started around six and stayed until nearly seven. I know because I heard her car start and looked out the window. That's what made me wonder what in the world could possibly take that much time to deliver a man's laundry."

"Hmmm, so that means she has an alibi," I mused.

"Oh, honey, that child couldn't hurt a flea. The doc on the other hand was mad enough to exterminate something or someone, that's for sure. Mmmhmmm. That Tina was up to something, all right. The question is what?"

"It certainly looks that way," I said, making another mental note to find out what Ms. Doolittle had been snooping for. She and the doc might both have alibis, but that didn't mean he hadn't been mad enough to hire someone to kill the librarian for him. It was a bit of a stretch, but the city girl in me couldn't help thinking big.

*Ding.* The timer on Lulubelle's dryer went off. Tracy came over to check out Belle's hair, then glanced at me and did a double take as though just now remembering something important. She stared at her watch in shock. "Oh dear."

"Oh dear?" I choked out. "As in 'Oh dear, your hair is going to look fabulous,' or 'Oh dear, I made a mistake and you're not going to want to look in the mirror'?"

Tracy hid her hand mirror behind her back, speaking volumes.

"Oh God," was all I said.

"God can't help you now, child," Belle pointed out. "I do believe you're the victim of a faulty timer."

"What does that mean?" I squeaked.

"Basically that your color stayed on way too long," Tracy clarified, and summoned one of her assistants. "Raoulle, take Sunny to the wash bin, stat! There might still be time to save her."

Raoulle jogged over, lifted the dryer, pulled back the foil, and let out a yelp that had me shaking in my chair. "Don't worry, honey, we can trim most of this right off. Come with me, and we'll fix you right up."

I stood and started to turn toward the mirror, but he threw a towel over my head and dragged me behind him. "Trust me, sweetie, you don't want to see what's under there just yet."

Hours later after washing and cutting and attempting to repair my hair, they tried to make up for it by plastering my face with makeup and giving me a complimentary mani/pedi.

"It's not that bad, really." Joanne looked at me, but the grimace on her face did not match the words coming out of her mouth.

I glanced in the mirror and could have cried. Forget looking like a cute, pixie Tinker Bell. I looked like a nearly bald Cinderella's fairy godmother. They'd butchered me. My hair was so short, my lovely golden blond highlights were gray, and my face looked like a drag queen's. Hell, I had the nails and toes to match. Add a skimpy outfit, and I would be ready to hit the streets.

"And this, my friend, is why I am *not* a salon girl. How am I supposed to go on a date like this?" I asked.

"Look on the bright side. I haven't met a woman Sean didn't like yet, so you should be good." Jo grimaced and added, "I'm so sorry."

"Sean liking me is the least of my worries. How am I going to get anyone to take me seriously like this? I'm supposed to be working on this case, but I look like a freak."

"Tracy said the lowlights will fade pretty quickly, and you said yourself that your hair grows fast. In a couple weeks, you can have them colored over. In the meantime, roll with it. It gives you attitude."

"It makes me look old." I moaned, but there was one positive outcome to my new look.

Maybe now Mitch wouldn't try to kiss me again.

# 9

❀❖✳❖✳❖✳✳❖✳❖❀

The sun shined bright in a crystal clear blue sky and sparkled off the snow surrounding the outdoor man-made ice rink in the park in the center of town. It kind of reminded me of a mini–Central Park.

I inhaled the clean, crisp air and felt rejuvenated as I sat on a wrought-iron bench next to a brass lantern and laced up my skates. The rink was pretty empty since kids were still in school and most people were working.

After my disturbing episode with the detective last night, I took Sean up on his offer and called him that morning. We decided to go ice-skating today, so I told him I would have Jo drop me off here after we had lunch. She hadn't let me go home to try to repair the damage from the salon, saying the look really complimented me now. Tracy had taken over for Raoulle and added some gel, giving me a spiky look that made the gray appear more like silver glitter.

She'd said the short, sassy look suited the angles of my face, making me appear more sophisticated. She'd even toned down my makeup, adding a touch of pink blush, pale green shadow that enhanced my eyes, and clear lip gloss that made my natural rosy lips shine. I had to admit I felt better about my new look now, and given the rare sunny day, my mood had definitely been lifted.

"Sunny?" Sean said, shading his eyes from the bright rays of sunlight and staring down at me in wonder. "You look amazing."

I couldn't help but grin like an imbecile, my mood was just that good. "Thanks. I feel amazing compared to earlier."

His brow puckered curiously, his dimples still peeking out at me.

"Don't ask." I snickered. "Race ya," I said, jumping to my feet and taking off on the ice at full speed.

I wore hockey skates, preferring them to figure skates, much to my mother's horror. Figure skates had always killed my ankles, and that had pretty much squashed her dream of seeing me in the Olympics. Just one more way I'd let her down. On the bright side, my father loved hockey, although he wasn't too fond of having a daughter who could kick all the local boys' butts.

"Hey, wait up," Sean yelled after me. He could skate, but he wasn't nearly as good as me.

We raced around the rink five loops, and I beat the pants off of him every time.

"I am the champion, my friend," I sang, laughing with my hands fist-pumping the air.

"You are a cheater, is what you are," he sang back, swatting me on the rump as he circled by me.

"Am not!" I knocked his hand away and pulled my puffy coat down lower over my jeans.

"I let you win." He crossed his arms over his leather bomber jacket, his eyes holding a teasing glint.

"Did not!" I shoved him back and skated over to the bench.

"I had a . . . what was it? Oh yeah, a pain in my side. Cramps." He repeated my excuse from the gym the other day. "At least I didn't wimp out and take a rain check."

"Funny. You can't admit I'm better than you." I unlaced my skates and pulled on my boots.

"You're good, lass, I'll give you that." He winked. "And I'll buy you a hot chocolate since you won."

I glanced up and saw Carolyn Hanes drive by with the lady from the Historical Society, who wore the wild leopard-print scarf.

"Deal," I said, staring after them. "Do you mind if we try out the café next door to the library? I heard it was good, and I've been meaning to check it out."

"Sounds like a plan."

Fifteen minutes later we were seated at a small round wrought-iron table with matching chairs by a window inside of Warm Beginnings & Cozy Endings Café, with a perfect view of the library. I ordered a white hot chocolate with raspberry cream, and Sean ordered a cappuccino.

"This is nice, Sean. Thank you for today. I needed it."

He blew on his coffee and studied me over the rim of his cup in a rare serious mood for him. "Things have been tough for you lately, huh?"

"That's the understatement of the year. I came here for a fresh start and now look at me. Everything's such a mess. I might be helping to solve this case, but I'm still a suspect. I don't have an alibi."

"I'll be your alibi." He touched my hand.

"I'm serious, Sean." I pulled my hand away. "I could be in big trouble if we don't find the real killer soon. Captain Walker said Mayor Cromwell wants this case closed, like, yesterday, and Chief Spencer is all over us to find some answers now."

"Come on, you can't be serious. Anyone who gets to know you can see you're not the murdering type."

"Anyone except Detective Stone." The chocolate curdled in my belly, and a sour taste hit the back of my throat.

"Mitch isn't so bad once you get to know him. He's just giving you a hard time because he's a cynic."

"Doesn't matter. I wouldn't put it past him to find a way to pin this whole thing on me, circumstantial evidence or not."

"Then we'd better get busy."

My eyes met his. "We?"

"Jo's not your only friend, love." Sean tweaked my cheek. "I meant it when I said I'm here for you. You need anything at all, let me know."

I reached out and squeezed his hand. "Thanks, Sean, that means a lot."

A movement outside the window caught my eye. A tall thin man got out of his fancy car, carrying a briefcase and wearing a suit. He headed into the library.

"Who's that?" I asked.

Sean followed where I looked out the window. "Oh, that's Pendleton. He's been trying to get the library closed down for the past year so he can use the land and put up a chain bookstore. Amanda Robbins was completely against it, but now that she's gone, who knows what will happen?"

"Why not just open the bookstore someplace else in hopes of driving the library out of business?"

"Divinity is very old-fashioned and against overbuilding. There isn't enough land available that's zoned for commercial businesses around here. The library is a nonprofit organization owned by the town, but the town needs money. Something like the bookstore would bring in more jobs and revenue, but the town was divided. Amanda Robbins was highly respected and a very persuasive person."

"I saw Amanda's neighbor, Carolyn Hanes, who also works at the library. She drove by earlier, and she had some lady from the Historical Society with her. I recognized her from the salon this morning. Couldn't miss her with that crazy scarf she wears. Do you think she's trying to stop Carolyn from keeping the library open?"

"I can't imagine Carolyn would be in favor of the deal. If the library closes, she is out of a job, but you never know. Why don't we go find out? I've been meaning to

127

browse the shelves. Now is as good a time as any, I'm thinking."

"You read?" I smiled slowly.

"Cute."

"I try. Now pay our tab, and let's get out of here. You still owe me for whooping your butt on the ice."

"Yeah, yeah. Head on over. I'm right behind ya."

"That's what I'm afraid of." I laughed and hurried outside, covering my backside. Sean chuckled from behind me, paid our tab, and quickly joined me. We headed across the street to the library.

It was smaller than I'd thought it would be, but scenic pictures of the Adirondack Mountains and rivers of upstate New York graced the walls. Light oak bookshelves stood in rows like a set of dominoes, and small tables were scattered about in strategic places.

It was pleasant and inviting.

Sean and I mingled among the patrons. He made a beeline for the romance section while I wandered over to the mystery aisle, trying not to giggle. The man was a piece of work but so stinking lovable.

"Can I help you with something, dear?" said a feeble feminine voice from beside me.

I turned and saw the little old lady from Dr. Wilcox's office. Donning a friendly smile, I held out my hand. "I'm Sunshine Meadows, but you can call me Sunny. I saw you in Dr. Wilcox's office the other day."

She straightened her crooked glasses and studied me with watery blue eyes, her hair as frizzy and blue-tinged as ever. "Hmmm, dear, I don't remember, but it's nice to meet you just the same. You have a lovely name." She held my hand in both of hers and patted the top, the sleeve of her overcoat nearly covering us both. "My name's Maude Sampson."

"I'm really enjoying the homey atmosphere of Divinity. Everyone is so friendly." Well, almost everyone, but she didn't need to hear me rant about one tall, dark, and ornery detective.

"Divinity is a wonderful place to live. Why, my Bernard has worked in the steel mill all his life and provided such a good home for me and my girls. They're all grown-up and off raising their own families these days." She looked a little sad, swiping away tears. "I miss them so." She sighed. "But not to worry. I still have my work to keep me busy."

"Work? But I thought your husband said you were retired."

She blinked, looking confused for a moment. Then her eyes widened with awareness, and she looked around the room as though just now realizing where she was. "Silly me. I worked at the library for so many years. I sometimes forget I don't work here anymore." She yawned. "Excuse me. I don't sleep well at night. Do you have the time?"

I glanced at my watch. "It's three thirty."

"Oh dear, I was supposed to meet Bernard for lunch today, and it completely slipped my mind. He's going to be so mad. I'll have to make it up to him by cooking him his favorite dinner. It was wonderful meeting you, Miss Meadows." She buttoned up her coat, and my eyes widened as I realized she still had her apron on beneath it.

"Please, call me Sunny," I said after her, but she kept

129

hurrying toward the door in her, dear Lord in heaven, mismatched shoes. And I thought I was forgetful. I shook my head with a chuckle and started browsing the latest titles when I overheard hushed voices from the other side of the shelves.

"What's taking so long? This should be a done deal by now," a man's voice said.

"She's a harder nut to crack than Amanda was, if you can believe that," said a woman's voice.

I quietly slid a book out of the shelves, and the smell of dust mixed with fresh paper drifted past my nose. I stifled a sneeze and peeked through the slot to the other side. The man was Pendleton, which wasn't really a surprise, and I immediately recognized the wild scarf of the lady from the Historical Society.

My jaw hit the book beneath it with a resounding smack. I ducked and waited a minute until they resumed talking.

At the salon, she'd made it sound like she was the one most responsible for stopping Pendleton from turning the library into a chain bookstore. She'd even feared Pendleton might have killed Amanda Robbins to make the deal go through. Yet here the old crone was whispering in secret to the man she pretended to despise. I was beginning to worry about Carolyn Hanes's safety.

"Maybe it's time we tried new tactics," said another female voice. "We're running out of time, but we can't talk here. I have a plan. I'll notify you both with your instructions soon."

I pressed my lips together and tried not to breathe as I slid the book back in place. I knew that voice. Footsteps sounded as the trio exited the other row, and I dug my iPod out of my satchel and slipped the earbuds into place just in time.

Bee-bopping my head to the music, I plastered a surprised expression on my face when Pendleton, the lady from the Historical Society, and Carolyn Hanes herself rounded the corner. Pendleton and the other woman kept walking and exited the library, while Carolyn stopped before me.

"Miss Meadows, fancy seeing you here," she said, looking a little stunned and . . . guilty.

"Huh? Oh, sorry." I pulled the earbuds out. "Can't hear a thing with these darn earbuds in. What did you say?"

She regained her composure. "I was wondering if you decided to become a member of our fine library."

"You know, I'm thinking I might. You have a great selection of books here."

She looked down to the mystery I held in my hand. "That's a good choice. I take it you like mysteries?"

"Love them." I clapped my hands. "There's nothing like trying to figure out who done it and discovering you were right."

"Hmmm, yes, I suppose that is quite thrilling. Well, I've got to run. So many things to do without Amanda here." She looked genuinely sad, which confused me even more. "Enjoy yourself, and good luck to you in figuring out the ending."

"Thanks." I wrinkled my forehead, watching her scurry away.

Sean drew up beside me. "What was Gladys Montgomery doing with Pendleton? She's head of the Historical

Society and has been trying to get the library declared a National Historical Landmark. The last thing she'd let a bigwig like Pendleton do is tear down one of her babies to put up something commercial."

"I'm not sure, but I intend to find out. She wasn't against the chain bookstore and neither was Carolyn Hanes, apparently. What I want to know is who is the 'she' that is more stubborn than Amanda Robbins was in regard to this deal with Pendleton? They could all be in cahoots and have committed the murder together."

"You really think so?"

"It's a possibility. Pendleton certainly seems angry and frustrated the deal hasn't gone through, Carolyn has small feet, and the Historical Society lady knows all the loopholes. I definitely have to do more digging on this angle. In the meantime, I'm pooped. Would you mind terribly if we called it a day?"

"Not at all. I have to work the night shift at Smokey Jo's soon, anyway, so I'll take you home." He juggled his armload of romance novels. "Let me check out these books, and we'll be on our way."

"Nice selection." I pressed my lips together. "Thanks, Sean. I really did have fun."

"Me too." He finished his transaction and then led the way outside and drove me home.


Once we got there, we were greeted by Morty, who was standing outside. The sun had already started to set, the rare sunshine fading fast, and the temperature began to drop. Soft snowflakes fell from the darkening sky once more. I couldn't afford a snow blower or a driveway service. I groaned. Looked like I'd have to shovel later. So much for getting some rest.

Morty meowed, bringing me back to reality.

"You left your cat out in the cold all day?" Sean asked.

"No. I don't know how the little stinker gets in or out, but he pretty much goes where he wants to. He even escaped from the vet's. I swear he's Houdini." *Or magical*, I thought, but didn't want to spook Sean.

Sean shrugged. "You're a pretty cool lad, aren't ya?" He knelt down and reached out to scratch the cat behind the ears. To my complete and utter amazement, Morty let him.

"He likes you," I sputtered.

"Don't sound so shocked. People aren't the only species I have a way with." Sean grinned and stood.

"I can see that. I'm just stunned. Morty is beyond finicky."

Morty stuck his nose in the air, sniffed, puckered his face as though he smelled something he didn't like, and then sauntered around to the back of the house like he owned the place. Oh, who were we kidding? He and I both knew he did. He was probably off somewhere killing his dinner and then sneaking back inside through some secret entrance. I had to admit, he kept things interesting.

"Thanks, Sean. We'll have to do this again some time." I held out my hand.

Sean smiled slow and sweet, took my hand, then pulled me into him. "Anytime, love. Now let me show

133

you how we say good-bye in Ireland." He bent his head, kissed me square on the mouth, and turned on his heel toward his beat-up SUV.

He was such a sweet, cute, fun guy, but I had truly felt absolutely nothing from that kiss. Not like when . . .

"If you're done goofing off and making out with Boy Toy, don't you think it's time we got to work?" said a deep voice from the shadows.

I whirled around and grabbed my heart. "Would you stop sneaking up on me like that? And we weren't making out, not that it's any of your business. He was saying good-bye."

Mitch grunted. "According to you and your stupid vision, it should be my business. Lucky for you, I don't buy into any of that. I don't like waiting around for twenty minutes," Mitch snapped. "You said you would be done with Boy Toy at four." He tapped his watch. "It's four thirty, Tink. Shouldn't you be turning back into a pumpkin by now?"

"Wrong fairy tale, and you are so not Prince Charming. Besides, the mice turned into horses and the pumpkin turned into a carriage. Cinderella was just trying to be herself. Kind of like me."

"Mice?" he said, scanning the tree in front of the yard. "Don't cats eat mice?"

I opened the door and went inside, realizing I'd either left it unlocked by mistake, or Morty really was a Houdini cat. "It's freezing out," I said to the detective. "If you want to talk to me, you're going to have to come inside, cat or no cat."

Several minutes later, the detective finally came inside

and closed the door behind him, his hand hovering above his weapon. "But I thought we could go get something to eat and go over our notes."

"I'm too tired to go anywhere else today. He's not going to get you, you big scaredy-cat."

"You're not the one he pulls those freaky *Exorcist* moves on." The detective followed me to the kitchen, his eyes darting around constantly. After a few minutes, he relaxed and sat down at the kitchen table.

"Quit being so grumpy. You want tea?" I asked.

"No, I want food, and I'm not grumpy," he growled. "I'm starving."

"This isn't a diner, you know."

"Relax, Tink." He barked out a laugh. "I'm not fooling myself into thinking you can cook."

"I can cook." I opened my pantry and realized I had nothing but the cat food I'd bought when I first moved here, the cat food Morty never ate. Hmmm, maybe . . . "Want some tuna fish?"

The detective peeked in the cupboard from behind me and that darn eyebrow of his inched up in the most annoying way again. "Nice try," he said sarcastically. "I'll take my chances with takeout."

He knew me too well already. I'd serve him cat food in a heartbeat and not lose a wink of sleep over it. "Suit yourself." I closed the cupboard. "So much for getting rid of the tension between us."

"Hey, you're the one who told me about your ridiculous vision." He shook his head. "If you hadn't read my tea leaves, there wouldn't be any tension between us."

I faced him head-on. "Thought you felt nothing?"

His eyes locked on mine and then dropped to my lips as he mumbled, "I didn't."

"Then why are you even grouchier than usual?"

He surged to his feet and squared off in front of me. "Because I'm hungry, dammit!" He stared at my lips again, definitely looking hungry, but I doubted food had anything to do with it. With a growl, he huffed off to my wall phone and ordered Chinese.

I opened another cupboard to make a cup of tea and sucked in a sharp breath. I quickly shut the cupboard door before Mitch returned.

"What's wrong?" he asked, frowning at me as he walked back into the room. "You look a little green."

"I'm fine. Just lost my pixie dust is all. Too much excitement for one day. I couldn't eat a bite if I tried. Can we do this another time?"

The lines between his brows deepened further. "Fine, but we need to compare notes no later than tomorrow. Call if you need anything."

I nodded, followed him to the door, and locked it tight, but Detective Stone was the last person I would call concerning this matter. I headed right back to the cupboard I'd opened for the tea and stared at the bottle of digoxin, with the name scratched off the prescription label, sitting right next to the canister.

Someone was setting me up.

# 10

❀✖❀✖❀

Early the next morning, the doorbell rang. I padded in my Elmer Fudd pajamas and Bugs Bunny slippers to the front door to see who had the gall to ring my bell this early.

I looked through the peephole and should have known.

Opening the door, I yawned and stepped back. "Morning, Mom. Dad. How's it hanging?"

"It isn't hanging, but *you* might be if you don't quit slacking off," my father said as he pushed his way inside while checking his pulse. He wore his black running suit and white sneakers as though he'd been out power walking all morning. Yet he still didn't have a hair out of place.

"We've let you play cops and robbers long enough, darling." Mom followed close behind, sporting a cream track suit, a matching visor, and sneakers as well. They looked like cover models for a seniors' fitness magazine. "It's time we got serious about solving this case," she continued. "I want to know everything. What you have, who you've talked to, where you're going."

"All before hot chocolate?" I asked. "Scratch that. Forget the cocoa, I'll take a cocktail. It must be five o'clock somewhere," I added, shutting the door behind them.

A hand slipped in between the wall and the door at the last second, pushing it back open until a head popped inside. "I'll take some coffee." Mitch stepped inside, looking fabulous in a matching soft gray NYPD sweat suit left over from his former glory days. "How about that talk we never got to have last night, Tink?" he asked. "You look like you're feeling better."

"And you guys look like the Three Stooges." I crossed my arms over my tank top self-consciously. It was 7 A.M. I wasn't exactly dressed for company. "What are you guys, the exercise brigade?"

"I heard you bailed on your exercise session. You should try it sometime. Like maybe shovel your driveway for a start." He stomped the snow off his sneakers.

"I was too tired last night, and you three are way too peppy this early. How did you meet up, anyway?"

"I bumped into your parents on my run this morning." Mitch shoved a hand through his hair. "One thing led to another, and we decided to continue in your direction and all work together. Kill two birds with one stone, so to speak." He winked.

I scowled.

The only reason he was in a good mood was because

he'd caught me off guard and he'd flustered me by bringing my parents over. I'd get him back, but right now I had no choice except to play along. I sooo couldn't function without my morning hot chocolate, and he knew it.

"It's déjà vu all over again," I said as I closed the door behind Detective Stone. "My life totally sucks."

"Sylvia, please. The good detective is only trying to help." My dad's face puckered like a dried tea leaf. "And it had better not be déjà vu." His eyes looked toward the kitchen. "I think I'll take my coffee out in the living room this time."

"Where is that albino rat of yours, anyway?" Mom asked, searching the room warily.

"He's around," I said, not bothering to correct her. It would do no good, anyway. "Do we really have to do this right now? I'm not even awake yet," I whined.

"Honestly, Sylvia, if I didn't know better, I would think you don't care if you have to do thirty years to life for murder."

I sighed. "Of course I don't want to do time for a murder I didn't commit. However, you all are making solving this case very hard on me." I walked toward the kitchen. "Anyone want tea?"

"Hell no," Mitch blurted. We exchanged looks, and his horrified eyes told me all I needed.

"How about we have coffee by the fire out in the living room?" Dad suggested.

Mitch's eyes narrowed. "You can't read coffee grounds, can you?"

"I'll never tell." I tossed a wink right back at him.

"You don't scare me, Tink." He leaned in until our

faces were mere inches apart, and my heart sped up. He glanced at the pulse throbbing in my neck, and the corner of his lip tipped up a hair. "Bet I scare the hell out of you, though, don't I?"

"Fine," I snapped, taking a step back. "You guys find a spot to sit, and I'll join you in a minute."

Mitch scanned the room even more warily than my mother had.

"Now who's the scared one?" I wrinkled my nose. "Morty is still upstairs if that's what you're worried about."

"Who says I'm worried?" he muttered.

"Um, your hunched shoulders and stiff neck."

He relaxed and stood up straight. "Nonsense."

"Whatever." I trudged into the kitchen and suddenly remembered I had been too tired last night to deal with the digoxin. It was still in the cupboard by the tea canister.

"Need any help?" Mitch said from behind me after following me into the room.

I whirled around, wide-eyed.

He studied me carefully. "I really do scare you, don't I? I was just kidding, Tink."

"I'm fine," I said, and put the coffee on.

He opened a cupboard to take out the mugs, and I nearly had a heart attack, yelping, "No!"

His hand froze, and he looked at me over his very broad shoulder.

I bit my bottom lip and peeked inside, but the digoxin was gone. Just a paw print remained from my furry Houdini friend. *Thank you, Morty*, I thought, and closed my eyes, wilting against the sink. When I opened them, I caught Mitch eyeing me critically.

"You're not fine," he said. "Something more than *me* is bothering you for a change, and I want to know what."

"It's just this case." I loaded up a tray with mugs, cream, sugar—Splenda for Mom, of course—and cocoa packs. "You're right." I turned to him. "We need to compare notes. Figure out a new lead before someone else gets hurt." I grabbed the coffeepot and headed into the living room with Mitch right behind me, carrying the tray.

Once we were all seated and sipping our brew, I began to feel more human and a little calmer. I had to figure out where Morty had hidden the evidence.

"Okay, ready to get started?" The detective rubbed his hands together and then took out his notebook and pen.

I gaped at him. "You carry a notebook on your run?"

"I always have my notebook with me, *especially* when I run. Exercise is a great way to sort things out."

"I'll take your word for it." I shook my head.

"With your aversion to exercise, you must have an amazing metabolism. You look great." Mitch's gaze roamed over my body.

"Thanks." I felt warm all over and didn't bother to cross my arms this time.

His eyes lingered on his way back up, and after an endless moment he met my eyes but didn't say a word. His smoldering look said it all.

"Let's start with what we know so far," my mother said.

141

The moment was ruined. I knew I couldn't have him, but that did *not* mean I didn't want him. And no matter what he said, I could tell he wanted me just as much.

We were so screwed.

"Right. Good idea." Mitch opened his notes. "Amanda Robbins went to see Sunny at five P.M. on the night she was murdered. Sunny read her tea leaves, and the reading revealed Ms. Robbins had twin tumors in her uterus and would be murdered by a man. Naturally, Ms. Robbins was upset. Sunny gave her some calming tea to drink later, and she left at six P.M. The coroner determined the murder took place at six thirty. Sunny called the police at seven, and I found the body around seven fifteen."

The detective took a sip of his coffee and scanned his notes before continuing. "Kip—that's the coroner—discovered Ms. Robbins had an allergic reaction to nuts that day, but that's not what killed her. She died from the tea she drank that was laced with digoxin and then hit her head when she fell. We found a set of small footprints outside of the deceased's window, but other than that there was no sign of a forced entry, leading us to believe Ms. Robbins knew the killer."

"Detective Stone brought me in for questioning shortly after that because the tea leaves laced with digoxin were mine," I interjected. "I was home at the time of the murder, trying to sort out my vision, but I don't have proof of my alibi. Yes, my feet are small, but I don't have access to digoxin. And the most important part of proving my innocence is that I don't have a motive."

I stood and paced. "I had nothing to gain from Ms.

Robbins's death. If anything, her murder has hurt my business. No one wants fortunes of doom and gloom. Mayor Cromwell is up for reelection, so he wants this case solved yesterday, and Chief Spencer told Captain Walker to use any means possible. So he made me partners with Detective Stone and ordered us to work together."

"She's my assistant, not my partner," Mitch clarified.

"Oh, would you let it go already?" I huffed, stopping before him with my hands on my hips.

"Just stating the facts." He looked up at me calmly and sipped his coffee. "When you prove yourself and earn the right to be my partner, I'll say so."

"Oooh, you are pigheaded. The last thing on earth I want is to be linked to you in any way. But I will prove I am just as good as you, mark my words."

"Consider them marked. Now can we get on with this? We don't have all day."

"Sit down, Sylvia," my mother said in full lawyer mode now. "As long as they don't find the murder weapon on you—digoxin in this case—then everything else is circumstantial."

"That's good," I responded, trying not to tremble. Now more than ever I knew Mitch couldn't find out about the digoxin that had been in my cupboard. He'd never believe someone was setting me up. He'd simply close the case and throw away the key.

"If that's good, then why do you look so shaky?" the far-too-observant detective asked.

"Because it's terrifying being the only suspect without an alibi," I answered, which was true. This whole situation had me freaked out. Yes, I wanted a new life in a new home, but preferably not one behind bars.

"They might have alibis, but they all have motive. Like you said, you don't. If you're telling the truth, then you shouldn't be so skittish," Mitch pointed out, waiting a moment, probably for me to reveal what else I wasn't telling him. He was a smart man. He knew something was up.

When I didn't speak, he continued. "Next up we questioned Carolyn Hanes. She was Ms. Robbins's neighbor and friend. She even worked at the library with her. Miss Hanes reported that Ms. Robbins was worried about the library's budget, having to let people go, and she had concerns about her love life, too. She was also afraid someone was stalking her at night, which probably has to do with the footsteps outside her bedroom window."

"Either that or there was a witness we don't know about," I added, still believing that was a strong possibility.

"Maybe," Mitch said, reading his notes once more. "Miss Hanes also heard Ms. Robbins arguing with a woman on the morning of her death. She didn't hear the whole conversation, but she did hear the woman say to stay away or she would be sorry. After the woman left, Ms. Robbins went to the doctor's office, which brings me to Dr. Wilcox."

"A fine young man, he is," my father boomed. "Good role model." He gave me a pointed look.

"He's not as fine as you think, Dad. After we had dinner with him, Detective Stone and I went to his office the next morning. He admitted he was in love with Ms. Robbins

144

but that she didn't love him back and never would. He offered to marry her and take care of her because of her poor health. Amanda turned him down flat, and he was furious. Yes, he has access to digoxin, and the whole waiting room heard him threaten that she would be sorry for turning him down, but his alibi checks out. Turns out he eats dinner every night at Papas at six P.M."

"The doc also said he treated Ms. Robbins for a nut allergy on the morning of her death. That's why she went to the doctor's," Mitch added. "He said she never would have eaten nuts knowingly and that all she'd eaten that morning was a banana muffin from Papas."

"That's right," I jumped in. "So then we went to see Callista Papas for lunch. She admitted she went to see Ms. Robbins on the morning of her death because she caters the library's book talks. They were discussing the menu, and she had Ms. Robbins try the banana muffin. She knew the librarian had a slight nut allergy, nothing life threatening, so she purposely ground up nuts and put them in, but she didn't know Ms. Robbins had been sick. Mrs. Papas wanted the librarian to suffer a little since the woman was sleeping with her husband, Damon. She warned her to stay away, and then she left."

"Do you think this Damon character is the killer?" my mother asked.

Mitch scanned his notes. "Maybe. Mr. Papas had tried to break things off with Ms. Robbins, but she wouldn't take no for an answer. She even tried to get pregnant to frame him, but that didn't work. He had a vasectomy, but his wife doesn't have a clue. She just thinks he's sterile and despises him because he can't give her a baby. They don't believe in divorce, so she lives to make his life miserable. She might have motive but doesn't have access to digoxin, and her alibi also checks out. She runs the dinner service at Papas every night."

"Her husband sounds like a real gem. I loathe people with no ambition," my father said, and I chose to believe he wasn't including me in that comment. I had plenty of ambition, just not in the fields he wanted me to. He went on. "What does the scoundrel do while his poor wife is working her fingers to the bone?"

"He keeps the books and plays school," I chimed in.

"Excuse me?" Mom asked.

Mitch's lips twitched. "Let's just say he dabbles in extracurricular activities. Like your daughter. He prefers starring in his own movies while she enjoys climbing trees."

I ignored him, taking over the conversation. "Damon Papas tackles the books during the day, then goes to the gym during the dinner shift. Except the guys at the gym haven't seen Damon in months. Turns out he's getting his workout in other ways. I followed him from the gym to a house on a dead-end street. During my stakeout—"

Mitch snorted. "That's one word for it."

I ignored his rude interruption and kept going. "I discovered he had already moved on to another fling. He's having an affair with the kindergarten teacher, Mary Kinkaid. Amanda was in love with Damon, but he was only using her because he's miserable with his wife. Yet he would never divorce her, either."

I finished the rest of my hot cocoa, finally feeling more awake. "So Amanda tried to trap Damon, but he broke it off with her and told her about his vasectomy. She wouldn't take no for an answer and kept hoping he'd change his mind. Even though Damon might have wanted to get rid of Amanda once and for all, he doesn't have access to digoxin, either, and his alibi also checks out. He was with Mary on the night of Amanda's murder."

"Then we're at a dead end, aren't we?" Mom asked.

"Maybe not," I answered. "Mrs. Papas did say something else. She said Dr. Wilcox might have an alibi, but what about his nurse? Rumor has it she has an even bigger crush on him than he did on Amanda Robbins."

"I tailed her—" Mitch began, but I cut him off.

"Really? Is that what you call it?" I blinked all innocent-like, and he ignored me just the same as I had him.

"But I didn't turn up anything out of the ordinary," Mitch continued.

"I had better luck at the salon," I said smugly. "Turns out Nurse Doolittle felt bad for the doctor, so she helped him out by bringing his dry cleaning home while he was at dinner. Except she spent an hour there on the night of the murder. Dropping off clothes doesn't take that long, so the real question is, what on earth was she doing that whole time?"

"If she was in love with him like you said, then she might have killed Ms. Robbins to get her out of the way and give herself a fighting chance with the good doctor," Mom said. "She would also have access to digoxin."

"It can't be her," I continued. "The doctor's neighbor saw her at the doctor's house at the exact time the murder happened. There's no way she could have killed

Amanda. Belle said she didn't have the stomach for it, anyway, but she also said the doctor was another story. He might have an alibi, but I do have to wonder if he could have hired someone to do it for him. You know, like a hit man."

Mitch rolled his eyes at me. "This isn't some TV show, Tink."

I sat up straighter. "It could happen."

He ignored my response.

"Let's forget about the doctor for now," Mom said. "Maybe it's time you brought his nurse in for questioning, Detective? Find out exactly what she was doing inside his house."

"Now, that's a smart suggestion, ma'am," he said, and I ground my teeth. Hadn't I just suggested that very thing?

"Good boy," Mom said, and they all carried on as if I wasn't even there. "And Donald, darling, why don't you make a dinner date with Dr. Wilcox?"

"Whatever for? He's obviously not the upstanding young man I thought him to be."

"No, but he *can* be of help in solving your daughter's case. I know you doctors have the whole doctor-patient confidentiality thing going on, but you have your ways, darling. See if you can find out what patients Dr. Wilcox has who are on digoxin."

"Brilliant idea, shnookums." My father beamed.

"Not bad," the detective admitted. "I'm impressed, Mrs. Meadows."

"Don't let my appearance fool you, young man. Others

have made the mistake before, hence the number of cases I've won. I'm a lot smarter than I look."

"I don't doubt that for a minute." Mitch tipped his head to the side once in salute.

My father puffed up his chest. "My wife's a real pit bull in the courtroom. I love watching her in action. In the meantime, it sounds like we all have our assignments." He faced me and nailed me with a stern expression. "You try to stay out of trouble, young lady. We've got everything under control."

"Believe it or not, I'm rather smart myself, Dad." I stiffened my spine. "I've got a lead of my own I'm following up on."

"Really, now," Dad said, looking as though he were about to yawn. "Do tell."

"Well, when I was ice-skating with Sean O'Malley," I said, ignoring Detective Stone's eye roll, "I saw Carolyn Hanes drive by with the head of the Historical Society, Gladys Montgomery."

"The library is housed in an old building that Miss Montgomery has been trying to have recognized as a historical landmark for some time now," Mitch pointed out. "It's not surprising they would be together now that Ms. Robbins is gone."

"No, but what is surprising is that when Sean and I went into the library later, we saw them talking to Pendleton."

Mitch blinked. "You mean the developer who was trying to get Ms. Robbins to vote yes? I know he was pretty desperate to convince her to turn over the library.

He wanted to put up a chain bookstore in its place in exchange for giving her a better-paying management position there."

"One and the same. After asking around town, I discovered Amanda was on the library's Board of Trustees and was even board president. The library's state tax revenue funding has dropped drastically over the past year, resulting in an annual shortfall. Amanda had been seeking additional support to no avail. She'd even cut programs, staff, materials purchased, and public hours, as well as doubling late fines and charging for interlibrary loans. Nothing was working, and the library was still on the verge of closing, anyway. And with the town's strict zoning laws, there isn't enough land available for commercial use." I paced, working the situation all out in my head.

"Gladys made it known to everyone that she was against the library closing and a bookstore going up in its place. Carolyn was Amanda's best friend and an employee of the library as well. You wouldn't think either one would be caught dead talking to that tyrant unless it was to tell him he could take his business proposition and hit the road, right?"

"Sounds logical to me," Mitch said.

"Wrong. I overheard the three of them talking about wanting the deal to go through but that some mysterious woman was an even harder nut to crack than the librarian had been. We just need to find the mystery woman and see how she's involved."

Mitch stared at me for a long moment and then finally said, "You done good, Tink."

I felt pride swell in my chest. Finally, some credit from someone. I had worked so hard to solve this case, but no one seemed to acknowledge my efforts.

"That's my girl," my mom said.

"A true Meadows through and through," my dad added.

All I felt was frustration as I looked at them. I was only good enough to be their daughter when things went right. But like it or not, I needed them. The sooner we solved this case, the sooner I could get on with my life.

# 11

❖❁❖

Later that day, after I was finally awake and showered, I decided getting on with my life might involve more effort on my part. The person who knew the most about this case was me, yet I hadn't even read my own tea leaves.

Nodding my head with conviction, I parted the strands of crystal beads and entered my sanctuary. Glancing around at the soft pale blue walls, a veil of calm settled over me. I closed my eyes and inhaled my aromatherapy oils, already feeling better.

I turned on some soft new age music, flicked on the light to my tropical-fish tank, and started a fire in the corner fireplace. Gathering my supplies, I sat at the table in the center of the room, surrounded by lush green plants. Glancing up at the constellations covering my ceiling, I prayed this would work and shed some insight onto the state of my future.

I took my canister of homegrown tea leaves, placed the loose tea leaves in a cup, and then set some water on to boil. Once the watered boiled and steam billowed into the air, I poured the water over the tea leaves and stirred them with a spoon as it brewed. Next, I drank the unstrained tea and thought about what exactly it was I wished to know. In my case, what my immediate future held in store. Would "getting on with my life" involve looking out my windowpane or looking out through a set of bars?

I held the cup in my left hand, swished three times in a counterclockwise motion, and then I tipped the cup upside down onto the saucer so the excess liquid could run out. Righting the cup, I pointed the handle toward myself and began to read the pattern of tea leaves.

Holding the cup level, I started at the handle and read the tea leaves in a counterclockwise direction from the top of the rim to the bottom of the cup. The first thing I saw was an anchor, which represented a lucky sign and success in business. A huge relief swept through me, although I had no idea when that success would occur. I might have to go through a lot more before that happened. I kept reading. Next I saw a heart representing love and pleasures to come, but immediately after I saw the mark of interrogation representing doubt and disappointment. And finally I saw a comet blazing through my teacup.

A sure sign of misfortune and trouble to come.

There was a loud knock on my door, as though someone had been pounding for a while. I jogged out to the foyer and looked through the peephole to find Detective Stone showered and in full detective mode.

I opened the door and looked at him curiously. "Did you forget something?"

"Yeah, you . . . partner." A smile hovered at the edge of his lips.

"Seriously?" I beamed, forgetting about my disturbing reading and deciding to see what I could come up with physically instead of psychically.

"For now. We'll see how it goes." He pointed his finger at me. "If you make me look bad, all bets are off. I'm only doing this because we need to pool our resources. This doesn't mean our working relationship is permanent. I still think you're a quack," he added with much less bite.

"That's okay because I still think you're a grump butt. I'm just glad you finally admit I have something worth contributing. And trust me, I don't want this relationship to be permanent any more than you do."

"Looks like we have a deal, then." He held out his hand.

"Deal." I jumped up and down, gave him a hug, and then quickly stepped back. "Sorry."

He nodded once but couldn't quite hide his cockeyed smile. "If you're ready, Tink, let's go bring Nurse Doolittle in for further questioning."

I grabbed my coat and followed him out to his car. Ten minutes later, we were standing in Dr. Wilcox's office, asking the receptionist if we could talk to Nurse Doolittle.

A slightly chubby, rosy-cheeked brunette with curly hair, pink polka-dot scrubs, and a puckered brow appeared, looking us both over critically. After a moment, she asked us to follow her out of the waiting room and into the nurses' station. "May I help you?" she asked.

"Well, that depends," Mitch said. "Are you going to tell me where you were the night Amanda Robbins was murdered?"

"I already told you I was home," she said, wringing her hands inside the cotton fabric of her shirt.

"Wrong. We know you were at the doc's house, delivering his dry cleaning," I chimed in, and her eyes widened for a second. Then she smoothed her shirt and looked away.

"Last time I checked it wasn't a crime to help a person out. I was simply trying to do something nice for Dr. Wilcox."

"Look, we know you had a thing for the doc, and we know you wished the librarian was out of the picture so he would finally notice you." Mitch put on his serious cop-guy attitude. "I think you killed her to get her out of the way. You certainly had enough motive."

"I would never do something like that." Beads of perspiration popped out on her forehead. "Besides, you just said someone saw me delivering the doctor's laundry. Doesn't that give me an alibi?"

"Well, yes, to a certain degree. However, it doesn't take that much time to deliver someone's laundry. Maybe you paid someone to take out the competition for you. I hate to point this out, but you do have access to digoxin," I said, pasting on my pitiful face and deciding to roll with the good-cop, bad-cop angle. "All you have to do is tell us the truth about what you were doing inside the doctor's house for all that time. I really don't want to have to bring you in, but I'm afraid this big bad meanie of a detective won't think twice about it."

"Well, I—"

"What is the meaning of this?" Dr. Wilcox stormed into the nurses' station. "Our patients are getting backed up. All of you, follow me. You're causing a scene." He led us into the nearest exam room. "We've already answered all your questions, Detective. What more could you want?"

"*You* answered all our questions. Your nurse, however, did not."

Dr. Wilcox turned to Nurse Doolittle with a raised brow. "Tina, what's going on? Why wouldn't you answer their questions?"

"They know I dropped off your laundry for you the night of the murder." She hedged, looking like she wanted to say more but couldn't quite bring herself.

"Exactly," the doctor said slowly, giving her a penetrating look. "You're a wonderful help to me, and I really appreciate everything you've done." He paused for a minute. "I don't see what the problem is, Detective."

"The problem is your nurse was in your house way too long on the night of the murder. You weren't home," Mitch said, "and I want to know what she was doing."

"Tina, you don't have to say anything more," Dr. Wilcox said, not sounding surprised that she was at his house for so long that night. "You have the right to remain silent, you know."

She sobbed. "I can't."

"Yes, you can." The doctor took her hand, but she slid hers out of his grip.

"Your nurse said she was being nice and helping you out," I added. "If she would confirm exactly what she was doing at your place while you were at dinner, then she wouldn't be in trouble. Don't forget, Doctor. You're still a suspect as well." I turned to Tina and placed my hand on her shoulder. "We want to help you clear your name. All you have to do is tell us what you were up to."

"I'm calling my lawyer," the doc said, and started to leave, but Tina put her hand on his arm.

"No. It's time. You didn't do anything wrong, and neither did I." She patted his shoulder and then turned to the detective. "I admit I was at the doctor's house for an hour at the time of the murder. And I truly was trying to help him. That morning in the office he and Amanda had a big fight. He was only trying to take care of her, but she wouldn't let him help. He got angry and said things he shouldn't have and then stormed out of the office. I saw him take her file with him, and I was afraid he was going to do something stupid. So I dropped off his cleaning when I knew he'd be gone, and I searched his house. That's all, I swear. Once I found Amanda's file, I left to return it to the office." Tina started crying. "I didn't want to see him hurt any more by that woman."

"I was angry, but I would never do anything as stupid as break a patient's confidentiality," Dr. Wilcox said, staring down at his feet. "I was only trying to scare Amanda into changing her mind about letting me take care of her, but when I called, she wasn't home. So I went to dinner with every intention of returning her file to the office later that night. Nurse Doolittle beat me to it."

"Why wouldn't Amanda let anyone help her?" I asked.

The doctor sighed. "Her tumors were cancerous. We caught it early, but she still needed treatment. She didn't want anyone to know because she didn't want them to replace her at the library. The library was everything to her. She had no family or anyone else to help her. I did so much for her, was willing to do so much more, but she turned me down flat. She was a very proud and stubborn woman. Yes, I was angry, but I wouldn't have broken my oath as a doctor." He stared Mitch in the eye. "You have my word on that."

"I really didn't mean to cause more trouble for you, Dr. Wilcox," Tina said. "Does this mean I'm fired?"

He smiled sadly. "No, I'm not going to fire you, Tina. You're a good nurse, and frankly, this office would fall apart without you. I know you were trying to save me from myself, but it all doesn't matter now anyway. Amanda's gone."

"But I'm still here," the nurse said quietly, and the doctor looked at her as though seeing her in a whole new light. Some men were so blind.

"Well, thank you for your time, Miss Doolittle," I interjected. I grabbed Detective Stone's arm. "We have a thing to go to, don't we?"

He looked down at my hand and paused. "A thing. Right." He reached in his pocket. "Here's my card. If you think of anything else, call me—"

"Day or night. I think they've got it." I dragged him the rest of the way outside, ignoring his scowl. "Can't you see they needed a moment alone? What do you do, order those things by the thousand? I think everyone in town must have one by now."

"Can it, pipsqueak. Your status of partner can be revoked at any time." Detective Grumpy Pants was back to being his grumpmeister self when his cell phone rang.

"Stone here," he barked into the phone and then looked at me.

"What?" I mouthed.

He held up his hands. "Yes, sir. We'll be right there." He snapped his phone closed and frowned.

"We?" I asked. "Right where?"

"Captain Walker wants to see us in his office immediately."


"Sunshine Meadows, I'd like you to meet Chief Spencer and Mayor Cromwell," Captain Walker wasted no time in saying after I followed Mitch inside the police station all the way into Walker's office.

"So nice to finally meet you both," I responded, and shook their hands.

Chief Spencer, a man with a medium build and a full head of salt-and-pepper hair parted on the side and trimmed to precision, looked me over thoroughly. "I trust you're doing your best to clear your name and help solve this case, young lady?"

My smile slipped under a glare as dark as overbrewed Fire Oolong tea. This dude meant business. I nodded vigorously. "Sir, absolutely, sir. I'm detecting lots of stuff." Like whom Detective Stone's role model must be.

The chief's frown put the detective's to shame, and then he nailed the detective with a disbelieving look. "Is she for real?"

"Affirmative, sir." Mitch stood tall with his hands clasped behind his back.

I snapped my spine straight and matched his stance. "That means yes," I couldn't resist adding. The chief's hard gaze whipped back to mine. "Sir," I added. He eyed me critically like he didn't approve of me working on this case any more than Mitch did, but with the mayor up for reelection, he would pretty much give him whatever he wanted.

In this case me, apparently.

"Good, good, young lady," Mayor Cromwell spoke up in a big booming voice. He was short and stocky with an oversized troll head of shocking red hair and small beady eyes. "That's what I like to hear. At least someone is enthusiastic about solving this case." He raised a brow at Mitch, and I could see the detective's molars grinding beneath his cheek.

"Oh, believe me, Detective Grum—uh, Stone—works harder than anyone I know." I patted Mitch's arm, and his eyes cut to mine.

"Good, then he won't mind telling me what leads have panned out."

The detective cleared his throat. "Well, none exactly. But I'm still looking into the Ms. Robbins's phone records and personnel files—"

"None?" Cromwell boomed. "What the devil have you been doing, boy?"

"My job," Mitch spat, giving Captain Walker a warning look. "These things take time."

"Detective Stone is one of the department's best," Captain Walker spoke up, and Chief Spencer nodded silently beside him.

Kari Lee Townsend

"Well, that's not saying much about your department, then." Cromwell scoffed. "Time is something we don't have. Maybe we should put Miss Meadows in charge. We'd probably get faster results."

"Oh, I couldn't." I thought about that. "Although he did make me a partner." I chewed my lip, and Mitch slapped his hands on his hips, his mouth ajar as though ready to read me more than a Miranda warning. "But no, no, no, I really couldn't." *Shut up now, Tink, you're making things worse,* I thought. The detective was so going to make me pay later. "We have brand-new leads we're going to follow now," I added, hoping to improve the situation.

"Really, and who came up with those, Detective?" Cromwell squared off against Mitch, and it was obvious the two didn't like each other.

Mitch's jaw bulged like it killed him to admit it, but he finally responded, "Miss Meadows."

"I rest my case," the mayor said, throwing up his hands.

Mitch's hands clenched into fists.

"That's right," I said. "We will put this case to rest for sure, Mayor. You can count on us." I grabbed Mitch by the arm and once again pulled him out of a room, calling over my shoulder, "We'll be in touch soon."

Once we were outside, Mitch blew me off and started to storm away toward his car.

"Where are you going?" I sputtered.

"You figure it out, Tink, since you're so good at detecting." He climbed in his car and started the engine.

"Fine, I will," I hollered back at him, but I doubted

he heard me over the splatter of kicked-up snow and slush as he drove away.

Having no clue where to go from there, I walked down Main Street like I had the night I first met Detective Stone. It was earlier but still just as picturesque as dusk settled over the old-fashioned town. Light snow fell in big fat flakes softly to the well-tended streets, the brass streetlamps flickering to life in the ever-darkening sky. I stopped at the now-familiar corner of Main and Shadow Lane and once again entered Smokey Jo's Tavern.

Dim lighting, soft music, and mumbled conversations filled the space. Just what I needed. A place to blend in and forget my worries.

"Hey, Sunny, you okay?" Jo asked. "You look like you lost your best friend."

"More like my partner." I sighed. "I don't even know what happened." I sat down at the bar since the tables were quickly becoming occupied by the dinner crowd. Besides, I was only one person, and it seemed silly taking up a spot meant for at least two.

"What can I get for you?"

"Iced tea, some chicken fingers, and fries." I was used to eating by myself, but it never failed to remind me how alone I was in this world. I sometimes wondered if it would always be this way.

"Uh-oh. Comfort food. That can't be good." She slid the glass of tea in front of me and put in my order. "This one's on me."

"Thanks." I took a long drink and then set the glass down.

"Well, if it isn't my favorite fortune-teller," Sean said with a big grin, looking hotter than ever in his snug baby blue T-shirt and faded jeans. He carried a bin of clean glasses through the swinging door in the back and restocked the shelves.

"I'm the only fortune-teller, you know." I laughed, enjoying flirting with the rascal. But I knew it would never amount to more than that with Sean. He was God's gift to women—*all* women.

"But you're still my favorite, lass." He winked, twirling a liquor bottle expertly like something right out of the movies. "So, how's the case coming along?"

The cocktail waitress brought out my food and then left to check on the ever-increasing customers. Bernard Sampson came in and sat at a table by himself. Guess he was still miffed at his wife, Maude, for missing their lunch date. I could relate to his mood.

"Not so good, I'm afraid." I dipped a chicken finger in honey mustard sauce and took a big bite, sighing as I chewed the sweet and tangy delight. My mother would be appalled. "I'm worried we're going to fail," I voiced my biggest fear.

"Only quitters fail," said a deep voice from beside me.

"Hey," I said to Mitch, swallowing hard as I peeked up at him. "You still mad at me?"

"That wasn't about you, Tink. Cromwell and I have a history. You wound up in the middle of it." He snagged a fry, dipped it in ketchup, and popped it into his mouth.

After he finished chewing, he looked me in the eye. "I'm sorry."

"Apology accepted," I said softly, sliding the plate between us.

"Thanks." He ordered a soda and then pulled out his notebook. "Contrary to one bonehead's beliefs, I *have* been working. I've been doing some digging."

"And . . . ?"

"Nothing. Not a blessed thing. Looks like we're back to the drawing board."

"This day just keeps getting better and better," I grumbled.

"As much as I hate to admit it, the mayor is right. We are running out of time and out of leads."

"Then maybe we should up our game."

He eyed me warily. "What do you have in mind?"

"I'm thinking it's time I became a babe."

# 12

❖❂❖❂❖❂❖

"So, what do I do again?" I asked as I sat at a table in Lulubelle's kitchen, not feeling like a babe in the least. There were a total of three tables, with four women at each one. Jo's group was winning, so she was at the head table in the dining room, while the rest of us were at the lower tables in the breakfast nook and island. I sat next to a black-and-white-cow cookie jar and Belle herself.

"You roll the three dice and hope they land on whatever round we're on. In this case, fives." She sipped her margarita and nibbled on a finger sandwich. "Don't worry, sweetie. Bunco is a lot of fun once you get the hang of it."

I rolled the dice but didn't land a single five. "Sorry. Hope I don't make your team lose."

"Oh, posh." She waved her hand. "It's all about the booze and the snacks." She threw her dice, bouncing them off the chest of the woman across from her. The women snorted on a laugh, and Belle let out a squeal while she tossed her hands up in the air, yelling, "Bunco!"

I clapped my hands, assuming her squealing was a good thing. "I like your bangs, by the way. How's Big Don?"

"Aw, thank you, doll face." She beamed, and then her smile dimmed a little. "Still just as big and blind as ever." She shook her head, and her chubby cheeks wiggled. "Cheers." She held out her glass.

"It's his loss, then," I said, clinking my glass to hers, but I didn't take a sip. She looked surprised and motioned for me to bottoms up. "I'm not really much of a drinker."

"Oh, come on, sugar, live a little. They weren't kidding when they said life's too short."

"Well, that's true." I tipped my margarita up and chugalugged. "Oh boy." My eyes nearly crossed. I'd have to pace myself, or I'd be calling one yummy detective to come tuck me in. Hmmm, then again . . . "No." I blinked. So not gonna go there.

"No what?"

"No way am I ever going to be as good as you, but thanks for letting me be an alternate," I said after she finished with her victory jig over her latest score.

"No problem. You and Jo actually helped us out. It takes twelve people to play two teams. Amanda Robbins was one of our regulars, poor dear. We still haven't replaced her."

"Who is the other regular?" I asked above the music and hooting and hollering women.

"Carolyn Hanes," Belle said around a mouth full of chips.

"Really?" I leaned in close, not wanting to miss a word. "I don't know her that well, but she doesn't seem the type to let loose."

"Oh, honey, that child is plenty loose—with her wallet, anyway." She snickered.

"Now that I think about it, her house was full of really nice things. She must like to shop."

"She loves to shop, so much so it's become a problem for her." Belle looked around and then leaned in even closer to me, her eyes sparkling bright as though she loved a good piece of juicy gossip. "I heard she has a shopping addiction. That Home Shopping Network can be deadly."

"Don't I know it," I agreed. "My own mother is addicted. So where is Carolyn tonight, then?"

"Working at Gretta's Mini-Mart. Poor Carolyn had to take a second job. It's a shame things didn't pan out for her, really."

"What didn't pan out?"

"Word around town is that she was next in line for the management position at the library. Once Amanda died, everyone thought Carolyn would be a shoe-in. Especially with Maude Sampson retiring. But the board filled the position with some young whippersnapper from out of town, leaving poor Carolyn in the dust. Why, I heard tell that young woman is barely old enough to wipe her nose, let alone run the library."

"Have you met her yet?"

"Nope, and I don't plan to. She won't be getting a neighborly welcome from many. No siree. We here Divinians are a loyal bunch. We look out for our own." Lulubelle nodded sharply, her eyes cutting to mine. Belle might look like a big, bubbly, fun-loving woman, but she was as sharp as the blade my father uses for surgery and as tough as the steak my mother attempts to cook.

I was suddenly aware I'd better tread carefully when following my lead on Miss Hanes. One thing this new librarian and I had in common . . .

I, too, was an outsider.

But that didn't stop the questions from running through my mind. Why didn't Carolyn Hanes get the library job? Was she hurting for money because of her shopping addiction? Was she desperate enough to betray her best friend by working with the bigwig? What had he promised her to make it worth her while? Even more baffling was why the town historian Gladys Montgomery would be in cahoots with a man like Alex Pendleton.

Maybe it was time I got acquainted with this town's past.


Early the next morning, the pounding in my head was unbearable. I'd only had the one drink at Bunco last night. I wasn't that much of a lightweight, was I?

The pounding grew louder, and I suddenly realized the noise wasn't coming from inside my head. It was coming from outside my front door.

I glanced at my bedside clock. Eight A.M. on a Sunday morning. Maybe if I ignored it, whoever it was would go away. The pounding continued, and Morty pounced on top of the mattress from out of nowhere. He stared me down. I stared back.

"Can't you twitch your tail and turn them into a pile of dust or something, big guy?"

He gave me a look that said, *You're on your own. I don't have time for you silly humans,* then made a noise somewhere between a purr and a growl right before he pranced away.

I threw back the covers. Grabbing my fleece robe and slipping my feet into my enormous bunny slippers, I slowly scuffed my way downstairs to the front door.

"All right already, I'm coming." I yanked open the door without even looking and then groaned. "Mom? Dad? Seriously?" We had to stop meeting like this.

Mom pushed her way right past me, dressed in her Sunday best. "Chop-chop, darling. It's time for church." She blinked at my hair. "Are you getting gray? You must take after your father. You should have that Tracy woman down at the salon fix it. I heard through the rumor mill she's pretty good. I'd never let her touch my own hair, mind you, but since you don't seem to care much about your appearance, I'm sure she could do *something* to help."

"Gee, thanks, Mom. I'll keep that in mind." I didn't even bother to correct her and point out it was Tracy and her salon that had turned me gray in the first place. Pushing those thoughts aside, my mother's words registered and I gaped at her as though she were from another planet. "Church? We haven't been to church in years."

"Yes, well, maybe that's the problem," Dad said. "We

need all the prayers we can get to clear your name. Dr. Wilcox has rescheduled our dinner twice so far."

"Can you blame him?" Mom chimed in. "He's probably still wary of all of us now that we know about his blackmail intentions. To think he even considered breaking his vow as a doctor." She tsked. "Now, that's a man who could benefit from a morning in church. He obviously hasn't gone to mass in quite some time."

"Not everyone is Catholic, Mom."

"Doesn't matter. Confession is good for the soul. You should try it. Father Moody is a lovely human being."

Poor man's ears would never be the same after listening to my mother's confessions, I suspected. I rubbed my temples. "And how did you hear about the librarian's file?"

"Small town, Sylvia." Dad grunted. "There's nothing too trivial for these people to gossip about."

Good Lord. I groaned, knowing he was right. Not to mention Divinity had a huge Catholic population. Half the town would probably be at nine o'clock mass to see if anyone knew what was in that file. Looked like I was going to church. I bit my lip, made the sign of the cross, and looked up as I mumbled, "Forgive me, Father."

Twenty minutes later we were headed to Sacred Heart Church on Mystical Drive a half hour early. We entered the small, quaint church with rows of pristine white pews and gorgeous stained-glass windows gracing the sidewalls. I had to admit there was something so peaceful about entering a church of any kind.

The pews were filling up quickly. The front rows were completely occupied by the Mad Hatters—aka the busybody church ladies who thought I was a devil-worshipping heathen just because I was psychic and hadn't attended mass since I'd moved to Divinity. Not to mention my first reading had ended in a little thing called murder. I had dubbed them the Mad Hatters because, frankly, they were crazy. Stubborn and opinionated and downright self-righteous.

Not even close to the churchgoing citizens they claimed to be.

I couldn't stand people who were hypocrites, and yet my mother chose to sit right behind them. "Good morning, Alice. Shirley. Mable." Dad followed close on her heels, tipping his head. "Ladies," he added as though they were all great friends.

Their red, purple, and green hats swung in our direction. They smiled a lovely smile at my mother and gave her a nod of approval, a charming smile at my father and showered him with expressions of adoration, then looked down their noses at me while turning their lips into a frowning purse of disgust. I just donned a sugary sweet smile and waved at them with my fingertips.

They harrumphed in return.

Then the most remarkable thing happened. Their pursed lips turned into nasty scowls as they looked toward the door of the church. I couldn't believe they'd found someone to dislike more than me. Craning my head around to look, I saw an average-sized woman with medium brown hair and plain features. Nothing unusual or outrageous about her clothes or makeup, either. I didn't understand what could possibly have caused such a negative reaction.

Until I noticed Carolyn Hanes. She'd focused on the newcomer, and a hurt look crossed her features. The hurt quickly turned to anger as she faced front once more, made the sign of the cross, and prayed to Jesus. The newcomer could only be one person.

The new manager of the library.

I'd heard the Historical Society was having a meeting that afternoon at the town hall. It was open to the public, so I decided to go and check it out. I slipped in the back as the meeting was in full swing, hung up my puffy coat on one of the last available coat hooks, and then slid into the last row in the back to listen to Gladys Montgomery.

"Calm down, people, I understand how you feel. I don't want to lose the library any more than you do. It's been a part of Divinity for ages, but we have to face the fact that it's not thriving. Alex Pendleton is a snake and only cares about making money. But he does have a point. The library is losing money. Our town is losing money. We need businesses to bring in revenue and jobs, but we just don't have enough land zoned for that sort of thing. And, frankly, we have other landmarks more worthy of saving. If we don't let him have the library, he'll take something else. It's all about compromise."

"What about the anonymous gift the library received?" someone asked. "I heard that will keep the library afloat for at least another year."

"And what then? What if there isn't another gift, and Pendleton has moved on?" Gladys asked. "Then the library closes and just sits there."

"Amanda Robbins would roll over in her grave to hear you talk like that," someone else said.

"I've spoken to Pendleton," Gladys went on, ignoring the comment about the librarian. "He would be willing to drop his pursuit of the old Divinity Theatre Hotel if we let him have the library. I know we don't want to lose the library, but like I said, it's not doing well anyway, and a bookstore would still provide books. Whereas the Theatre Hotel is ancient. It's been around much longer than the library and is therefore a more desirable candidate for National Historical Landmark status." Gladys's eyes lit up.

"Don't you see? We are so close. The National Park System Advisory Board has already had their meeting and has recommended the hotel to the secretary of the interior for potential landmarks. His final decision should be made in a couple of weeks. If we don't give the library to Pendleton, then he will most certainly petition the secretary to try to stop the hotel's landmark status so he can put his bookstore there. The hotel would make a wonderful museum, and once it becomes a landmark Pendleton won't be able to touch it. I know we have some tough decisions ahead, but what choice do we have?"

"A lot of our citizens are hurting for money, too, not just this town. How do you think they will be able to pay for books or afford to go to a museum?" someone else chimed in. "At least with the library open, our citizens have some sort of free entertainment. And think of the children. The library hosts wonderful programs for the children and gets them interested in reading. The kids won't read half as much if their parents can't afford to pay for books."

"Don't forget the seniors," Maude Sampson said. "For some of us, the library is all we have left."

"The library can't close down," Bernard Sampson added, sitting tall and solid by his wife's side. "Those who are retired have no place else to go." He glanced at his wife, and his jaw worked beneath his skin. He jingled the change in his pocket. "My wife needs that library, plain and simple."

"You may not have a choice, Ms. Montgomery, but I do," said Ms. Smith, the new manager of the library. "I now have Amanda's vote and am proud to say I agree with her decision. The library stays."

"I'm sorry, Mr. Sampson." Gladys straightened her spine and burned daggers from her eyes at Ms. Smith. "As president of the Library Board, I've called for a revote."

"But Ms. Robbins was the deciding vote, and Ms. Smith said her vote still holds. The results will be the same," yet another citizen pointed out.

"You never know. Some votes might be swayed after today's meeting," Gladys said.

"My thoughts exactly," said a tall blonde in an expensive suit, carrying a tiny dog in her purse, as she entered the back of the town hall.

No one recognized the stranger, save one. Gladys's pale face gave away all. This had to be the mystery woman she, Carolyn, and Pendleton had been trying to sway with no luck.

"That's why I've decided to double my gift to the library," the woman finished with a satisfied smile, chorused by several gasps around the room and an eruption of cheers. "That's right, good citizens of Divinity. My name is Lucinda Griswold III. Your library might be running out of funds, but my pocketbook is not. I have a huge soft spot for libraries, and your town is simply divine." She locked eyes on Gladys. "I think I'll stay for a spell."

Gladys gripped the podium, looking like she might be sick.

Grabbing my coat off the hook, I slipped out the back of the town hall as quietly as I could. I decided to walk and think for a while. Passing the ice rink in the center town park, I strolled down the business district and ran into Detective Stone.

"Hey, Tink, I was looking for you. Where are you coming from?" He fell into step beside me.

"Church with my parents and then the town hall meeting."

"Church?"

"I go." I hoisted my chin high in the air. "Just not as much as I'd like to since I've been here."

"I'm not questioning that or judging you. I simply can't imagine you sitting in a pew with your parents like one big happy family."

"Trust me, there was a lot of praying involved." I snorted.

"So how'd the meeting go?"

"Very interesting." I told him about all the details that had come out during the meeting. How Gladys wanted to trade the library to Pendleton in order to keep the hotel in hopes of making it a landmark. And how Pendleton had promised higher-paying jobs to library employees, which explained Carolyn's interest. Then I finished with, "I still think the three of them were in cahoots to get rid of Amanda since she was the deciding vote to keep the library open. They probably hadn't counted on Carolyn not getting the manager position at the library, and they especially didn't count on the anonymous gift."

Mitch looked thoughtful as we walked. "What I don't understand is this Griswold woman. She has more money than she knows what to do with, obviously, but why Divinity? Why this small library?"

"That's what I keep wondering, too. There has to be more to this story. We're missing something."

"Agreed. We need to find a possible link to digoxin for the trio and look more into Miss Griswold's background. Friends, enemies, grudges, et cetera. Anything or anyone to connect her to Divinity."

"I'll see what I can come up with. How about you? Anything new?"

"More dead ends. What about your father? Any luck with the doctor?"

"Not yet." I blew out a breath. "I'm still worried. What if none of these leads pans out?"

Mitch stared at me for a long, intense moment. "We don't have any hard evidence on you, Tink. Unless the murder weapon suddenly shows up at your house, you're fine."

I swallowed, my throat suddenly dry. "Right," I said, shoving my hands in my coat pocket, and then I went into a coughing fit.

"You okay?" Mitch patted me on the back, and I jerked away.

"Fine, fine. I don't like to be touched when I'm coughing." That sounded ridiculous to my own ears, but I could not let the detective get too close to me.

He held his hands up. "Oh-kay. Whatever you say, Tink, but just for the record, you're acting weird again."

"Don't you know by now that weird is my middle name?" I faked a smile. "It's a trendy city thing."

"Yeah, let's go with that." He slid his sunglasses over his eyes, but that still didn't hide his expression. *He must think I'm totally whacked.* "I'm going to look into the public records. Do some digging. I was going to ask you to dinner, but you don't look so good. Maybe you should lie down."

"Good idea." I kept my hands in my pockets. "Catch you on the flip side." I turned on my heel and took off as fast as I could until I rounded the dead-end road to my house.

Stopping, I glanced around several times until I was certain I was alone. Finally, I pulled my hand out of my pocket, tightly holding the contents.

Just as I suspected. Another small bottle of digoxin like the one that had been in my cupboard. There was no name on the prescription. It had been scratched off just like the other bottle as well. But how on earth did it get there?

I had taken my coat off in the town hall during the meeting and hung it up on the coatrack in the back. Someone at that meeting must have slipped the digoxin inside. A chill ran over me. The real killer was trying to set me up to take the fall.

Everyone in town knew I was a suspect with no alibi

but also no murder weapon. If they could get Detective Stone to find me with the evidence on my person or in my house, then I was screwed. We'd formed a truce of sorts, but he still thought I was a quack, and he didn't trust women. He wouldn't hesitate to haul me off to jail, case closed. I had to up my game and solve this case before the situation spiraled out of control.

Things were about to get ugly.

# 13

Later that night, I walked into Smokey Jo's to grab a bite to eat. A little freaked out over the whole killer-stalking-my-every-move thing, I didn't feel like being alone. Even big, bad, spooky Morty could sense something was off and had disappeared—and he was far from a coward. Meanwhile little ole fraidy-cat me was a nervous wreck, and I couldn't even share it with anyone.

I couldn't tell my parents because they would stick to me like wet tea leaves even more than they already were or, knowing them, hire a bodyguard. And I couldn't tell Mitch because he wouldn't believe me. He'd confiscate the digoxin as the proof he needed to arrest me. I didn't dare tell Jo or Sean because I didn't want to involve them or give the detective an excuse to arrest them as accomplices. So, basically, I was on my own.

I found a spot at the bar and tried to decide what to

eat for dinner. Glancing around, I noticed the place looked pretty empty tonight. Just a few locals, and—

My jaw fell wide-open.

Detective Grumpy Pants and Lucinda Griswold III?

It hadn't taken him long to find another dinner date. I set my jaw and narrowed my eyes in his direction. I knew when he'd said he was going to ask me to dinner, he hadn't meant as a real "date." But it still irritated me that he'd moved on so quickly.

My rational side knew the detective in him was just checking her out, but my emotional side suspected the man in him was checking her out in another way. He looked so relaxed, leaning back in his chair, his arm draped over the back and his knees spread wide. Lucinda said something, and Mitch threw back his head in a laugh. The grin that crept across her face was sexy as hell and full of promise. Even worse, Mitch smiled a real and genuine full smile with crow's-feet and all.

Something in my chest, that I refused to put a name to, tightened. Like it or not, I realized, my vision was coming true. The heartache had begun, and I was terrified there was nothing I could do to stop it.

"Hey, lass, why so down?" Sean tapped my cheek, capturing my attention.

I jumped, placing a hand on my aching chest and then inhaling deeply. "Sorry. It's been a weird couple of days."

"Is there anything I can do?" He leaned across the bar, his firm biceps fully flexed and on display. "Say the word."

"You already have." I squeezed his arm, the corners

of my mouth lifting along with my spirits. "You always cheer me up, Mr. O'Malley."

He placed his hand across his heart. "Then may the gods bless me as I slip peacefully into the night knowing I have accomplished my sole mission in life."

"You are such a devil." I shook my head but couldn't stop grinning. He really had put me in a better mood. Then again, he always did.

"And you, my love, are an angel from above." He held both my hands in his. "You've stolen my heart. You do know that, don't you?"

"You have a heart?" I teased.

"Aye, and it belongs to only you." The look in his eyes was anything but teasing.

I didn't need to be psychic to see he was actually telling the truth. I pressed my lips together. He felt for me the way I felt for Mitch, and heartache or not, I couldn't stop him from falling any more than I could stop myself.

My gaze was drawn to where Mitch sat with Lucinda, but they were gone. I tore my eyes away from their empty chairs, trying not to wonder if they'd left together, and glanced back at the bartender. "Sean . . . ?"

His gaze shot to where mine had been and then back to me with a dawning expression of realization. Regret and disappointment flashed across his features, but then his expression quickly changed to a carefree, fun-loving one. "No worries, love. What can I get for you?" He straightened and started wiping the bar as if the entire exchange had never happened.

Relief swirled through me. I wasn't ready to deal with

my feelings or lack thereof. I needed to make a move. Do something to shake this case up a bit. Maybe if I forced the killer to act, he or she would get sloppy. All I knew was that I was sick of waiting around and doing nothing.

Let my partner sneak off to play footsie under the covers with some floozy. I planned to do a little undercover work of my own. I had a case to solve and a killer to catch. If he could work alone, then so could I.

I looked up at Sean with a determined expression. "Give me your biggest burger, a plate of fries, and a vanilla milk shake."

Sean's mouth grew slack, and then he nodded and saluted me as he went in the back to place my order.

I would need sustenance for what I had planned.

I'd heard Alex Pendleton was a gambling man. Word around town was he liked to live large and live hard. There was a weekly game in the back room of Nikko's Restaurant.

Nikko's was an Italian restaurant in direct competition with Papas Greek restaurant. Papas did more business, so Nikko came up with the weekly gambling game as a way to up the competition. Church on Sunday morning and gambling on Sunday night.

Gotta love small-town living.

And to top it all, Alice, the ringleader of the Mad Hatters, was married to Nikko. She turned a blind eye and made it sound like a prayer meeting was taking place behind closed doors. As long as Nikko made money off the gambling, Alice would find a way to justify it. The world might come to an end if she couldn't afford more hats.

I repeat: hypocrite.

The game wouldn't start until after the dinner crowd ended, so I had time to catch Pendleton before he left. I hadn't realized the weather had gotten so nasty out. I didn't own a TV, but investing in a radio might not be a bad idea.

I cruised the streets in my VW bug until I found his BMW parked in Divinity's only hotel. A large brick building a few stories high with a patio on the rooftop so the summer tourists could watch the Fourth of July parade down below. Right now it was loaded down with a couple feet of snow.

Pendleton didn't live in Divinity. In fact, I'd heard no one knew exactly where he lived because he traveled around so much, checking on several projects in various stages of development. It was rumored his suitcase and a hotel room were pretty much his home.

I parked my bug down the block at the Laundromat to disguise my real whereabouts. Everyone knew the bug was mine since no one else in town drove one. And living in Vicky, no one would question that my washer had gone out, and I had to use the Laundromat.

Locking my car, I weaved in and out of the shadows on foot until I crouched beside the BMW once more. Detective Stone might have finally accepted I would be working with him, even if he still didn't like it, but that didn't mean he would lend me any supplies. I wouldn't be getting a gun anytime soon—which was fine by me because I hated guns—but I could use handcuffs and pepper spray. I'd simply "borrowed" them from his apartment, along with the bugging devices.

First I had to break into Pendleton's car, and then I would plant the device. Something told me a lot of his more interesting conversations took place in the privacy of his car. I held my breath and pulled a bobby pin from my hair. I'd taken to pinning back the strands at my temples since this new cut made it stick out in every direction. Removing the pins, I had to look like Tinker Bell with her finger in a light socket and the strands sticking straight out. Hopefully, I wouldn't run into anyone I knew.

Straightening the bobby pin, I tried jiggling it in the lock on the driver's side door. I had no clue what I was doing, but I had to at least make an attempt. I wished I'd paid closer attention to the carjacking I'd witnessed firsthand when I'd lived in the city. If only I'd grabbed one of those coat hangers I'd seen through the Laundromat window. Those always worked in the movies.

I was thinking about going back for one when it suddenly dawned on me. The car alarm hadn't gone off. Could it really be that simple? I tried the door, and it opened. Guess this really wasn't the city if even Pendleton wasn't concerned with crime.

I climbed into the backseat and shut the door, holding my breath until the inside light went off. Lying down on the floor in the back, I reached my hand under the driver's side seat and planted the bug. Feeling pretty smug, I was about to get up when the front door opened.

I remained perfectly still as Pendleton slid inside and

shut the door. Firing up the BMW, he pulled away from the curb. Hopefully, my instincts were right and he was headed toward Nikko's and not out of town.

His phone vibrated. Cursing softly, he answered with a sharp, "What do you want?" He swore again, then said, "Hang on a sec, my phone's about to die."

He reached his hand in the back, and I shrank down as low as I could, sucking in my stomach as his fingers missed me by a mere inch.

"Wait a minute, I might have to pull over to find my charger."

My eyes bugged. I could not let him pull over and find me hiding in the back. No telling what he would do to me. Squirming, I felt something under my tailbone. I reached beneath me and snagged the end of a cord and then slipped it out from underneath my back. Sliding it onto my stomach, I lifted the edge as Pendleton made one final swipe.

"Yes," he snapped. "I've got it . . . Okay, I'm plugged in. You were saying?"

I wilted in relief.

"No, that's not going to work. I can't risk them finding out the truth. You know I'd never survive behind bars. I'm really close to making the deal. Stay calm, and I'll be in touch."

He disconnected as he pulled into a parking lot. Once again I held my breath as he opened the door and got out. I heard his footsteps crunch on the snow outside as he walked away, and I nearly cried in relief. Sitting up carefully, I peeked over the backseat through the front window.

187

Nikko's.

Keeping low, I climbed out of the car and closed the door quietly. Then I tiptoed away and stood upright as though I'd been out for a stroll. I hadn't planned ahead and Nikko's wasn't anywhere near the Laundromat. Zipping my coat up all the way, I shoved my hands in my pockets and headed for the road for the long walk back to my car.

"You're Sunshine Meadows, aren't you?" said a sultry female voice from behind me. "I don't think we've met."

I turned around slowly and made myself smile, even though the sight of this particular woman made me want to tear her hair out. "You can call me Sunny. And you are?" I feigned innocence.

"Lucinda Griswold III." She locked up her Aston Martin and faced me, smiling politely, but not quite hiding the sharp, assessing gleam in her lavender eyes. Her sleek black cocktail dress hugged her perfect curves beneath her faux fur coat she'd left open.

She looked fabulous and I felt frumpy as hell, which made me like her even less. "Well, it's nice to finally meet you. I heard about your generous gift to the library. And then doubling the funds? You must really love to read."

"I love libraries, especially old ones. I find something so charming about them. And Divinity is simply divine. I want the citizens to accept me. As a fellow outsider, you should know all about that."

"Hmmm, yes. Some people are harder nuts to crack than others."

"I can only imagine." She paused, staring me down. "Especially being a murder suspect and all. Why, you simply must be traumatized. I know I would be."

"Well, lucky for you, you're not a murder suspect." Somehow I doubted even a murder allegation would intimidate this woman. She might play the innocent rich socialite, but something told me she knew exactly what she was doing. "Must be nice not to have to worry about anything except keeping the library open."

"You'd be surprised. We all have to worry with a murderer still on the loose."

"I'm sure Detective Stone is doing all he can to close this case."

"Yes, Mitchell has been wonderful about easing my fears. I hope I'm not next on the killer's list because of my gift." She shuddered, but I'd bet my freedom it was forced.

"Speaking of *Mitchell*," I said between clenched teeth, "I heard you two had dinner together, so why are you at Nikko's now? Let me guess, the detective is a cheap date. He didn't feed you enough?"

"On the contrary, everything he fed me was absolutely delicious." She leaned in close and fairly purred, "And dessert at his place was to die for. A man with good taste who can cook. He's a rare gem, that one."

"Ah, yes, he's something." My jaw ached from clenching it so tight. "Then why are you here?"

"For the game, of course."

"But I thought it was a gentleman's game only."

She arched a shapely blond eyebrow. "Darling, I've got money to burn, and I'm quite entertaining. What gentleman do you know who would turn me down?"

I couldn't argue with her there.

"The more intriguing question is, what are you doing here, standing by Mr. Pendleton's BMW?"

"Admiring the model. Although this vehicle isn't half as impressive as your car."

"Thank you for noticing. I'm rather fond of Martin myself. Wasn't that your adorable little . . . bug . . . I saw back at the Laundromat?"

I smirked. "Why, yes. Yes, it was my cute little bug. At least my good ole Punch is reliable, unlike my home appliances. My washer broke, so I was doing some laundry."

"I get that, but that still doesn't explain why you're here."

"I took a walk while my clothes are drying."

"Impressive. That's quite a ways to walk, especially at night with the streets being unsafe and all."

"Don't you worry. I can take care of myself. Or if I get into any real scrapes, I'll simply call *Mitchell.*"

"Hmmm, well, lucky you."

"Aren't I, though?" I wrinkled my nose.

Her smile stiffened, and then she tipped her head slightly to the side. "It was a pleasure, Ms. Meadows. If you'll excuse me, I have a game to win."

"Good luck."

"Darling, didn't your mother teach you anything? Luck has nothing to do with it." Her tinkling laughter trilled out behind her as she strutted into the restaurant with a walk she must have been perfecting all her life.

I spun on my heels and stomped away, counting to one hundred. Mitchell had some explaining to do. Dessert at his place? I mean, come on. That was going a little above the call of duty in my book.

I kept marching along, realizing the walk was much farther than I had first thought. The snow was coming down in droves now, a storm beginning to rage outside, matching the one churning in my insides. I really needed to get some snow tires. My bug would have a hard time getting me home in one piece at this rate.

I inhaled deeply and tried to take my mind off the weather and one truly infuriating detective. I thought back to the phone call Alex Pendleton had received. It had sounded like whoever was on the other end of the line had been pressuring him to make the deal go through.

Had Alex been desperate enough to kill for it? After all, he had said the truth could not come out and he would never survive jail. I still needed some hard evidence to link him to the murder. Hopefully, the device I'd planted under his seat would turn up something more concrete. In the meantime, I'd keep digging.

A weird feeling crept over me, like someone was watching me. I had almost made it back to the Laundromat, but I could swear someone was following me. I'd been too distracted to notice before, but I was definitely getting that eyes-burning-into-my-back kind of feeling now.

I picked up the pace. I couldn't even call for help. In my haste to sneak into Pendleton's car, I'd grabbed the bugging device but had forgotten my cell phone at home. Not too smart for a detective. Then again, no matter what Captain Walker said, I wasn't a real detective. Just an amateur sleuth. Launching myself into a jog, I glanced behind me and was certain I saw a shadow duck behind a building.

My jog became a sprint, and I dropped my keys as I

dug them out of my pocket. Unlike Pendleton, I still locked my car even in Divinity. Force of habit I was regretting at the moment. Scrambling to pick them up, my hands shook as I unlocked my bug. I checked the backseat to make sure I was alone, then threw myself inside. I slammed the door, quickly locked it, and frantically searched the street but didn't see anyone.

I took a moment to wilt down in my seat. When I caught my breath, I turned the key in the ignition and thanked the good Lord for letting my old bug sputter to life. I pulled away from the curb and began to navigate the snow through town toward my house. Looking in the rearview mirror, I did a double take. A car was following right on my behind. I couldn't get a good look at the make or model or even the driver, so I decided to test my theory.

I turned down a random street, and sure enough, the car followed. A few blocks more, I turned down another street, and once again, the car followed. My heart thumped wildly in my chest. I hadn't imagined anything. Someone really was following me.

Stomping on the gas, I barreled down another street and tried to lose my stalker. I wasn't even sure what street I was on anymore, I just knew I had to get away. My windshield wipers whipped wildly back and forth now, but I still couldn't see through the blinding snow very well.

I turned onto what I thought was another side street, went right over the median in the center of town, and into the park. I clipped a tree, went into a 360-degree sideways skid, and ran smack-dab in the middle of an enormous snowbank.

The car behind me stopped, and someone got out. I could barely make out the shape of a human being walking toward my car. I yanked on the handle and heaved my body against the car door, trying to open it. Finally it gave way, and I jumped out, slamming myself into the guy until I lay flat on top of him.

I raised my fist and got ready to pummel him good when a deep voice said, "Tink, what the hell are you doing?"

"D-Detective Stone?" I stuttered in shock, staring down into dark eyes that haunted my sleep, and then I scowled. "Me? What I'd like to know is what the hell are *you* doing . . . *Mitchell.*"

# 14

❖✳❖✳❖

I scrambled off the top of Mitch and got to my feet to inspect my car. "Great," I said as I circled her, and then gasped. "Oh my God, look at the dent in the side. The pink flower is all crinkled."

"Relax, Tink. Big Don can pop that right out." Mitch stood and brushed all the snow off his jeans. "Why were you driving like a bat out of hell in this weather?"

"Because you were chasing me. Not too smart in this weather, Spanky. I could have ended up crashing through the ice, and it would have been all your fault." I jabbed a finger in his direction. "I thought you were the killer."

"My fault? You shouldn't have been out in these conditions, anyway. I was making a final round to ensure no crazy fool was in trouble. I should have known better." He threw his hands up in the air and then paused. "Hold on, back up a minute. Why would the killer be after you?"

"Hello, I am still a suspect, and I was the last person to see Amanda Robbins alive. Maybe the killer is afraid she told me something incriminating before she died."

His face grew concerned. "Has anything else happened?"

"Um, well, no." I couldn't tell him about the digoxin in my cupboard and pocket. It sounded too suspicious for even me to believe. But I could tell him about my stalker. I would feel better if at least one other person was aware I could be in danger. "Someone was following me when I was walking from Nikko's back to the Laundromat, though."

"Are you sure?" He studied me.

"Positive. I saw their shadow duck behind a building."

"Are you crazy, Tink? You have no way of protecting yourself." He glared at me, shoving a hand through his hair. "You must be trying to get yourself killed."

"Oh please. I was fine." I wasn't stupid. I had the pepper spray I'd borrowed from his apartment, but I couldn't exactly tell him that without suffering the consequences.

"You weigh nothing." He gestured toward my body with his hands. "A strong wind could break you in two."

"Um, no, that would be my mother," I said, feeling a warm rush wash over me following the path of his eyes. "I enjoy food way too much."

"You'd never know it." He started pacing, and I could literally see the wheels turning in his mind. "Speaking of food, who was with you at Nikko's?"

"Wouldn't you like to know?"

His eyes cut to mine. "Actually, I would, since I asked you to dinner and you said you wanted to rest."

"Well, you certainly didn't waste any time in replacing me," I snapped back.

"What are you talking about?"

"Oh no, don't you go acting all innocent on me." I stabbed my finger in his chest. "I saw you at Smokey Jo's with Lucinda Griswold III."

"You were there?" His eyes widened.

"Ha! So you don't deny it."

"Of course not." He looked confused. "I was checking her out, but don't worry about her. She's fine."

"I'll bet. You certainly looked like you were enjoying yourself."

Dawning washed over his face like soapy water over my teapot, when everything becomes crystal clear. "I know what this is about. You're jealous."

"Am not." I stepped forward and snapped my spine straight. "We've already established there's nothing between us and never will be."

"Exactly." He stepped forward as well and shoved his face close to mine. "Then why are you so angry?" he asked softly, and I could feel his warm breath on my cheeks.

"I-I'm not angry." I stumbled back a step. "I don't think taking Lucinda back to your apartment is necessary to figure her out. It's not very professional, and she might get the wrong idea. And how do you know she's fine? We still don't know why she wants this particular library to stay open."

"Trust me on this and never mind about her. She's rich and bored, that's all."

I knew him well enough by now to know there was

something he wasn't telling me. Some partner he was. Well, if he could keep secrets, then so could I. I'd keep the little matter of a certain conversation one Alex Pendleton had to myself as well.

"You still didn't say why you were at Nikko's if you already ate at Smokey Jo's," Mitch pointed out.

I lifted my hands in the air. "My washer broke so I was doing laundry. I went for a walk while my clothes were drying."

He glanced in the back of my VW bug. "Then where is your laundry basket?"

"Trust me on this and never mind about that." I threw his words back at him. "It's fine."

He narrowed his eyes but didn't press the issue. "Better call for a tow before we freeze to death. I'll drive you home."

"Aye aye, Grump Nazi," I muttered, and grabbed his cell.

"Hey, what are you doing now?"

"I left my phone at my house."

"And you think you can take of yourself." He walked away to further inspect my car while I made arrangements for the tow truck to take my bug to Big Don's Auto Body.

Hopefully, the damage wouldn't be too much to fix. Without working and with this case taking longer than expected to wrap up, my savings were dwindling fast. Although, lately, going back to the city was looking better and better.

Something I never thought I'd live to say.

* * *

"What's the damage, Big Don?" I asked the next morning as I stood beside the giant of a man in his auto-body shop. He had to be at least six foot six, nearly as tall as Wally, with a waistline even bigger than Lulubelle's and a head the size of a basketball.

"Hmmm," he grumbled while rubbing his thick beard. "I'll try to keep her under a thousand, but you did a number on her. She's no spring chicken, you know."

"Great." The detective should have to go halfsies with me on this one, considering he scared me half to death. If he hadn't been following me, I never would have whirled off the road like a spinning top in the first place. "Go ahead and fix her. She might not be much, but she's all I've got."

"Done."

"Good. Belle says you do great work, by the way."

His face flushed crimson, and he nodded once. "Belle's a good woman," was all he said, and then he headed back into his office. I doubted Belle had any idea that Big Don actually had noticed her and, if I wasn't mistaken, was a bit sweet on her. He just needed a push to make a move.

I turned to leave, and a big old station wagon came rolling in, looking even older than my bug. I stifled a chuckle when the driver climbed out. I should have known Gladys Montgomery would be the driver, she being into old things and all. She got out of the car and made a beeline straight into Big Don's office.

Glancing around, I realized no one was watching me, so I nonchalantly walked over to the station wagon and peeked inside. The back looked empty as far as I could tell, other than a bunch of real estate listings from Rosemary on various properties in town, all of them zoned for business.

Wandering around to the front passenger's side, I tried the door, and it was unlocked, squeaking open as if it were a sign. I poked my head inside, flipped the visors open, and then ducked my head down to the floor mat to peek under the seat. My eyelids opened wide.

Gladys was packing?

"Excuse me, may I help you?" her voice said from right behind my backside.

I jumped and hit my head on the dash, yelping in pain.

"What in the world are you doing in my car, young lady?" She puckered her face like a sour pickle.

"Admiring it?" I said in question format. "I love old cars, too, if you haven't noticed. I took a peek inside to check out the upholstery and dashboard, when I lost my earring under the seat."

"You're not wearing an earring in the other ear." She squinted. "In fact, I don't see any earring holes at all."

"It was a clip-on. Wearing only one earring is a trendy big-city thing." I cleared my throat, and she eyed me warily.

"It's Sunny, isn't it?" she asked with a smile that looked way too bright to be natural.

"Yes, ma'am, and you must be Gladys." I held out my hand and shook hers. "Great speech you gave the other day at the town hall meeting."

"Why, thank you." She beamed, relaxing a little. "Some people don't understand what this town needs to survive, let alone actually thrive for a change. God forbid if we get out of the red." She bristled. "But don't get me started on that."

"Change is hard for anyone. I know from firsthand experience. You really think this deal with that developer, um, what was his name?" I watched her carefully.

"Alex—er, Mr. Pendleton."

"Right. Mr. Pendleton." You could tell a lot about a relationship from the way people addressed each other. "You really think the deal will be good for Divinity?"

"Absolutely. We need this deal as much as we need our national landmarks. Turning the library into a bookstore will bring in money and jobs. Turning the hotel into a museum will also bring in revenue."

She went on a rant, arms flailing about like something right out of a puppet show. "As much as I love the library, we can't afford for anything to be free in these hard times. Why can't she see that? Someone needs to make her see it, is what I say. I know the people are hurting, but our town is hurting more. Stupid woman is going to ruin it all. I just know it."

"Who is?" I had realized a long time ago it was better to let people talk. They often revealed more than if you asked them questions outright.

"Huh?" Gladys looked startled, as though just now remembering she was talking to me and not herself. "Oh my." She smoothed her hair. "Sometimes I get carried away over things I'm passionate about."

"That's okay, I'm the same way." I nodded. But there

was a fine line between passion and obsession. "You were saying?" I tried to encourage her to keep talking, but then Big Don popped his head out the office door.

"Gladys, your ride's here," he boomed.

"Thanks, Don." She waved at him, grabbed her purse, and said, "Nice to meet you, Ms. Meadows," as she hustled to the door.

She might not have said the name, but I was pretty sure Lucinda Griswold III was the "she" Gladys had been referring to. The bigger question was, how exactly was Gladys going to *make* her see the error of her ways?

The gun she was packing beneath her seat?


"Sylvia, honestly, you haven't tried on a single thing." My mother walked beside me down the street, frowning on the inside, I was sure. God forbid she wrinkle her face any more than her clothes.

After lunch, we had gone into almost every single one of the quaint little shops Divinity had to offer. Unlike most of the female population, I did *not* enjoy shopping. I led a simple life with simple needs. My mother could not seem to wrap her brain around that and insisted on dragging me shopping with her every chance she got. She was determined to reform me one day, and no matter how many times I claimed that would never happen, she refused to give up.

"I haven't found anything worth trying on, that's why," I responded.

We entered a designer dress shop, and Mom went to work, determined to find something for me to try on. While she was browsing the racks, I bumped into someone.

"Whoops, sorry." I turned around and looked straight into the face of Mrs. Sampson. "Maude, hi. So nice to see you again. You didn't miss lunch with Bernard again, did you?" I teased.

She stared at me blankly. "I'm sorry, do I know you?"

"It's me, Sunny. From the library."

"Ah, yes, the library. I must get back to work. I'm late again." She fled without another word.

"But you're retired," I hollered after her to no avail.

"Who was that?" my mother questioned.

"One poor, confused lady, I'm afraid," I answered, staring after her when my eye caught sight of a store across the street. "Hey, Mom, I saw a shop back there that I wanted to check out."

"Really? Well, that's wonderful. I'll go with you." She started to put the outfit in her hands back on the rack.

"No!" I yelled, and she scrunched her forehead together. I hastened to explain before she got suspicious and followed me. "I mean, it's vintage clothing. Not really your cup of tea. You finish trying on that outfit, and I'll meet you outside when I'm done."

"Well, okay, but you better not take off on me. I know a very good detective who will hunt you down." She tried to look stern, but I saw her slight smile.

"Ha, ha." I grinned back. It felt good. It wasn't much, but it wasn't an argument, either. "See you in a few minutes."

I slipped outside and crossed the street, heading straight into Eddy's Gun Emporium. Hunting was big in these parts, so it would make sense that one of the most thriving businesses in town was a gun shop.

The walls were lined with rifles and shotguns and bows and arrows, the shelves loaded with of all kinds of ammo and knives. Stuffed heads and full bodies of deer, bear, birds, and rabbits occupied every available free space, and huge big-game fur pelts covered the floor. My head swam. This shop wasn't exactly my cup of tea, either, but I had no choice. I had some questions that needed answering.

"May I help you?" a man in his forties with a polite smile and kind eyes asked from behind a display case. "You look a little pale. Are you sure you're in the right store?"

"You caught me. This isn't really my thing." I studied him. "Although this doesn't really look like your thing, either."

He chuckled. "At one time, it wasn't. I used to be a big-city accountant, but the pressure got to me and I gave it all up. After moving to Divinity, I tried hunting. Best decision I ever made. I don't believe in hunting just for the sake of the sport. These animals will die off for sure if we don't thin out their numbers. Hunting with respect to nature is a wonderful thing." He leaned his elbows on the case. "I don't sell my weapons to just anyone."

"I admit that makes me feel better." I smiled sincerely. "I'm Sunny, and you're Eddy, I take it."

"Edward Jones at your service." He shook my hand. "I'm taking a wild guess that you're not in here to take up the hobby."

"No. But I do see you sell handguns."

"Sure, but you have to have a license to carry one, and it has to be registered."

"Oh, it's not for me. No offense, but I really don't like guns."

"None taken, but I still don't get how I can help you."

"Well, I was wondering—you know, with a killer on the loose and all—have many people come in to buy a handgun?"

He looked thoughtful. "A few of the men. You mind my asking why you want to know?"

"Just wondering if maybe I should buy one for my, um, mother. She's a city girl through and through. Any other women in town buy one lately?"

"I'm not sure," he said.

"Oh." My shoulders slumped.

"But I can check for you."

"Really?" I brightened.

"Hang on." He ducked down below the counter and minutes later came up with a book in his hand. Scanning the pages, he finally said, "Little Bobby Jo Sawyer did, but then again, she's about to enter the police academy."

"That's it? You're sure? No other women?"

"I'm sure. Here, see for yourself." He turned the book around to face me.

I scanned over the list of recently purchased handguns, and Gladys Montgomery's name was not on there. That didn't really mean anything, though. She could have bought a gun from anywhere and had it for years. Still, I was desperate to find a lead of any kind. My eyes halted halfway, locking on one name in particular.

Alex Pendleton.

Could Alex have bought the gun for Gladys to off Lucinda? No, that didn't make sense because he wouldn't want to be linked to the murder. Or could Gladys have stolen Alex's gun, intending to frame him for the murder of Lucinda? Or even scarier, were they the ones trying to frame me for Amanda's murder? After all, Alex had said he couldn't let the truth come out because he would never be able to handle jail. I needed to find the link that would tie them to the digoxin and soon, before they used that gun on me instead.

"Thanks, Eddy. You've been a big help. I think I'll stick with my original plan and avoid guns altogether."

"Something tells me that's a smart decision. You take care now, Ms. Meadows."

I marched back out on the street in time for my mother to exit the dress shop across the road. Her eyes flittered to mine, but then she read the name of the shop behind me and a horrified look crossed her face.

I quickly crossed the street to join her and held up my hand. "No worries, Mom, I didn't buy a gun. I went in there to give him a good scolding about how dangerous guns are."

"Right." She gave me a calculating look that warned me to be careful and not do anything stupid to jeopardize this case. "Well, if you're done with your lecture, I'd like you to meet a new friend of mine."

I looked around but didn't see anyone. "Where is she?"

"Inside, buying the outfit I picked out for her. She's my new protégée. At least someone welcomes the advice I give them." My mother sniffed sharply.

A woman exited the shop and came to a stop beside

my mother. "Thank you so much for all your help. It's nice to finally meet a friendly face around this town. I swear everyone thinks I'm the devil."

"I know exactly how you feel," I said, glad to know the Mad Hatters had taken the focus off of me.

"It was my pleasure, dear," my mother said and then swept her hand in my direction. "This is my daughter, Sylvia Meadows." She turned to me. "Darling, this is the new manager of the library, Holly Smith."

"It's Sunny," I corrected, and held out my hand.

Holly shook it, her handshake firm and tough, nothing at all like her average, slightly mousy appearance. Her sharp eyes met mine, and I swear a warning of *Back off* was very clearly written in them. Then they changed so quickly, I questioned if I had imagined it. Either I needed glasses, or there was more to this woman than met the eye.

Last I checked my vision was twenty-twenty.

# 15

❖✳✳✳✳❖

"It was great meeting you, Sunny," Ms. Smith said as though she hadn't just given me the look. "And again, thank you for the help, Mrs. Meadows, but I really must be going. My shift at the library starts at five." She waved and then walked off.

"What a nice girl," my mother said.

"Hmmm, she seems nice enough, but she's hardly a girl, Mother," I said. I couldn't get that look out of my head. I knew I hadn't imagined it, but I didn't know what it meant, either. "I have to go, too," I said, needing time to figure out what to do.

"But we're not finished. What could possibly be more pressing than spending time with your mother?"

"I, um, have to meet with Detective Stone to go over the case."

"Oh, well then, by all means get going. We need

something to break in this case soon." My mother looked worried, like the kind of worry I see on the faces of the people whose tea leaves I read after I tell them I see a pistol. A pistol represents disaster, and right about now disaster pretty much summed up my life. My mother never looked worried. That was not a good sign.

I gave her a quick hug and air kiss, and then I drove home in my rental car. It was almost four o'clock. I had to hurry if I was going to get to the library before Holly Smith. Maybe she was hiding something in the office. But how was I going to sneak in with Carolyn Hanes around?

I let myself into the house, tossed my bag on the kitchen counter, and then hit the message button on my answering machine.

"Hey, Tink, where are you?" A pause filled the line, and then Mitch's smooth, deep buttery voice continued, "We need to talk. Call me."

Morty rounded the corner and hissed.

"Oh, so now he wants to talk. Ha!" I said to Morty, feeling like hissing myself. "Too little, too late. I have plans." I looked at Morty and sighed. "I just haven't figured them out yet."

Morty stared at me for a full minute, and I couldn't look away. If I didn't know better, I'd swear he could hear my thoughts. He meowed and then headed for the stairs. When I didn't follow, he ran back, rubbed up against me, and meowed again. Louder this time. Then headed for the stairs once more.

I needed to change my clothes, anyway, so I followed. When I reached my bedroom, Morty was sitting on my mattress. I eyed him curiously. "What are you up to, boy?"

His nose wrinkled, and it seriously looked like the corners of his mouth tipped up. Then he stepped to the side, revealing a teddy bear behind him.

My jaw fell open. "Where did you get that?" I sputtered.

When I was little, my mom had a nanny cam that looked just like this. She used to watch my babysitters to make sure they weren't behaving badly. When I grew older, she still had a nanny cam to keep her eye on me. I hadn't seen a teddy bear like this in years. It couldn't be the same one . . . could it?

"How on earth did you get this?" I asked, gaping at Morty.

He sauntered off as if to say, *You simple, simple girl.*

My grin came slow and sweet. I didn't understand how it had happened, but I didn't really care, either. This nanny cam was the perfect solution to my problem.

I changed my clothes, putting on a flowy skirt and soft sweater, and then I grabbed the bear. Once downstairs, I stuffed it inside my bag and glanced around. "Thanks, Morty, wherever you are." The little stinker was as elusive as ever, his food and water still untouched. I shook my head and headed out the door.

Ten minutes later I was parking my rental car at the library. I glanced at my watch. Only thirty minutes until Holly Smith showed up. I had to work fast.

Locking up my car, I headed inside right to the circulation desk. "Excuse me," I said to the woman behind the counter.

"Yes?"

"Do you know where Miss Hanes is?"

"In the office in back."

"Thanks." I headed in that direction and knocked on the closed door.

The door opened, and Carolyn stared at me in surprise and then wariness. "Ms. Meadows?" She looked beyond me as though looking for Detective Stone. "Are you alone?"

"Oh yes." I waved my hand. "This is an unofficial visit. I have a request that might sound strange, but I was hoping you could accommodate me. You know, just between you and me. Detective Stone will never have to know."

"It's not anything unsavory, is it?"

"Oh, heavens, no." I held my hand to my chest. "It's just I feel so bad about what happened to Ms. Robbins. When she came to me for her reading, she mentioned how much she loved teddy bears." I had no clue if she really did like teddy bears or not, but I was winging it. "Anyway, I thought it would be a nice tribute if I could keep this teddy bear in here in her honor."

"Well, I don't see why not. I had no idea she was so fond of teddy bears, but that's very kind of you."

"Do you mind if I have a moment alone?" I forced my voice to hitch and my eyes to water. "I just want to say I'm so sorry for what happened to her and say good-bye."

"I guess that would be okay. But only a minute. This office is for personnel only." She slipped out the door, and I got to work.

I reached inside the bear and turned the camera on.

Then I climbed on the office chair and placed the bear on top of the bookshelf. The eyes stared right down at the desk.

Perfect.

I hopped down as Carolyn Hanes came back in. I dabbed my eyes, thanked her, and left. Mission accomplished. Just before I reached the door, I ran into Holly Smith.

She stopped short and blinked when she saw me. "Miss Meadows?"

"Ah, Miss Smith. So nice to see you again. I stopped in for a book, but you don't have it, so I'll be on my way." I tried to step around her.

"What's the title?" She blocked my path. "I'll see if we can order it."

"Oh, that's okay. I'm in a hurry." I tapped my watch. "I've got a date." I wagged my brows. "Can't keep the man waiting." I giggled, then darted by her and slipped out the door.

Back at home, I snuggled down in my pj's and sank my teeth into a gooey slice of veggie pizza. I sat on my living room sofa with a roaring fire going and surveyed the items on the coffee table before me. The audio device for the bug I'd planted in Pendleton's car and the video thingy for the nanny cam I'd placed in the library office sat front and center, beckoning me to check them out.

I never could resist a good beckoning.

"Let's see what you're up to, Alex," I said as I pressed the play button and sat back to listen, sipping my iced tea.

At first a lot of static filled the line, and then Pendleton's voice came in and out, telling me more than I wanted to know about the man. He sang Beatles songs with a voice that wasn't actually half bad. He cursed out other drivers, having a bit of a temper and not much patience at all. He had a surprising fast-food addiction and loved to listen to talk radio.

I yawned, getting bored and thinking bugging his car had been a waste of time. I reached forward to shut off the device when his phone rang.

"Pendleton here," he said. "Are you sure?" A pause. "Maybe we should drop this project and move on to another location in another town. They're getting too close." Another pause. "I know we've got a lot invested in this one, but I'm telling you, something doesn't feel right." A loud bang sounded like he had slammed his fist on the dashboard. "Okay, we'll wait awhile longer, but if this deal doesn't go through soon, I'm out."

He disconnected, and then a sound like keys dropping echoed through the device really close. There was some shuffling, and then I heard, "What the hell is this?" followed by a curse. Then the sound went dead.

I choked on a piece of my pizza, and Morty appeared at my feet, staring up at me with what looked like concern. I took a sip of my tea and reassured him. "I'm fine, my little hero."

He flipped his tail and lay down at my feet, apparently not moving until he deemed everything was okay. Physically, I was okay. Mentally, not so much. I'd worn gloves when I planted that bug, but I wasn't sure I'd done everything else right. What if Pendleton figured out I was behind the bug somehow?

Detective Stone wasn't going to be happy with me.

To take my mind off that little mess-up, I decided to turn on the video device. Carolyn Hanes wandered in and out a couple more times, doing normal office-type work. But she paced, looking worried about something.

Next, Holly Smith and Lucinda Griswold III came in together to join Carolyn and locked the door behind them.

"How are you holding up?" Lucinda asked Carolyn.

She took a shaky breath. "I'm doing okay, considering."

"It won't be much longer. Everything will work out, it always does," Holly added.

I didn't understand any of this. Holly had taken the position meant for Carolyn, and Carolyn had acted like she despised her in public. Yet here they were chummy-chummy. And what about Lucinda? Carolyn had told Gladys and Alex she was with them in trying to get the deal to turn the library into a bookstore to go through. Then why did she seem to be in cahoots with Lucinda as well?

Maybe it was like *Survivor*. Carolyn was playing both sides to see which ally would get her further in the game.

Lucinda's phone vibrated on the desk, and she answered it. A moment later, she looked straight at the nanny cam and then said, "Got it," and hung up. She tipped her head to the side and asked Carolyn, "Cute bear. Where'd you get it?"

"Sunny Meadows brought it in as a tribute to Amanda. Wasn't that sweet?"

Holly and Lucinda locked eyes, and then Holly said, "Very." Two seconds later, the bear all but forgotten, she said, "Speaking of Amanda, did you hear the latest?"

Lucinda paused a beat. "Okay, I'll bite. What?"

"Right before Amanda died, she was seen out on the town talking to Alex Pendleton." Holly shrugged. "It might mean nothing, but don't you find it odd they would meet in public together? Everyone knew they despised each other."

"Really," Lucinda said. "I wonder what they were talking about?"

"Where did they go?" Carolyn asked, looking confused.

"That new karaoke bar."

"Karaoke?" Carolyn frowned. "That doesn't sound like Amanda at all."

Holly lifted her hands, palms up. "Hey, that's what I heard. I think Pendleton likes to hang out there."

"That would be a good place to talk in private considering most of the locals prefer Smokey Jo's," Carolyn said.

"Hmmm. I wonder if the police are aware of the rumors," Lucinda speculated.

"Well, I'm sure the detective is looking into every lead." Carolyn stood, twisting her purse string in her hands. "If we're done here, I really need to go home now."

"Almost. We need to go over one more thing," Holly said.

I sat forward, my eyes glued to the screen, and then

the screen went all fuzzy like a snowy white blizzard. The bugger flicked off. Unbelievable. I never thought to check the battery. I blew out a breath, still processing everything I'd heard.

Not only were these women allies, but Carolyn had still acted nervous when they'd mentioned the case. Especially the part about Pendleton. The detective wasn't the only one following leads. I'd been given a new one myself.

Maybe it was time to do a little singing of my own.

The Song Bird was a new Japanese karaoke bar on the edge of town. I'd changed out of my jammies and had decided to check out the place, maybe ask around and see if anyone might have seen Amanda and Pendleton. Possibly overheard their conversation.

I asked Jo to come along, but she refused to step foot in her competitor's door. Besides, she had to work. They were swamped, so Sean had to work as well. That meant I would have to go solo. I was used to going solo, and I loved karaoke. Everything would be fine.

Then why was I shaking in my knee-high suede boots?

I pulled my rental car into the parking lot, missing my bug. Hopefully Big Don would call soon, saying she was fixed. Stepping inside the bar, I didn't see anyone I knew. I recognized some people from town but no one I knew personally. Not like at Smokey Jo's, anyway.

Jo had *nothing* to worry about.

This place was filled with eclectic people with bizarre tastes in music, strange clothes, and weird food I didn't even recognize. It kind of reminded me of being back in the city. Not in a good way. I agreed with Carolyn Hanes's statement: this place did not seem like the sort of bar Amanda Robbins would visit, so Pendleton must have made it worth her while.

I made my way over to the bar, tucking my skirt beneath my legs as I sat on a stool barely big enough to fit beneath my bottom. I ordered a club soda with lime. That way I could keep my wits about me, yet no one would know I wasn't drinking. I needed to keep a clear head and find some answers.

"Hi there, I'm Sunny," I said to the bartender. "I'm new in town. Someone I met at the library recommended this place."

The bartender was a petite Asian woman with long black hair twisted in a knot at the base of her neck. "That's nice. I'm Kim." She looked me over curiously. "You don't look like our usual crowd. We get more outsiders than we do locals."

"Really? That's odd. My friend said her coworker, Amanda Robbins, used to come here a lot."

"I heard about that poor librarian. That's awful what happened to her." She shook her head. "I don't ever remember her coming in here."

I sipped more of my club soda, completely baffled now. "Are you sure you've never seen her in here with some man?"

"I'm here a lot, and I've never seen Amanda Robbins in here by herself or with anyone else. Why don't you ask Cole?"

"Who's Cole?"

"The big guy at the end of the bar with the leather jacket and tattoos. He's one of the few locals we have. Works as a carpenter and did a few jobs for us when we first opened. He's been here every night since."

"Thanks," I said, and slid off my stool.

"Careful now, he doesn't mix well with strangers," were her departing words, but I kept walking.

Taking a deep breath, I plastered on a smile, shook my spiky hair out, and sashayed over to this Cole character. "Hey there, big guy. Come here often?"

"Seriously?" He looked at me as though I had three heads. He was intimidating as hell with his five o'clock shadow, buzz cut, and muscles to spare. No wonder he sat alone. His look said step back or die.

"Lame, I know. Sorry. I don't do the whole bar scene."

"Then why are you here?"

I snorted. I tended to do that when I was nervous. "To practice my karaoke, of course. I can sing, you know."

"If your songs are anything like your pickup lines, you'd better keep practicing." He sipped his longneck.

"Like you could do better?" I challenged him, hoping to get him to sing like a canary in more ways than one. Besides, I was good, darnit.

His eyes were orbs of steel, but I didn't so much as flinch. He grunted, stood up without a word, and then climbed the stage and took the mic from the man who was singing. The man scurried off the stage without a single protest.

The big guy opened his mouth, and I fell off my stool. The most amazing voice poured out of his vocal cords as he crooned a beautiful love song, staring off into space. It was like he was in his own world, singing to someone specific who wasn't there to hear it anymore. Pain and sorrow flashed across his face for the briefest of moments.

I sucked in a breath.

When the song ended, he turned back into the unapproachable intimidating beast at the end of the bar. He took his seat and chugged his beer once more, ignoring the roar of applause and requests for more from the crowd.

"That was incredible," I said in awe.

He jerked his head at me. "Your turn."

"Oh, I don't think so. How am I supposed to follow that?"

"Doesn't matter. You said you were better. Prove it."

"But—"

"Look, you've got balls. We both know this isn't your scene. You're obviously here to ask me something." He stared me down, but I didn't deny it. "If you want answers, then sing. It's as simple as that. Unless you're chicken . . ."

"I'm gonna make you eat those words," I grumbled.

His eyes twinkled and lips wobbled as though trying not to laugh. "You can try."

I marched up onstage and grabbed the mic from some other guy, who grabbed it back and yelled, "Hey."

Cole stood up, growled with clenched fists, and suddenly the mic was back in my hands. I saluted Cole with it, told the woman what song I wanted, and then closed my eyes and began to sing a beautiful love song like Cole had. I poured all I had into that song and really felt the emotion. The song ended, and I felt really good . . .

Until I opened my eyes!

The entire room was speechless. Mouths gone slack, ears plugged, painful facial expressions, and no clapping to be had. I felt my face flood with heat and bit my lip, handing the mic back to the man, who refused it as if it was now tainted.

"Oh, come on, I wasn't that bad," I said.

"No, Tink, you were worse," came a deep voice that never failed to rattle my insides. "Care to tell me what the hell you're doing?"

# 16

"No, pal." Cole surged to his massive feet and barked. "The question is, just what the hell do you think *you're* doing? I suggest you get your hands off my woman now before I remove them permanently."

"Your woman?" Detective Stone and I sputtered simultaneously, and then we stared at each other.

Cole shot me a knowing wink and nodded his head slightly.

"That's right, you heard the man," I said, yanking my wrist out of Mitch's hand and sliding my palm into Cole the Carpenter's meaty paw. I smiled up at him and fluttered my lashes.

He looked down at me and raised a thick brow much like the detective would have.

Ugh. What was it with these herculean men?

Mitch started laughing from deep in his chest, which

wasn't as large as Cole's but was impressive just the same, I had to admit. "You expect me to believe you and Sasquatch here are an item? Since when?"

"Watch it, buddy." Cole took a step toward Mitch.

I put my arms around the big guy's waist since it was all I could reach. "Now now, honey. Just ignore him. He's just a big hairy ape."

"No, you watch it," Mitch said back to Cole, ignoring me as he put his hands on his hips making his gun clearly visible. "Do you know who I am?"

"I know who you are, Detective, but I don't really care. No one treats a lady like that." The carpenter's arm draped over me, and I could barely breathe from his hug.

"Easy there, big fella. This lady must have air," I wheezed, patting his tree trunk of an arm until he lifted it slightly.

"Trust me, she's not a lady, she's a pain in my"— Cole's warning glare caused the detective to change course midsentence—"unmentionables. Now step aside. I'm taking her in for obstruction of justice."

"Whaaat?" I shrieked, stepping out from under Cole's humongous arm. "You're the one who is obstructing justice. I was just about to . . . to . . ." Oh shoot, I hadn't meant to say that much.

Both men paused, looked at me, and then crossed their arms and waited.

Finally, Sasquatch turned to Detective Stone and said, "She's all yours, pal. She's more trouble than she's worth."

"You have no idea," Detective Stone said, and then proceeded to hoist me over his shoulder and haul me out of the bar, much to the delight of the patrons based on all the hoots and hollers.

I could feel his muscles bunch and flex beneath me as he marched across the snow-packed parking lot. He smelled fresh and clean and manly. I shut off my senses and focused on how mad I was as he tossed me unceremoniously in his car and practically did a donut, he was driving so fast out of the parking lot.

"But my rental," I wailed, staring back through the tinted window.

"I'll send someone back for it." He looked straight ahead, not hesitating in the least.

"Where are you taking me?" I whined.

"Like I said, I'm taking you in." His face showed no emotion, the rat. "Maybe locking you up would do you some good."

"You can't be serious," I yelled. "You are *not* taking me back to the station again. I won't allow it. And you have no grounds to lock me up." I yanked on the door handle, but the door wouldn't open.

"I tried things your way, but you never called me back," he pointed out in a calm, irritating manner, as though he were talking to a child. "I meant it when I said we needed to talk. Maybe doing things my way will get some results."

"I want a lawyer." I set my jaw and ground my teeth.

"Fine." He paused, his eyes meeting mine for a brief moment as he dropped the bomb. "I'll call your mother."

I gasped, and a satisfied smirk settled over his face.

"I'm sure she'd love to know what you were doing with Sasquatch in the Song Bird as much as I would."

He looked back at the road. "Last I checked with her, she said you told her you had a meeting with me tonight to discuss the case." He jerked his head to the side. "Basically I'm just following your wishes."

"My wishes do not involve metal bars and a key," I spat out sarcastically.

"Did Sasquatch know that? He looked like the kind of guy who was into metal."

"Ha, ha. You really have no clue what you interrupted. I was on the verge of something big, but you had to go and ruin it."

"No you weren't, and no I didn't. Hell, I saved your scrawny behind."

Finally, a bit of emotion. "I highly doubt that." I snorted. "It's more like I saved your big ole behind from getting pummeled. If you hadn't noticed, that guy was huge."

"Bigger doesn't always mean better, babe." I opened my mouth to give him another scathing comeback, but he cut me off. "If you would have called me back, we could have avoided all this." He clenched his teeth, and a muscle in his jaw right below his jagged scar pulsed. "Quit being so damn stubborn and independent, Tink. We're supposed to be working together."

"Exactly!" I threw up my hands in frustration. "But someone kept me out of the loop. You left me no choice but to venture out on my own."

"And you leave me no choice now," he said, back to being calm and in control. "You're a danger to yourself and to others." He hesitated and chewed the inside of his cheek as though trying not to laugh. "I heard you sing."

"Oh, you make me so mad, you overgrown arrogant . . . turd."

"Turd?" A deep V formed on his forehead. "That's the best you've got?"

I crossed my arms and looked out the window, refusing to let him bait me anymore. The man made me want to pluck every black hair out of his oversized head.

Finally he said, "Okay, fine. I won't lock you up in jail if you agree to talk to me."

I made him wait for several minutes, and then I jerked a shoulder. "Fine. Where?"

"My place."

"Oh, joy." House arrest with Grump-o-liscious . . . hot but ornery as hell.

"Take it or leave it, Tink. I don't trust your place." He shuddered. "You've got backup."

"Someday, you're going to appreciate that backup."

"Maybe in another lifetime."

"That can be arranged," I couldn't help adding.

His eyes cut to mine. All he said was, "Don't even think about it, or I'll haunt your dreams." He pointed his finger at me.

The scary thing was, as much as I hated it, he already did.


"It's time to pony up and come clean, Tink. It's the only way we're going to solve this case. Why were you at the Song Bird tonight?" Mitch asked, handing me hot chocolate and taking the chair across from the couch this time.

227

Still, it was a little too close for comfort. The last time I'd been inside his apartment, we'd drunk hot chocolate and coffee, creating a mocha kiss I'd never forget. I squirmed, adjusting his tiger fleece over my legs.

I finally started talking. "Fine. Anything to get this night over with. After I bugged Pendleton's car, I—"

"You what?" Detective Stone's hand paused halfway to his slightly parted lips.

"You gonna let me finish or not?" I waited all calm and patient-like. Hey, I could play this game, too.

"I can't believe you went through my stuff. I was wondering where that went," he grumbled and then took a sip of his coffee. "Go on." He waved his hand and sat back. "I can't wait to hear the rest."

"As I was saying, after I bugged Pendleton's car, I placed a nanny cam in the office of the library."

"Wait." He wrinkled his forehead. "I don't have a nanny cam."

"I know." I wrinkled my nose at him. "This one was all mine."

"Where the hell did you get it from?"

"Morty."

He gaped at me. "Your cat?" He cursed. "What else can that thing do?"

I held up a hand. "You don't want to know. Anyway, we don't have time for that."

I rubbed my hands together and leaned forward, resting my elbows on my knees as I tried to remember everything I'd discovered. "Okay, so we already know Pendleton, Gladys, and Carolyn are working together to make the library deal go through. Pendleton wants that bookstore bad, and Gladys wants the hotel to be her national landmark. I thought Carolyn wanted money to pay for her Home Shopping Network addiction, but now I'm not so sure anymore."

"Why do you say that?" He studied me as though seeing me in a whole new light. Good, maybe he'd finally realize I had something to offer in solving this case.

"I'm pretty sure Lucinda is the mystery woman who is a hard nut to crack. She doubled her gift to the library and swayed the vote toward keeping the library in return. Then there's Holly Smith. She snagged the new librarian position, so you'd think Carolyn would be furious with her, right?"

"Makes sense to me."

"Then why did my nanny cam show all three together, locked in the office, talking about something almost being over and everything being okay? Holly voted the way Lucinda wanted her to in favor of keeping the library open." I sat back and finished my hot chocolate. "I swear Carolyn is working with them on something, but what and why, I don't know."

"That still doesn't explain why you were at the Song Bird with Sasquatch," Mitch grumbled, setting his empty cup on the coffee table between us.

I gaped at him in shock and then threw his words back at him with pleasure. "You're jealous."

His look pierced through me straight to my core. "Am not," he returned the favor, and we stared each other down.

"Whatever." I looked away first, feeling suddenly warm and kicking off his tiger fleece. "Anyway, Holly said she'd heard Amanda met with Pendleton at the Song Bird before she died. And Sasquatch, whose real name is Cole by the way, sang a love song that was so touching. You could tell he was really sad. He's a local. I think he might have overheard Amanda and Pendleton's conversation." I beamed, thoroughly proud of myself, thinking, *Top that, Grump-a-dump!*

"Wrong." Mitch looked bored.

"Excuse me?" I sputtered.

"I said you're wrong, Tink. W-r-o-n-g." He punctuated each word as though I really were a dunce. "I didn't tell you about Lucinda earlier because I didn't have all my facts yet, but it appears you won't stop causing trouble until I come clean."

"It appears that way, doesn't it?" I sat patiently, hands folded in my lap, fluttering my lashes and waiting.

He rolled his eyes. "Lucinda Griswold and Holly Smith are cops," he said point-blank, and it was like getting hit with a bullet to the chest.

I reeled back. "Crazy Detective say what?"

"You heard me. That's why I said not to worry about Lucinda, that she was fine. When you saw us laughing and talking so easily at Smokey Jo's, it was because we were reminiscing about my old department in the city. We know a lot of the same people even though Griswold and Smith are FBI."

"No way!"

"Yes way." He made a funny face and a set of air quotes. "I'm not sure what they are doing here, but I *am* sure they want to keep it undercover."

"So that's why Holly gave me a back-off look. I really

don't know what she wanted me to back off on, though. And Carolyn must be working on the inside with them. But I still don't get something."

"Really? Seems to me you know everything."

"Funny." I smirked. "Seriously, though, what was up with the librarian meeting Pendleton at that karaoke bar? That doesn't make any sense."

"My guess is the FBI knew you planted the nanny cam, and so they sent you on a wild-goose chase to throw you off."

I gasped. "Oh my God, Lucinda did look straight at the camera at one point." I wrinkled my brow. "But what about Cole? He is a local, and he certainly looked sad. Maybe he was sad to hear Amanda was murdered when he possibly could have stopped it if he'd gone to the police."

"He should be sad. That's Cole West. Why do you think he hangs out at the Song Bird instead of Smokey Jo's?"

"I was wondering that myself."

"His wife died in a motorcycle accident a year ago, and he was the driver. Hasn't driven one since, and he pretty much keeps to himself these days. Local bars just remind him of what he lost."

"Oh, poor guy." My heart went out to him. "Well, I feel like a total idiot."

"Don't," the detective stated matter-of-factly. "You probably gave him more entertainment than he's had in a long time. I can't believe you took the stage and sang like that."

"Like what? I love karaoke."

"Were we in the same room? You had to have heard

and seen the reaction from the crowd. Trust me, Tink. Karaoke does not love you."

"You're all crazy." I refused to believe I was that bad. I had ears.

"If you say so," he responded, then added half under his breath, "but I'd get my hearing checked if I were you."

"Whatever." I shook off my irritation with him and focused. "What do we do now?"

"We figure out what Lucinda and Holly don't want us to know."

"Sounds like a plan, partner. So are we good now?"

His eyes met mine and held. "Yeah. We're more than good."

My stomach flipped. There was a world of meaning in that one sentence. The question was, what was I prepared to do about it?

Turned out I didn't have to worry about it. Mitch's cell phone went off. He answered, gave me a sharp look, and then said, "I'll be there in a minute." He stood.

"No, we'll be there," I pointed out, standing as well.

"No, I'll take you home, and then I'll be there. Grab your coat."

"But you said we were good." I grabbed my coat and joined him by the door. "What's up, *partner*?"

He slipped his jacket back on and grabbed his gun. "You're going to follow me if I take you home, aren't you?"

"Now you're catching on." I patted his chest.

"Fine, let's go, you pain in my unmentionables. But you're staying in the car." He harrumphed and opened the door. "Pendleton got pulled over for a speeding ticket as he was headed out of town. He freaked out, took the officer hostage, and is spouting off something about a conspiracy and big brother watching him." He gave me a pointed look.

I bit my lip. "You think it had anything to do with him finding the bug I planted?"

"Gee, not at all. I repeat, let's go before you cause any more trouble."

He didn't have to ask me twice. I jogged to his car and climbed inside as he locked up his apartment and joined me in seconds.

When we arrived at the scene on the side of the road, Lucinda Griswold III and Holly Smith were already there, looking nothing like a rich socialite and mousy library manager. They were fully armed and ready to rock and roll as they used their car as a shield from Pendleton.

"Stay put," Mitch barked at me as he got out of the car. Of course I followed him.

"What's the status?" Mitch asked as he arrived by their sides in the standoff and then growled when he spotted me. He shoved me down behind the car and pointed a warning finger in my face.

I nodded and crossed my heart in a signal promising I would behave. Too bad he didn't see the other fingers crossed behind my back. I was desperate enough to do anything at this point if it meant solving this blasted case.

"Pendleton was making a run for it," Lucinda said.

"Why? Didn't he just get stopped for a speeding violation?" I asked, feeling vulnerable and wishing I'd bought that handgun from Eddy right about now.

"Not quite," Holly answered.

"What the hell are they doing here?" Pendleton shouted. "This isn't a freak show."

The officer he held at gunpoint said something to him that seemed to calm him down for the moment.

"What's really going on, Agent Griswold?" Mitch asked.

"We've been watching Alex Pendleton for years for money laundering. The bookstore would have been a front for his biggest site yet. Only this time we have proof."

"What proof?" Mitch asked.

"The bug Ms. Meadows planted. He spilled everything in detail. That's some partner you have there," Holly said.

"Assistant," Mitch mumbled. "She's been demoted."

"Hmmm, well, all I can say is she does good work," Lucinda added. "He smashed the bug, but that didn't erase all the conversations recorded on the audio device we found in her living room."

"You broke into my house?" I sputtered. "Are you crazy? You didn't let my cat out, did you?"

"You have a cat?" Holly asked.

"No," Mitch corrected, "she has a demon."

"If Morty didn't stop you, then he wanted you to find the evidence," I jumped in. "I guess this means the library deal is off."

"Yes. Pendleton is going away for a long time, just as soon as we take him down." Lucinda's eyes lit up. "I've been waiting for this day for a long time."

"I'm not going back to jail. I can promise you that,"

Pendleton shouted again. "Let me go or your friend here will get hurt."

"What about the officer he's holding hostage?" I asked, concern filling me.

"Pendleton's no murderer," Lucinda said.

"Maybe not, but even to my untrained eye, he sure seems like a loose cannon," I pointed out.

"Pendleton's no match for Officer Harlow," Mitch said with conviction. "Harlow is waiting for the right moment. He's been highly trained in hostage situations. Besides, we've got his back if he needs us. He knows that."

"What about Gladys Montgomery?" I asked, focusing on something else so I wouldn't think about Screw Loose Pendleton sporting a gun.

"She might have gone about things the wrong way, but she didn't do anything illegal," Mitch said. "Though I can't imagine the Historical Society or the Library Board will allow her to remain president."

"And what about Carolyn Hanes?" I asked.

"She's the one who called us right after Gladys and Alex approached her," Holly said. "She might be hard up for money, but she truly did love her friend and was only trying to do right by her. She'll get the manager position at the library once Pendleton is caught."

"And what about Amanda Robbins's murder?" Mitch asked.

"That's your department, darling. Not ours," Lucinda purred, and then winked at the detective.

"No, I'll never agree to that," Pendleton screeched, backing away from Officer Harlow and pointing his gun at him. "You'll never take me alive!"

A commotion sounded, and all the law enforcement on the scene drew their weapons in a ready position. I ducked and covered my head, peeking under the car as a scuffle ensued.

Officer Harlow ducked as Pendleton started frantically pulling the trigger, creating a sound like teakettle bubbles popping at a full boil. Bullets pinged off the sides of several police cars, including the one I was hiding behind. I yelped, and Mitch dove on top of me, covering me with every inch of his godlike body.

I felt safe, warm, and protected as I watched the scene unfold before me in awe. Officer Harlow crouched down like a football player, juking left and right until Pendleton hesitated for one brief second. But a second was all Harlow needed as he dove forward and tackled Pendleton flat on his back. He wrenched the gun from Pendleton's hand and then flipped him over and cuffed him in seconds.

"It's over, Tink," Mitch whispered in my ear. "You okay?"

"Fine," I wheezed. "Just hard to breathe."

"Sorry." He rolled off of me and stood. "You can get up now. Pendleton's been caught." He reached out a hand to help me up.

"That's it?" I asked amazed as he pulled me up.

"Told you Harlow was good."

Lucinda nodded at me and then winked at Mitch. "It's been a pleasure, Detective," she said, and wandered off to apprehend her perp from Officer Harlow.

I suddenly realized that might be it for the FBI, but things were far from over for me.

"This puts us right back at square one, doesn't it?" I said to Mitch. "Pretty much all of our suspects have fallen through."

"Except you," Mitch said, studying me in a way I did not like.

"You can't be for real."

"Oh, I'm very real. And you'd better get your thinking cap on, Tink. Time's running out."

# 17

"Thanks, Big Don." I handed him a check in exchange for my car keys as the phone rang in his office.

"Ma'am." Not a man of many words, that was all he said as he saluted me.

The answering machine kicked on, and Lulubelle's voice rang out loud and clear. Don jumped and then flushed. "I, ah, better get that," he said, and hustled off in that direction at a brisk pace, not waiting for my response. Guess he was finally noticing Belle now, though he still probably hadn't clued her in.

I climbed in my bug, settling into the creaky seat, loving every lump and bump as much as I loved sugar in my tea. Pulling out of the garage, I turned onto Main Street and headed home, thinking this really was starting to feel like home. All I'd ever had back in the city were my parents and a couple of acquaintances I wouldn't even call friends.

Divinity had brought me so much more.

I had Jo, who was turning out to be a great friend. Sean, who was also a friend and maybe a little more. Even Detective Stone, who was . . . well, I didn't really know. And finally, I had my house, my car, and my cat. The thought of losing them all if we didn't solve this case scared me to death.

I pulled my bug into my driveway and found a man waiting for me. He stood tall in his sports coat and jeans, his black hair thick and wavy, his dark sunglasses firmly in place, and his expression as grim as ever. Detective Stone. My traitorous heart sped up same as it always did when I saw him.

"What's up?" I asked as I stepped outside, acting as though he didn't affect me in the slightest.

"We got a call at the station from Bernard Sampson." Mitch's face looked graver than normal. "He says his wife never came home last night, and he's worried sick about her."

"Oh my gosh, that poor little old lady." My heart thumped for a totally different reason now. "You don't think anything awful happened to her, do you?" I fidgeted and paced. "It was freezing last night, and the killer is still on the loose."

"Let's not go there, Tink. Calm down and let's try to find her, all right?"

I took several deep breaths. "Okay."

We got in his car and cruised the town. We went to the library with no luck. No one had seen her. We went to the shopping district but still no luck. No one in the restaurants or at the church had seen her, either. After an hour of searching, we were headed back to my house when I spotted a movement off the side of the road.

"Wait a minute, back up," I blurted.

"What?" Mitch slammed on the breaks.

"Back there. I think I saw something."

He backed up his cruiser. I searched the street by Carolyn's house and Amanda Robbins's old house, which still had the yellow tape around it.

"I don't see anything," Mitch said, scanning the area.

"I swear I saw something." I opened my door.

"What are you doing?"

"What do you think I'm doing? I'm getting out to investigate. Isn't that our job? Jeesh." I stepped out of the car and closed the door.

"Get back in here, you crazy-headed fool," he snapped through the window he'd rolled down. "It could be dangerous."

"Yes, and poor Mrs. Sampson could be hurt." I crouched down and started zigzagging across the yard toward the librarian's house like I'd seen in the movies.

Detective Stone hopped out and jogged until he caught up with me, tapping me on the shoulder of my humongous puffy coat. "What are you trying to do, scare the bad guy off by line dancing?"

"Ha, ha." I continued my crazy movements. "Aren't you supposed to run in a zigzag pattern when chasing someone?"

"No, you only do that if you are the one being chased and the bad guy is shooting at you with a gun." He ran right along beside me. "Stop doing that, you look like a fool." He snagged his arm around my waist and pulled me back against him.

"Oh." I stopped moving, enjoying the warmth of his wide, hard, sculpted chest for a moment, then came to my senses and stepped out of his hold to stand up straight and march up the driveway.

"Now what the hell are you doing?" He snatched my hand and yanked me to a stop. "You don't want to advertise your approach, either."

I looked down at our hands and pulled mine from his, crossing my arms in front of me and tapping my boot. "Okay, smarty-pants, what am I supposed to do?"

"Let me go first. You don't even have a gun."

"I won't argue with that."

"That'd be a first." He grunted. "Stay close."

I stepped behind him and followed closely. So close that when he stopped short by the corner, I bounced off his back, grabbing his hips so I wouldn't fall. He craned his neck around and scowled down at me from over his shoulder.

"Not *that* close," he snapped.

"Sorry." I winced and backed off a step. Okay, a baby step, but after the standoff with Pendleton, I wasn't taking any chances. I wanted to solve this case, but I didn't want to die in the process.

The detective searched the area, made sure it was safe, and then peeked around the corner. He quickly stood up and holstered his gun. "There she is. I think she's alone, but—"

That was all I needed to hear. I raced around him and

242

ran to the old woman's side, glancing over my shoulder. He threw up his hands and followed, shaking his head the entire way. She sat at the base of the librarian's bedroom window, exactly where the footprints had been that night. She had her apron on, as was her habit, I was beginning to see, but at least this time her shoes matched. And thank God she'd worn a heavy coat.

"Mrs. Sampson, this is Detective Stone. Can you hear me?" Mitch asked.

She sat there staring straight ahead, looking dazed.

"Maude, it's Sunny. I'm so glad we found you." I touched her cheek.

She turned to look at me. "Sunny? Have we met?" she asked.

Sadness filled every ounce of my body and darkened my soul like tea filling my cup and staining the water black. "Yes, a couple of times. Bernard is looking for you."

"Oh dear, did I miss our lunch date again?" she asked. "My shift at the library takes up so much of my time."

"I know, but I'm sure they'll understand if you want to take a break." I held her hand. "Bernard is really worried about you. Would you like to go see him?"

"Oh yes. He's a good man. He works so hard for all of us. Where are my girls?"

"They're fine," Mitch said, giving me a funny look. Once he recaptured Maude's attention, he asked, "Are you ready to go, Mrs. Sampson?"

She gnawed her bottom lip. "Am I in trouble?"

"No, no. We're just going to have Dr. Wilcox check you out." Mitch helped her to her feet. "Make sure you're okay."

"I told Bernard I was dying, but he wouldn't listen to me." She sighed. "He never listens to me."

I looked her in the eye and squeezed her hands. "Something tells me he'll listen to you now."


Dr. Wilcox came out of the exam room, sending Maude home with her husband, Bernard. Bernard stopped at the exit to the waiting room and turned to the detective and me. He cleared his throat and said, "Thank you for bringing my wife back to me. I don't know what I would have done if you hadn't found her."

Mitch nodded once in return.

I said, "You're welcome, Mr. Sampson. Please take care of her. She's a little fragile."

Bernard replied, "I know all about my wife, Ms. Meadows. I've always looked out for what's mine." The lines in his face looked deeper today, like the worry and stress had finally taken its toll.

"That's my Bernard," Maude said, patting his arm. "A real trouper." She looked exhausted. He held her hand tight, and they walked out together.

Dr. Wilcox reentered the waiting room and called Detective Stone and me into his office.

"Well, what's the verdict, Doc?" Detective Stone asked, leaning a hip against the wall.

I refused a seat as well, too keyed up to sit.

Doc sat on the edge of his desk and rubbed the bridge of his nose. "Mrs. Sampson is worse off than I had originally thought."

*Gee, ya think?* I wanted to shout. I was no doctor, but

even I could tell she wasn't exactly all there. Instead, I smiled politely and inquired, "Really? How so?"

"She's always complained of being tired, but that's a natural part of aging. Forgetting some minor things is also an inevitable part of growing old, but I think Mrs. Sampson's forgetfulness has gone beyond the norm."

"What do you mean?" Mitch asked.

"Well, she's not just forgetting simple things. Part of her short-term memory is going as well. At times she seems to think she still works at the library. And she often forgets she's met someone a day later."

"I can attest to that," I said. "I've met her several times, yet she never remembers. And she always forgets to take her apron off, sometimes even mismatches her shoes."

"I'm afraid it's the early stages of Alzheimer's," Doc Wilcox admitted. "Bernard isn't going to be able to take care of her on his own for much longer. It's a shame. Last I heard they were planning to retire in Florida. That's not likely to happen now. His daughters live a couple of hours from here nowhere near Florida. Without their help, I don't see how Bernard can swing it."

"Thanks, Dr. Wilcox." Mitch stood up and shook his hand. "I'm glad she's safe. The last thing Divinity needs is for someone else to die."

"I couldn't agree more," Dr. Wilcox responded.

"Thank you, Doctor," I said and followed Mitch out to the car. "So where to, Detective?"

"The library. I'm in the mood to do some reading." He looked at me as he started the car. "You in?"

"Um, okay, sure." I fastened my seat belt. "What kind of reading?"

"Personnel files."

"But I thought we pretty much ruled Carolyn Hanes out," I said.

"Carolyn's not the one I'm interested in. I never checked out Maude. Something seems off about her retirement, and then there's the fact that we found her by the librarian's window." He rubbed his jaw while turning down the road for the library. "I want to know why."

"Hasn't she been through enough?" I felt really bad for Mrs. Sanders. She was so confused, and she seemed to be getting worse every day. With her daughters gone and her husband working a lot of overtime, she was virtually alone.

"Tink, I'm not saying she's guilty." Mitch's voice was low and gentle. "I'm just saying she might need more help than we realize."

"Fine, I'm in." I was on a mission now. I pointed my finger in the detective's face. "But only to prove there's no way that sweet little old lady could be a murderer."

"Fair enough."

A few minutes later, Mitch pulled into the parking lot of the library and cut the engine. I followed the detective inside, and we headed straight to the circulation desk where the new manager, Carolyn Hanes, was talking to one of her employees.

"Good afternoon, Miss Hanes," Detective Stone said. "You mind if we have a word with you?"

She looked warily at me, but she nodded, excused herself to her employee, and then to us said, "Follow me." She led the way in the back to her office and closed the door behind us.

I scanned the room but didn't see any signs left over

from Lucinda or Holly having been there. Carolyn had definitely put her stamp on the room. "I noticed the teddy bear I left is gone," I said. "What happened?"

Carolyn shrugged. "Ms. Smith said it was a fire hazard. I guess it fell off the shelf and landed on her desk next to a candle and then burst into flames."

"No kidding? Imagine that," I said.

"I know. It could have burned down the whole library. That's why I issued a new policy." She locked eyes with me, and I wondered if she'd somehow found out the bear held a nanny cam. "No gifts that aren't of monetary value are to be accepted."

*I'll bet you did*, I thought, but said, "Hmmm. That's a shame."

"Isn't it, though?" Carolyn turned to the detective. "How can I help you?"

"I need to see the personnel records from when Amanda Robbins was manager here," the detective answered.

"But you already looked through them."

"Not all of them," he explained.

She looked confused and a little troubled, but she complied. What choice did she have if she didn't want to look guilty and uncooperative? "Certainly. You can use my office if you'd like."

"Thank you. That would be wonderful," I said all sugary sweet.

A few minutes later Detective Stone and I sat at Carolyn Hanes's desk with a large box between us. He took half of the files, while I took the other half. We decided to pore over every one once more in case he had missed something the first time around.

Finally he came to Maude Sampson's file. "This can't be right."

"What?"

"It says here that Maude didn't retire." He looked up and met my eyes. "She was fired."

"You're kidding." I leaned forward and scanned her file. "Why would her husband lie about it?" I wondered aloud.

"Like he said, he's always protected her. He probably didn't want the scandal or embarrassment to taint her name." Mitch read on. "You're not going to believe this one. Carolyn Hanes was the one who got her fired. Her report on Maude says she was incompetent, forgetting things, and messing up the catalog system."

"You know," I said as something occurred to me. "Maude worked there much longer than Carolyn. If Maude hadn't gotten fired, she would have been in line for the management position. They might not have been able to discriminate against her because of her age, but the fact that she was incompetent was a whole different matter. I think Carolyn was desperate for a higher-paying job because of her shopping addiction. While she might not have murdered her best friend, I doubt she was above getting Maude fired."

My cell phone buzzed. "Hang on, Detective, I've got to take this." I answered the call.

"Hey, Dad, what's up?" I listened in shock. "Are you sure?" He filled me in on all the details. "Wow, okay, I'll tell him." I hung up and stared at Mitch with my mouth hanging open.

"What the hell is it?" Mitch sat forward.

"Dad finally got the doctor to talk." As much as it pained me to say this, I knew I had no choice. "Maude Sampson was on digoxin for an irregular heartbeat." I blew out a breath. "I guess that means she could have committed murder, especially if she was angry at Amanda for firing her. She loved working at the library. It was her life, especially after her girls left."

"Don't jump to conclusions, Tink. What else did your father say?"

I thought for a minute and then brightened a little. "He did say the pharmacy revealed Amanda Robbins used to pick up Maude's prescription for her because Bernard worked overtime at the mill. Amanda would bring it to the library and give it to Maude at work before she was fired."

"Carolyn would have had access to it," Mitch pointed out. "She still could have been playing both sides and given it to Pendleton to use on Amanda when the bookstore deal didn't go through. And then jumped ship with the FBI when things started to look bad for Alex and Gladys. And hell, for that matter, I think Gladys Montgomery would do just about anything to have one of her treasures declared a national landmark."

"Do any of them have an alibi?" I asked.

"They all claimed to be each other's alibi, hashing out the details of the deal and what the repercussions would be if it went through," he answered. "But no one saw them."

"You know what that means, don't you?" I asked.

"Yeah." He grinned. "We're back in the game. I'll see if we can get Pendleton to talk."

"And I'll talk to Maude's husband, Bernard. Maybe

he can clarify if one of his wife's bottles was ever missing. He might also be able to explain more about his wife's condition. Help give her an alibi."

"Sounds like a plan, Tink. Maybe you'll make it through this investigation after all."

"Gee thanks, ye of little faith." I smirked.

"Hey, everyone's a suspect in my eyes until a case is closed." Mitch's smile dimmed, and the detective in him took over full force. "Including you."

# 18

I pulled my bug up to the large mill on the outskirts of Divinity and parked next to old man Sampson's pickup truck. It was nearly lunchtime, so I figured it was as good a time as any to have a word with him. I chose not to talk to him at home because I didn't want to risk Maude being around to overhear our conversation.

A loud whistle blew, and a minute later the doors opened and workers filed out for their lunch break. Some would remain on-site to eat, while others needed a break from the daily grind. I'd taken my chances that Bernard was one of the latter.

Turned out I was right.

Bernard was one of the last to exit, his shoulders slightly drooping, and his gait a bit heavy. He approached his truck and then stopped short when he saw me. I hopped out of my car and walked over to him.

"Hi, Mr. Sampson. Remember me? Sunny." I held out my hand.

He shook it warily. "I remember you. What do you want?"

"Wow, you get right to the point, don't you?" I giggled, but his mouth flattened to a thin line. I stifled my awkwardness. "I'm sorry, I don't mean to intrude on your lunch hour, but I was wondering if I could have a word with you?"

"About what?"

"I was worried about Maude and wanted to see how she's doing."

"She's fine." He started to walk around me.

"There's more." I stepped in front of him, pulling my coat closer together. The temperature was below freezing today.

"You know where I live, why not come to the house?"

"Because I don't want your wife to overhear us."

He hesitated for so long, I wondered if he'd had a stroke. Finally, he huffed, "Fine, but I eat in my truck."

"In your truck? But it's so cold out."

"I like the cold. Besides, it's the one place that's all mine where I can relax and feel at peace." He climbed into the driver's side without another word.

I could relate. My sanctuary gave me the exact same feeling. I could only hope I'd get to start up my business again soon. Share a piece of me with the world. I slipped inside the passenger's side of Bernard's truck, but somehow felt he didn't quite want to share a piece of himself with me.

"I truly am sorry for invading your space, Mr. Sampson, but I really am worried about your wife."

His old-fashioned metal lunch box sat open on the worn cloth seat between us, his sandwich already half eaten. He slowly lowered the rest of his sandwich to his lap and looked at me. "I don't mean to be so gruff, Ms. Meadows, but it's been a long couple of weeks. What do you want to know?"

"For starters, how is Maude?" I asked, full of sincerity. I truly cared about what happened to her.

He jerked his gray head to the side. "As good as can be expected."

"Does she remember anything from over the last couple of days?"

"She's fine now, but she doesn't remember anything from when she wandered off." He looked pained and frustrated. "She has her good days and her bad, but then again, so do all of us."

"I hear that," I said softly, and then I asked the question that I dreaded but needed to be asked. "Your wife didn't retire from the library. She was fired, wasn't she?"

His eyes whipped up to mine, looking startled and a little afraid, but then he stared off into the distance. "She had just started to forget things at that time, but it wasn't that bad. We both thought it was part of getting old. We'd worked so hard so we could enjoy our golden years, but then it looked like we wouldn't have any golden years at all. Maude kept saying something was wrong, but I kept insisting she was fine. That maybe if she read more or did crossword puzzles or something, she would get better."

"But she didn't get better, did she?"

"Nope. Things got worse, but I was in denial. When she got fired for being incompetent, I couldn't bear for anyone to think less of her, so I said she retired. Ms. Robbins felt horrible about having to let her go, so she agreed to tell everyone publicly that Maude retired."

"But officially she had to put why she was fired in the records, didn't she?"

He nodded, looking sad.

"Don't take this the wrong way, because I really do want to help your wife, but where was she the night of Amanda Robbins's murder?"

"Truth is, this is not the first time Maude has wandered off and not remembered where she was. I've covered for her in the past, but this time she was gone too long. I was afraid something really bad had happened to her, so I had to call the police." He looked at me with pleading eyes. "I swear my Maude would never hurt a fly. You have to believe that."

"You didn't answer my question, Mr. Sampson," I reminded him softly. "Where was your wife on the night of the murder?"

He sounded worn-out and exhausted. "I don't know."

"You don't know? What do you mean?"

"I came home from work at supper time, but she was gone. I drove around looking for her for hours, and then I went home. She showed up at ten P.M. with no memory of where she'd been."

I touched his arm, and he flinched. "Thank you," I said. "I know that was hard, but I promise you, I believe you about Maude not being capable of hurting anyone. I have to question her, but I will do everything I can to clear her name. We *will* find the real killer, I promise you."

He looked down at his lap and nodded. The whistle on the plant blew, signaling the end of the lunch break. "Well, I gotta get back to work."

"Thank you, Mr. Sampson. I'll be in touch." I climbed out of his truck and looked back, but he just sat there, staring at the steering wheel, looking dejected. I vowed right then and there to find a way to help him get his wife back.

Later that afternoon, I went to the police station. I passed Captain Walker in the hall.

"Ms. Meadows. How's the case coming along?"

"We're getting there," I answered.

"Good. Glad to hear it. Mitch is in his office, down the hall and on the right."

"Thanks."

"Anytime." He saluted, rounding the corner toward his own office.

I walked through Mitch's door and closed it behind me. The room was nothing like his apartment. His home had class and good taste and atmosphere. This room was all business, devoid of any homey touches. No pictures, no knickknacks, no anything. Just a desk and a couple chairs. It was like he didn't want anyone to know he was actually human, had feelings.

"You don't knock?" he asked, not looking up. He sat at a simple desk, organizing his notes in front of him.

"Sorry." I rolled my eyes. "Knock knock."

"Who's there?" he asked.

"Oh, come on."

His mouth twisted into a cockeyed half smile, and he finally looked up. "Have a seat, Tink. You get to talk to Sampson?"

I sat in a chair across from him and dropped my bag on the floor, feeling as exhausted as Bernard had looked. This case was taking its toll on me. "I caught him on his lunch hour at the mill."

"And?"

I fiddled with the tassels on my bag. "And you were right. Maude definitely needs more help than we thought. She wandered off the evening of the murder and didn't come back home until ten that night." My eyes met his. "And she can't remember where she was during that time."

"That doesn't mean she's guilty, okay?"

I nodded, feeling hopeless. Things were not looking good for poor Maude. "How about you? Any luck with Pendleton?"

"Lucinda said they interrogated him, but he's not breaking. He swears none of them killed Amanda Robbins. He admits he did go see her the night she was murdered. He tried to get her to change her vote, but she wouldn't budge. They argued, and then he left. He met with Carolyn and Gladys right next door but says they didn't hear anything."

"That's still just his word." I brightened. "Any one of them could have killed her, or they could have planned it together, and Amanda could have had some of Maude's medicine left over in her house. Anything is possible."

"That's right, but we still don't have any solid proof. The trio had motive and possible access to digoxin, but we can't place them at the scene of the crime for sure. Mrs. Sampson had motive and access to digoxin, but we can't place her at the scene of the crime, either. You might not have motive, but you don't have an alibi, either, and you were the last person to see Ms. Robbins alive. All we have for sure are your tea leaves laced with digoxin. Your father is a cardiologist, Tink."

My eyes met his and held for a full minute. "After all we've been through together; you can't seriously believe I'm capable of murder."

He studied me for a moment. "My gut tells me you're innocent, but I don't trust anyone fully. Make no mistake, I *will* do my job, no matter what that entails."

My heart squeezed tight. That stung. He cursed softly. He wasn't as impartial as he wanted me to believe, no matter what he said.

"You want to clear your name or not?" he finally asked.

"Gee, no, I'd rather rot in a cell."

"That can be arranged."

I clenched my jaw. "What now, Detective? I wouldn't dream of standing in the way of you doing your job . . . whatever that entails."

"Good. Glad we're on the same page," he said rather loudly as he stared me down, and a muscle in his jaw throbbed. He took a deep breath and continued in a calmer, quieter voice. "I think it's time we talked to Maude herself."

No matter how frustrated he made me or how much it hurt to think he still had doubts about my innocence, I knew he was right. We were running out of time. "Do you think questioning Maude is wise? I don't want to upset her or make her condition worse."

He scrubbed his hands over his face, looking as though this case were taking a toll on him like the rest of us. "She still has many cognizant moments, Tink, and at this point we're desperate. I think she's the one who left those footsteps outside Ms. Robbins's window the night of the murder. Maude Sampson is either our murderer or an eyewitness. Either way, if she can remember what she saw, she might be the proof we need."

"Okay then, let's do it."

We covered all of our bases when it came to questioning Maude Sampson. We went to her house, a big old colonial with a country-style decor, instead of the police station to make her more comfortable. We sat in her living room and let her serve us coffee and tea. She actually looked pleased to have the company.

Her husband was present for moral support and had insisted on calling a lawyer to protect her rights. Dr. Wilcox was in the room to assess her state of mind and be there should she need any medical assistance. Hell, even my lawyer was there to protect my rights (my parents were sitting in the back of the room).

"Go ahead, Detective Stone," Dr. Wilcox said. "Mrs.

Sampson is fully aware and here of her own accord. She's not here under duress, and she wants to cooperate."

Mitch nodded once and then turned to Maude, who sat on the couch beside her husband. "So, how are you, Mrs. Sampson? You feeling okay?"

"I'm feeling great, dear. How's your coffee? Can I top you off?"

"I'm good. The coffee's great, thank you." He smiled kindly. "Do you remember Amanda Robbins?"

Maude's face fell. "I remember Amanda well. I worked with her for years at the library. It's such a tragedy what happened to her. After my girls moved away, Amanda was like a daughter to me. She was so good about bringing me my medicine, and I always looked out for her as well. I miss her terribly." She wiped away a tear and sipped her tea.

"You okay?" Bernard asked, looking strained. "We can take a break if you'd like. You don't have to do this, you know."

"No, no. I'm fine." She patted his hand. "I want to do this, Bernie. I won't feel right until we know what happened to Amanda."

He squeezed her hand briefly and then nodded for the detective to continue.

"Mrs. Sampson, do you remember why you don't work at the library anymore?" Mitch asked.

She glanced at Bernard with a questioning look.

"It's okay," he said. "They know."

She looked back at Mitch. "I left because I was fired."

"And how did that make you feel?"

"Sad. I loved working at the library. Bernard and I

had such plans for when we retired, but I needed to work there a bit longer for us to afford it." She sniffed. "Poor Amanda didn't have any choice after Carolyn turned me in. But it wasn't Carolyn's fault, either." She shook her head. "I was forgetting simple things like what a stapler was used for, and I kept making mistakes in the catalog system. Everything was a mess, and none of us wanted that."

"What did you do after you stopped working at the library?"

"Oh, I kept busy around the house, and I visited the library often. After all, I still had to look out for Amanda, though I guess I didn't do a very good job."

"On the day of Amanda's murder, what did you do?"

"Well, I remember having breakfast with my church group, and then I did some volunteer work down at the food pantry. I had a doctor's appointment in the afternoon, and then I stopped into the library. I remember Carolyn was there, and when I asked where Amanda was, Carolyn said she couldn't make it in because she had to go to the doctor's. I figured I would swing by her house later to check on her. I went home and made dinner for Bernard and some chicken soup for Amanda."

"And did you go see her?" Mitch asked.

Maude's face puckered up and she looked off into the distance for a few minutes and then looked back at Mitch. "I'm not sure. I remember leaving the house, but I don't remember anything after that until I got back home at ten P.M."

"Are you sure? Think really hard."

"I wish I could help, but I can't. I'll take a lie detector test if that would help."

"You'd pass with flying colors, Mrs. Sampson. We don't question that you're telling the truth. It's not much help if you can't remember."

"I'm sorry. I wish there was some way we could know for sure."

"There is," I spoke up.

Mitch looked at me in question, then his eyes narrowed as his grump-o-meter went off and Detective Grumpy Pants took over. "Oh, hell no."

"Just because you're a nonbeliever doesn't mean I'm not the real deal," I muttered.

"What is it?" Mrs. Sampson asked. "I'm open to anything. I just want to help."

I knelt down before her and looked her in the eye as I said, "I could read your tea leaves."

Mutters of mixed emotions broke out throughout the room, my parents being among the loudest.

"No," Bernard said rather firmly from beside Maude. "I won't have it."

"Why not?" I asked curiously. "I might be able to help clear your wife's name, Mr. Sampson. Isn't that what we all want?"

"Help? I doubt that will happen. Look at what happened the last time you read someone's tea leaves," he sputtered.

My eyes shot to Mitch's for a brief moment as I thought of the vision I'd had and the kiss that had followed. I knew Bernard was talking about the time I'd read Amanda Robbins's tea leaves, but Mitch's reading hadn't helped, either. My readings always came true, but they sometimes caused more trouble than they were worth. For the first time, I considered giving up my passion. Maybe I was doing more harm than good.

"Yes, I'll do it," Mrs. Sampson said, surprising us all.

"But—" Mr. Sampson started to speak.

"You don't get to decide everything, Bernard," Maude announced with conviction. "I believe the decision is mine, right, Detective?"

The detective looked from her to me and back to her. "If you think it will help, we'll do this thing," he said to Mrs. Sampson and then locked eyes on me. "But I want to be there."

"Good. We'll meet tomorrow at noon in my sanctuary, and I'll introduce you to my world," I stated.

He rolled his eyes. I vowed right then and there that no matter the outcome of this case, I wouldn't rest until I made that man a true believer.

Tomorrow was only the beginning.

# 19

❖⟡✦⟡❖

I opened my front door to find Detective Stone and
Maude Sampson on time at noon the next day. I made
eye contact with Detective Stone and raised my brows
questioningly. He glanced at Maude and then gave me
the thumbs-up sign, meaning today was a "good" day
for her.

"Where's Bernard?" I asked, glancing beyond them.

"He's at work. I told him not to take the day off
because I didn't want him with me." Maude nodded once,
sharply. "No negative juju at my reading."

"Hear that, Detective?" I arched a brow at him. "No
negative juju. Think you can handle that?"

He held up his hands. "I won't say a word. I'm here
to observe."

"Good." I stepped back and let them in. "Follow me."

I led the way into my sanctuary. Everything was set.

I'd already fed my fish, watered my plants, and started a fire in the corner fireplace. I sprayed lavender around the room and flicked on some new age music, then gestured for Mitch to have a seat out of the way. After he sat, I pointed to the chair across from mine at the old-fashioned tea table in the center of the room.

I dimmed the lights until the constellations on the ceiling glowed their mesmerizing hue and the blue paint on the walls turned a bit deeper, calmer. Setting the mood and getting the seeker to relax was imperative for the seer if they wanted to produce a good session.

I gathered my tea leaves and kettle from my supply shelves in the corner and carried them over to the table, setting them down in the center. Taking the seat across from Maude, I held her hands in mine gently. "Ready to begin?"

She nodded, looking more curious than afraid.

"Good. I normally get an indication from the person whose fortune I'm about to read as to what psychic tool will work best in helping me see the prediction clearly. In your case, you're a tea leaf person just like Amanda Robbins was."

"Why, that sounds lovely." Maude leaned forward as if telling me a big secret. "I think tea is wonderful, you know." Her eyes sparkled.

I smiled and leaned forward as well. "Me too." I winked.

She giggled, and Mitch arched a brow. But staying true to his promise, he didn't utter a word.

"Okay, the first step in the process is for you to brew

the tea yourself. I've already boiled the water, so all you have to do is place the loose tea leaves in the cup."

She did as I told her, with precision, I might add. "There, all done. I really do hope this works."

"It will," I said with conviction, and I could have sworn I heard a soft grunt from the far side of the room. I tipped my head to the side and narrowed my eyes at him, but he just whistled softly and looked around the room—everywhere except at me.

Grrr.

"Now you pour the water into the cup in front of you and stir the tea leaves as it brews," I said to Maude.

"Okay, I'm good at stirring. I love to cook." Maude's bright smile faded a bit. "I don't get to cook as much these days now that the girls are gone, but Bernard still needs to eat. He doesn't have much of an appetite lately. I worry sometimes that there's something wrong with him, too. It's no fun getting old."

"Now I'd like you to drink the unstrained tea," I said, steering her mind back to the task at hand and away from her depressing thoughts. Then again, I wasn't sure what we were about to discover wouldn't be just as depressing. "Think about exactly what it is you wish to know. In this case, where you were on the night of Amanda Robbins's murder."

"Okay, dear. I can handle that." She sipped daintily. "Oh my, this is simply divine."

"Thank you. I grow my own, you know." I smiled, and she kept sipping. "When you only have about a tea-spoon of liquid left, stop."

"All set." She held up her cup. "This is exciting. What next?"

"Well, now you hold the cup in your left hand, and then you swish three times in a counterclockwise motion." She did as I said. "Now tip the cup upside down on the saucer, and let the leftover liquid drain." Again she did as I said. "Okay, now you hand me the cup, and I read your future, well, past in this case."

She stared down at her cup, looking nervous. "I'm not sure I want to know what you see, but I know it's the right thing to do." She slowly handed me the cup and nodded. "Okay, I'm ready."

I carefully took the cup from her hands and pointed the handle in her direction. "It will be okay," I said reassuringly to her.

I looked down at the cup and turned the cup in the opposite direction from what I normally would. Clockwise. Leaves to the right of the handle represent the future, which we didn't need to know just yet. I was more concerned with first looking at the leaves to the left of the handle, which represented her past.

Images in the white space were positive and good, while images that appeared in the tea leaves were negative and bad. I breathed deep and stayed focused, so I could concentrate on the shapes that appeared before me. There was the love, happiness, and contentment she and Bernard had shared throughout their marriage when their girls were little. Maude smiled fondly as I retold the story she already knew. Then her smile faded, as I knew it would, when I got to her recent past, which was filled with nothing but tea leaf images, the negative and bad.

"I see a cloud that would explain the health problems you're going through," I said gently. "Headaches, mental problems, the mind, thoughts, a serious trouble. There's also a mountain indicating the many obstacles you must overcome. Followed by a wavy line showing the uncertain path you must follow." I hesitated.

"What is it?" she asked.

"A mask. You stumbled upon something hidden. Wait, there's a lamp at your side."

"What does that mean?" she asked.

My eyes met hers and then moved beyond her to lock on Mitch's as I said, "Secrets revealed."

"Am I responsible for Amanda Robbins's murder?" she asked in barely more than a whisper.

"I'm getting a strange reading of both yes and no."

Mitch rolled his eyes, shaking his head. I ignored him.

"That doesn't make any sense," she said.

"I'm thinking it means you're somehow indirectly involved."

My vision blurred into tunnel vision and I stared into the past, looking through Maude's eyes on the night of Amanda Robbins's murder. I was outside, wandering aimlessly until I reached the librarian's house. I could feel Maude's concern for Amanda because she'd gone to the doctor that morning.

I lifted my hand to knock, but I heard shouting from inside. Someone was arguing. I walked around to Amanda's bedroom window and looked inside. I could see her trying to get a man to calm down, but he wouldn't listen. I couldn't see the man clearly, but he was angry at her because she wouldn't be reasonable. She was the one who wouldn't listen.

Suddenly, he shoved her hard. She tripped and fell back, hit the side of her head, and collapsed on the floor, blood seeping out all over her carpet. I could feel the man's alarm, as though he hadn't meant for that to happen. He left the room and came back with digoxin and a towel. He added some of the heart medicine to Amanda's teacup and then poured the liquid down her throat, breaking her cup on the carpet when he was finished. He wiped down everything with the towel, erasing his fingerprints, and then left through the front door as though he'd never been there at all.

I snapped out of my trancelike state and retold exactly what I had just seen. "The digoxin was just a cover-up. I couldn't see the man's face, either. It was blurry. But I'm pretty sure it had to be Pendleton. Amanda wouldn't change her mind on the bookstore deal, so he got angry and shoved her out of frustration. He hadn't planned on her dying. So he found and used the digoxin she must have picked up for Maude." I looked at Mitch. "Don't you see? This proves I'm innocent and Ms. Robbins was killed by a man like I first claimed."

"That doesn't prove anything," Mitch said. "You could have made the whole thing up just to clear your name."

"Are you kidding me?" I stared at him, seeing the doubt all over his face. "This also proves Maude's innocent. You already have your man locked up. At least give him a lie detector test, then you'll see I'm not lying."

"That might work," Mitch said, and sent a text to Lucinda, I assumed. "At the very least it will put an end to your little storytelling. You can't go around messing with people's emotions, Tink."

I could tell he meant the reading I'd given for him, and the havoc it had wreaked on both our lives.

"Just because you won't admit—"

"It's all my fault," Maude said quietly.

We both stopped arguing and looked at her with concern. Her voice sounded so dejected.

"If I had been stronger, maybe I could have saved her." She shook her head sadly. "If only I had remembered, I could have gone to the police immediately." She looked up at me. "What's going to happen to me now?"

"Well, I'm not sure." I reached out and squeezed her hand.

"Can you see my future as well?"

"I really don't think—" Detective Stone started to say.

"No offense, young man, but I didn't ask you," Maude said.

I pressed my lips together to keep from grinning. Mitch held his hands up and then sat back quietly. I picked up her teacup and this time turned it in a counterclockwise direction.

"I see a knife, which indicates a hidden enemy, but I think it's safe to say we just found out who that was. At least we know he's locked up, so you're safe. I also see . . ." I stared at the image before me and bit my bottom lip.

"What is it?" Maude asked. "Please don't keep anything from me. I need to know."

Mitch's cell phone rang, and he stepped out of the room.

"I see a nail, which means pain and anguish. Next to that is an hourglass, which means time is running out and you should proceed with caution." My gaze met hers. "You are in imminent peril. And, last, I see a ladder, which signifies turmoil and evolution. A rise or fall in life. It's a sign of travel. You're going somewhere soon. Where, I don't know. That's all."

Mitch stepped back in, looking a little pale and disturbed.

"What's the matter?" I asked.

He glanced at Maude and then back to me as he said, "Alex Pendleton has just escaped from jail."

Mitch took a disturbed and upset Maude home and stayed with her until Bernard finished his shift at the mill. Then Mitch came back to my place to discuss our next move. I was pulling my suitcase out of the storage area in the basement when Mitch walked back in.

"Going somewhere?" he asked.

"I thought I should stay in a hotel or something until you catch Pendleton again. If he finds out I gave Maude a reading and that we're on to him, he might come after me."

"Relax, Tink, you're not going anywhere. Just because he escaped from jail doesn't mean he killed Amanda Robbins. I'm still not buying what you think you saw in the teacup. We need hard evidence, not fairy tales."

"You are so infuriating," I snapped, and stomped my

foot. "Just because you don't believe, it doesn't mean it isn't true. I'm telling you I am in danger. I can sense it."

"You are," he pointed out. "You're in danger of me locking you up if you try to leave town. You're still officially a suspect until this case is closed."

The shutters on my house shook, and Mitch looked around warily.

"Careful," I said. "You're upsetting Morty."

Mitch's phone rang, and he frowned at me as he answered it. A minute later, he snapped it closed and walked over to the coat closet and grabbed my coat. "That was Captain Walker. Bernard called and said Maude ran off again. She was upset and kept saying something about it was all her fault, and she was a danger to everyone. Then Captain Walker said he got a call from Maude herself, saying something about the reading triggering her memory. She remembers that night and wants to identify the killer, but then her phone went dead. They are all out looking for her now."

"Oh no."

"Oh yeah. See what you've done to the poor woman with your nonsense?"

"It's not nonsense. It helped her remember, and now she's trying to do the right thing. We have to help her before Pendleton gets to her." I grabbed my coat from him and the pocket wacked against a table, making a loud clunk. I sucked in a sharp breath.

"What the hell was that?" Mitch asked, his face riddled with suspicion.

"Nothing."

"What are you hiding, Tink?" He reached for my coat.

"I said nothing." I jerked away from him.

He sighed, took a step forward, and easily took my coat from my hands. His eyes never left mine as he reached inside the pocket and pulled out the contents. His face grew hard, and he looked at his hand to confirm what he obviously suspected. Then he stared me down, looking angry and disappointed at the same time.

"You know, you almost had me convinced," he said quietly, gazing at the bottle of digoxin. "But my past experiences should have clued me in. Women can't be trusted, especially frauds from the city like you."

"That's not fair. That's not even mine. Someone has been trying to set me up. You have to believe me."

"Life's not fair, and I'm not buying anything you say anymore." He grabbed my arm and hauled me outside and then stuffed both me and my coat into his car. "I'm taking you in."

"But what about Maude?"

"You let the department worry about her. Our partnership is officially terminated."

"What are you going to do to me?"

"Make sure you don't leave town, which is probably what you were about to do. In fact, I wouldn't be surprised if you and Pendleton have been working together from the start. I think you're the one who needs a lie detector test. I'm taking you both down."

I sat quietly, looking out the window, unable to process what had just happened. I couldn't believe Mitch actually thought I was guilty. After all we'd been through, that hurt. My instincts were right. Falling for him was such a bad idea.

"Now you get quiet?" he grumbled through his teeth, the muscle in his jaw knotting with frustration.

"I plead the Fifth until I talk to my lawyer." I had to wonder if he'd cared about me at all. He was angry because he thought I'd duped him, but that didn't mean he was hurt or brokenhearted.

"It must be bad if you're willing to call your mother."

Oh, it was bad all right, but I had no intention of calling my mother. I did, however, have every intention of defending myself. Just as soon as I found a way to escape. We rode in silence for the next couple of blocks, and then he turned down a side road that was a shortcut to the station.

"Look, over there." I pointed out his window. "I think I see Maude!"

"Where?" Mitch turned his head to look out his window, and I grabbed the wheel, yanking it to the right.

"What the hell?" Mitch said, fighting for control as the car spun wildly in a wide 360-degree turn.

I screamed, unbuckling my seat belt and opening my door all in one motion while the car was still spinning.

"Wait, you're going to kill yourself," he shouted, but it was too late.

He lunged for me, but I tumbled out the door, hitting the ground hard and rolling into a ditch. Seconds later I heard a loud crash and looked up to see his car wrapped around a tree.

"Oh my God," I whispered, climbing to my feet and hobbling in his direction, battered and bruised.

I'd only wanted to escape. I hadn't counted on the roads being that slippery or, God forbid, him getting hurt.

I reached his car. The radiator hissed steam into the frigid air. I managed to crank his door open and pressed my lips together as I looked at him. His head rested against the steering wheel with a bump and trickle of blood oozing from it. I slowly reached my hand out and touched his neck, wilting with relief when I felt a pulse. His chest rose and fell with steady breaths. He would not be happy with me.

I'd knocked him out cold.

I called 911 from his cell phone and then left it turned on inside his car. He had a blanket in the backseat, so I covered him up. Once I was sure he would be okay, I kissed his cheek and whispered, "I'm sorry," then shut his door and took off running.

My house wasn't that far away, but it felt like forever in the ice and snow. Opening my front door, I flew inside and grabbed my suitcase. Running upstairs, I tossed it on my bed and started throwing essentials inside. I didn't know who I was more afraid of at the moment: Pendleton or the Grumpster. Either way, sticking around now was not an option.

I was officially a fugitive.

I had no clue where I was going to go, but I figured anyplace was better than here. I only prayed they found Maude in time and that she could identify the killer. I needed time to figure out how to prove my innocence. I had no connection to the killer at all, but Mitch was determined to find one somewhere.

When the police hadn't ruled Amanda Robbins's death a suicide, Pendleton must have tried to set me up since I was also a suspect. He knew I was getting too close, and now he'd escaped from jail. If he caught Maude, I was a goner for sure.

I turned toward my bed and blinked. Morty had appeared out of nowhere as usual. He sat on top of my suitcase like he didn't want me to go. I picked him up and deposited him on the bed.

"I'll be back. I promise." I petted him behind the ears and then picked up my suitcase and headed for the stairs.

Morty jumped in front of me and hissed.

"What is with you?" I nudged him out of the way, and he scratched me with his paw. "Ow!" I rubbed my hand. He'd drawn blood. "Naughty boy. Why'd you do that?"

He licked his lip and kept staring at me, the hair on his back raised. He really didn't want me to go out the door, but I didn't have time to figure out why.

"I'm sorry, Morty. I'm not abandoning you. I have to go away for a little while, but I will be back. You have my word on that." I hoisted my suitcase and kept moving. When I got to the top of the stairs, Morty was already at the bottom, staring up at me and meowing.

It was a strange and eerie meow.

I stopped in my tracks and pursed my lips at him. "Morty, this isn't funny," I said, but then I heard it.

A noise coming from downstairs.

# 20

Oh my God, what if someone was breaking into my house?

Was it Pendleton coming to kill me? Or maybe Mitch seeking revenge? Or the police coming to lock me up and throw away the key? None of the options were favorable, but I didn't have a clue what to do.

I listened a minute, but didn't hear anything more. I didn't want to call the police on a false alarm, yet I wasn't foolish enough to open the door. Maybe if I peeked out through the peephole, I would see something. I looked outside and almost fell over with relief. As I unlocked the door and yanked it open, a gust of wind filled with snow swirled around my legs. "Goodness, Maude, you scared the wits out of me."

She gave me a look almost as creepy as Morty's meow had been, and for a brief moment I wondered if maybe she were the killer. But that was crazy. The vision had clearly shown the killer was a man, although it had also revealed that Maude was indirectly involved in some way. I wasn't so sure I wanted to invite her in.

"Are you okay?" I asked when she stood there, her eyes wide and glazed, giving me a funny look.

"No," she said, shaking her head, looking as though she were in shock. "Everything is a mess."

"But I thought everything was clear, and you were going to identify the killer."

"I was."

"The police are looking for you. I was on my way out. I can drop you off at the station, or near it, anyway." No way was I getting too close to a jail of any kind.

"I can't go anywhere." Her eyes met mine sadly. "And neither can you, I'm afraid."

"Why not?" An uneasy feeling settled over me, and I took a step back.

"Because I won't let you," said a menacing male voice from just outside the door.

I looked around for a weapon, but it was too late. The door swung open wide, and I saw a man holding a gun pointed at Maude, only it wasn't Alex Pendleton. . . .

It was her husband, Bernard.

I gasped. "Mr. Sampson? What on earth are you doing?"

He pushed Maude all the way in and shut the door behind him. "What I should have done from the beginning. Get rid of the evidence."

It finally sank in. "You're the killer?"

He scowled. "I'm not a killer. What happened with Ms. Robbins was an accident."

"Okay, then help me understand." I looked around for Morty, but I didn't see him. Some watch cat he turned out to be. If I could keep Bernard talking, it would buy me some time to figure out what to do.

"I don't have to tell you anything," he spat. "It's because of you we're in this mess right now."

"Me?" I took another step back. "What in the world did I do?"

"You and those stupid tea leaves. If you'd left well enough alone, Pendleton probably would have taken the wrap. But no, you had to go and help Maude remember with all your psychic mumbo jumbo. All this time I been taking care of her, and now she has to up and get sane on me. It's not fair. None of it is fair."

"Not fair?" Maude snapped. "You're not the one losing his memory. Your life will go on. Soon I won't remember mine at all. How is that fair, Bernard? Huh? You tell me." She started to cry. "I might as well be dead."

"See, that's just the thing," Bernard ground out. "Save your tears, woman. I worked my whole life taking care of you and the girls. We saved and we planned, and now it was supposed to be our time. We were going to retire and move to Florida where I could fish every day if I wanted. But no, you had to go and lose your mind. When you got fired, it set us back financially. I had to postpone our retirement and take care of you. I'm exhausted, Maude. I can't do it anymore."

"But I didn't get sick on purpose, Bernie. And why kill Amanda? You knew how much she meant to me," Maude said on a sob.

"I went to her and pleaded with her to give you your job back. She refused to listen. Said she was sorry, but her hands were tied. I got so angry. I could feel all my rage and frustration build in me until I couldn't stand it anymore. So I pushed her. I swear that's all I did, but she was so dang small. She fell back and hit her head, and just like that she was dead."

"You should have called the police right then and there," I interjected in a calm voice. "You'd be in far less trouble. You still will be in less trouble if you call now."

"I panicked. Haven't you ever panicked?" He looked at my suitcase. "Seems to me you were doing just that when I got here, so get off your high-and-mighty horse."

He had me there.

"Besides, even if Amanda's death was an accident, I'd still do time. I'm too old to do time." He looked back at Maude with pleading eyes. "You've got to understand my situation. What it will be like for me once you don't remember."

"You should have killed me instead of her, then." The look on her face was pure anguish. "I'm obviously dead to you already."

"I told you I didn't mean for it to happen, but it did and that's that. So be it. I had picked up your prescription for digoxin before stopping by her place. After the accident, I poured some in her cup and thought people would assume she'd committed suicide on account of everyone knew something was wrong with her. I forgot all about the stupid note, though. I meant to leave one. When they declared her death a murder and suspected Miss Meadows, I tried to help that theory along by framing her." He looked at me. "No hard feelings, ma'am."

"No hard feelings?" I sputtered. "It's just my life you were messing with!" The man was insane.

He raised his hands in the air. "I was desperate. When that didn't work, I came clean about Maude's memory loss and figured they might think it was her." He glanced at her and winced. "I'm sorry, Maude, but like you said, soon you won't remember anything, so what was the harm? A nuthouse or a nursing home, you wouldn't know the difference, anyway. I've already done my grieving for you after I first found out about your condition. Don't you want me to have the retirement I deserve?"

"You can't be serious. You deserve to rot in hell," Maude said. She looked at me, heartbroken and beaten down, like she didn't have the strength to go on. "I can't believe I ever had children with that monster."

"Shut up," he yelled. "I gave you everything. We haven't been in love for years. We've gone through the motions so your precious town wouldn't be scandalized. I stayed by your side for the sake of our girls. I took care of you all. Now this is the thanks you show me?" He waved his gun about. "You're the one who deserves to rot in hell. And I'm in just the right frame of mind to send you there." He cocked his gun and aimed it in our direction.

Oh my God, we really were going to die!

Maude and I huddled together, and suddenly the front door burst open. Mitch came barreling through with his gun drawn and pointed straight at Bernard.

Bernard moved faster than I'd ever seen a human being move, let alone a man of his age. He spun in Mitch's direction, ducked as Mitch fired off a shot, and then pulled the trigger on his own gun, shooting Mitch in the arm. Mitch dropped his gun and grabbed his arm on a howl of pain.

"I spent four years in the Marines right out of high school before I got hired at the mill. Not to mention I've been trophy hunting since I was fourteen, son. I'm an expert marksman. Now get on over there with my wife and that quack."

I scoffed, my jaw falling open. What was with everyone?

Mitch stumbled over to me, blood pouring out his arm, taking my mind off nonbelievers. I ripped off the hem of my skirt and wrapped it around his arm. Then I ripped off another piece and wrapped it around his still-bleeding head.

"I thought you'd be in the hospital by now," I said quietly. "I called 911, you know. And I'm sorry, by the way."

"I woke up right after you left, called off 911, and then followed you." He gave me a sarcastic look. "Believe me, I planned on making you sorry."

"Yet somehow I managed to make you even sorrier," I said on a wince. "Story of our relationship."

He grunted and then turned to Bernard. "You'll never get away with this, Sampson."

"Says you. Everyone thinks I'm out looking for my poor wife. Pendleton breaking out was a happy coincidence. I've got enough retirement money for one, and I've already set up a secret account. I hear Mexico is as nice as Florida."

"Then why didn't you simply leave town earlier today?" Mitch asked, scratching his head. "You could have been long gone by now."

"I had intended to . . . until Maude remembered the night of the murder." Bernard glared at his wife. "I saw it plain as day when she looked at me with horror in her eyes, and then she ran off. I knew I had to follow her and put an end to her misery and mine. If she lived, she would rat me out. If she died, I'd just look like the grieving widow who ran away to drown his sorrows in Mexico. Suited me just fine."

"Bernie, you don't want to do this," Maude pleaded with him. "Think of our girls."

"I *am* thinking of them. If I don't take care of you, they'll have to. They have no idea what it's like to have you look at them blankly with no recollection whatsoever." He stood up straight and nodded once as though he'd made up his mind. "I won't put them through that."

"Mr. Sampson, you can't be serious. An accidental killing is one thing. But premeditated murder is a whole different matter," I said. "Can you honestly kill us all, kill your own wife in cold blood?"

His bottom lip quivered, and his cheek pulsed, but he refused to waver. "My mind's made up. Move to the living room, all of you." He gestured with his gun.

We all moved into the living room and lined up on the couch where he was pointing. He faced us like a one-man firing squad. He stood rigid with his back to the bookshelves against my wall.

"I'm sorry, folks, really I am. I wish things could have

been different, but they're not. So be it." He took a breath and lifted his gun.

Vicky began to shake, her walls rattling violently, my knickknacks clanking against one another. Pictures tipped sideways, and the floor beneath our feet rumbled while the pipes creaked and groaned.

"Oh my goodness, what's happening?" Maude asked. "I think we're having an earthquake."

"Or the house really is haunted," Mitch muttered.

"More like a Morty temper tantrum," I clarified.

"You're kidding, right?" Mitch raised his brows at me.

"Um, no. I told you that you'd thank me for my backup one day," I said and watched Detective Stone's eyes bug.

"What are you all blabbering on about?" Bernard asked, looking around uneasily.

"Behind you," I yelled, pointing up.

"I'm not falling for any tricks," Bernard said. "Just for that, you're going first." He pointed his gun straight at me. He cocked the hammer and started to squeeze the trigger.

I let out a terrified wail and covered my mouth with both hands, my gaze locking onto Mitch's. He didn't hesitate. He jumped in front of me, wrapping his good arm around me with his back to Bernard.

An eerie meow echoed through the room, and Bernard yelled, "What in blue blazes is that?"

Mitch loosened his hold a little but still didn't let go of me as he turned us so we could both see.

Bernard had spun around, eyes wide with fright and disbelief as he stared up at a glowing Morty. Literally, his fur was an iridescent white, his eyes blacker than coal. Bernard lifted his gun in the cat's direction. Morty sat on the very top of the bookshelf, ready to pounce. At the last second, he leapt in the air with a loud howl and landed on Bernard's head. Bernard bellowed, dropped the gun, and latched onto the cat, who had his claws sunk deep into his skull.

Mitch grabbed my hand and instructed me to hold Maude's hand, and then he pulled both of us out of the way just as Morty launched himself off Bernard and followed close on our heels. A bleeding Bernard faced us once more with rage in his eyes. He bent over to pick up his gun, and the bookshelf teetered precariously as though some supernatural force were helping it along.

Looking up in shock, Bernard never had the chance to utter a single word. The bookshelf came crashing down on top of him, and my hardcover volumes buried every inch of his body.

Mitch picked up his gun and scrambled over to the shelf. He found Bernard's arm and felt for a pulse, then looked at us with relief. "He's alive but barely."

Maude picked up a book, then stared toward the heavens with an angelic smile on her lips. "So be it," she said quietly, and I was sure we were all thinking the same thing. Amanda Robbins, ever the librarian, was with us in spirit, and Bernard had gotten exactly what he deserved.

Maude sat down in the corner to wait for the police and started to read, looking strangely at peace. Morty appeared by my side, purred, and then licked the spot he'd scratched earlier. I petted him on the head in forgiveness.

"Guess you make a pretty good watch cat, after all," I said.

He gave me a bored look that said, *Was there ever any question?*

I giggled, then wandered over to check on Mitch's head and arm. "You okay?" I asked.

"No, I'm not okay." He stared at me for a moment, full of raw emotion blazing from his normally unreadable eyes. Then he pulled me into an awkward embrace with his good arm, his injured one still hanging uselessly at his side. His face looked pinched as his gaze roamed over my features tenderly; then he cursed softly and his head swooped down to mine.

His lips were firm as they pressed against mine, then softened as they began to move. My lips parted, and he slipped inside, possessing my very soul. Warm tingles traveled down my spine all the way to my toes, and heat flooded my every cell. My arms wound around his neck, and I stepped on his toes, pulling him even closer. I plunged my hands into his hair and kissed him back with all my heart.

When we were both out of breath, we broke apart and rested our foreheads against each other. Morty walked in circles around our entwined legs, purring and rubbing up against us both.

Mitch looked down and scoffed. "Oh, so now you like me?"

Morty looked up at him, flicked his tail, and then walked off regally, with his nose in the air as if to say, *That will so never happen.* Mitch chuckled.

"So does that mean you finally believe me?" I asked quietly.

The corner of one side of his mouth tipped up slightly.

"I believe you're innocent, if that's what you mean. I always did, Tink. I just had to keep you on your toes."

"That's good to hear, but that's not what I mean." I studied him, waiting.

"I believe your cat is . . . different . . . if that's what you mean."

I set my jaw and took a step back, crossing my arms. "I agree, Morty is unique, but that's not what I mean, either."

Mitch sighed, running a hand through his thick dark strands and then scrubbing his palm over his five o'clock shadow. "I believe that *you* believe you're psychic. Isn't that enough?"

I searched his eyes and knew in my gut that it wasn't. As much as he moved me, I wanted someone who believed in me fully. I wanted someone who accepted me for who I was, who embraced me and all that I represented. I said sadly, "No, it's not enough. I'm sorry, but I want it all."

"That's what I was afraid you were going to say," he said grimly. "Sunny, I—"

My breath hitched. "Say it again."

He looked at me funny. "What?"

"My name." I smiled softly, touching his cheek. "That's the first time you've called me by my name."

He coughed, removing my hand from his cheek and holding it in his own. "I don't know what to say."

"You don't have to say anything." I slipped my hand from his and patted his arm. "I already know."

He puckered his brow. "But how?"

"My vision, remember."

"Ah, right. Your vision." He made a set of air quotes, and we could hear the sirens right outside my door now.

"Friends." I held out my hand.

He stared at me for a moment, shook my hand, and then shoved his hands in his pockets. "Sure. As long as we're not partners, we can be anything you want."

"I *will* make you a true believer one day."

He tweaked my nose. "Not if I prove all your fortune-telling stuff is nonsense first."

I narrowed my eyes. "Game on."

He matched my expression. "I always did like a good challenge."

"Good," Captain Walker said as he followed the ambulance crew into my living room. "Then you're going to love what I've got planned for you both."

"And what might that be?" Mitch asked, all joking aside and traces of humor erased from his expression.

"The challenge of working together on a permanent basis." Captain Walker grinned wide.

"Excuse me?" I asked, striving to comprehend what was happening. "I thought our working arrangement was only temporary as a way to solve this case and clear my name?"

"No way in hell am I working with an *amateur* on a permanent basis," Mitch snapped. "Captain, you saw what a disaster this last case was."

"What are you talking about?" I gaped at Mitch. I couldn't believe after the conversation we'd just had, he was throwing me under the bus the first chance he got. "This so-called amateur solved this case."

"Are you kidding me?" Mitch poked me in the chest with his good hand. "You nearly got yourself killed."

"I nearly got us killed?" I poked him right back. "If you hadn't come barreling in like Rambo, you wouldn't have gotten yourself shot."

"And we're back," Captain Walker said on a grin. "There's the dynamic duo I know and love. You two have great chemistry. You're so competitive, that's what keeps you sharp and makes you work harder to outdo each other. In the process, cases get solved, and isn't that the point?"

"But she—" Mitch started to say.

Captain Walker held up his hand. "Keeps you on your toes. Presents a challenge."

"And he—" I started to add.

Captain Walker held up his other hand. "Pisses you off. Gives you something to prove."

Mitch and I both started shouting at once.

"Silence, you two!" Captain Walker swiped his hand through the air. "Once again, you don't have a choice. Mayor Cromwell is a true believer and thinks Sunny is the breath of fresh air this town needs to crack down on crime. And Chief Spencer is behind him one hundred percent. So from here on out, Miss Meadows will be your unofficial partner, Detective Stone. A consultant of sorts to help solve future crimes in Divinity. You should feel lucky."

"Lucky? This is a disaster in the making, and you know it. You can't force her to do this, you know." The detective faced me. "Be reasonable, Sunny. You know you're not up for this. Tell them no. They can't make you work with me."

"Oh, don't you call me Sunny, you Grump Butt."

"Enough with the grump overkill, already." He put his hands on his hips and stared me down.

"If the adjective fits . . ." I crossed my arms over my chest and stared right back.

"Since you're so bubbly all the time, what's that make you—Bubble Butt?"

"I'll take that as a compliment. They don't call me Sunny for nothing."

"Yeah, well, I never did like my eggs sunny side up. They're way too runny, kind of like your runaway mouth every time we investigate. Face it, Tink. You don't have a clue what it takes to be a real detective."

I narrowed my eyes, seething and more determined than ever. "Just for that comment alone, I'm going to prove you wrong." I looked Captain Walker dead in the eye and simply said, "I'm in."

"Fine, it's your funeral," Detective Stone grumbled.

"Careful, Detective." I smirked. "It just might be yours."

He threw his hand up, cursing under his breath, and marched away mumbling, "That's what I'm afraid of."

"Better get some help, stat," I yelled after him. "You're gonna need it."

# Epilogue

❖⊱❁⊰❖

"Bye, Mayor Cromwell," I said from my front door as the man walked to his car. "I'd say good luck in the upcoming election, but we both know you won't need it." I winked.

"Thanks, Miss Meadows," he said from the end of my driveway. "Same time next week?" he asked. "I have a few more questions I need answered."

"I'll check my calendar and give you a call. I'm sure we can squeeze you in somewhere. Business is booming these days."

"I'm sure it is. Then again, I never had any doubt you would be a huge success."

"And that, good sir, is why you make such a great politician. You're very charming."

He saluted me, then climbed in his car and drove away.

My parents pulled into my driveway, doing a double

take as the mayor drove away. "I see you're coming along quite well," my father said as he walked up the driveway, escorting my mother. "Wasn't that Mayor Cromwell?"

"One and the same." I beamed proudly. "And yes, business has picked up tremendously now that the case has been solved. Would you like to come in?"

"No, no." My mother glanced around, looking for Morty. "We're fine right out here on the front porch."

"But it's still winter," I pointed out.

"Ah, yes, but the sun is shining," my father boomed. "It's a fine day for farewells."

I blinked. "Are you serious? You're leaving?"

"Well, don't look so thrilled, darling." My mother sniffed sharply.

"Mom, I didn't mean it like that. I just mean we all know we get along much better from a distance. Think how great Easter will be after going all those months without seeing each other." I stretched my mouth wide until my teeth ached. One could dream. "Besides, I really want to make it on my own this time. For real."

"I suppose she is getting rather old not to be doing something with her life, Vivian," Dad said, patting her on the back.

"Gee, thanks, Dad." *I think*. But hey, whatever it took to make them leave, I was up for. It wasn't that I didn't love them. I knew they cared about me in their own unique way, but I needed my space. I think we all did.

"I suppose you're right, Donald." Mom dusted off her suit. "Before we leave, I thought you might like to know that Pendleton fellow was caught trying to cross the Canadian border."

"Oh, well that's a relief," I said. "And just so you know, Mrs. Sampson is moving in with her oldest daughter and her family, who, unlike Bernard, seem only too happy to have her with them."

"Yes, well, must be nice to have daughters like that." Mom inspected her fingernails. "Anyway, I admit, it appears as though you really can take care of yourself. So I guess we'd better be on our way."

"Does that mean you believe in my gift?" I asked quietly. No matter how old I became, it still seemed so important to receive my parents' approval.

My father stared hard at me for a long time. Then he finally nodded once. "Well, I don't know how much I truly believe, but logically, a lot happened that can't be explained. It would seem there might be something to this nonsense after all."

"Close enough." I hugged him hard. It wasn't a full admission, but it was a start. And at this point, I'd take what I could get. He patted my back awkwardly, then walked off to start the car. Mom gave me an air kiss and joined him without a word. I waved and watched them leave, feeling renewed somehow.

I looked down, and Morty was there. Just there. Out of nowhere, by my side, steady and true. I laughed out loud. He tipped his head and looked as though he were raising a brow. I scooped him up and gave him a good rub as I walked back into Vicky. My cat, my house, my business.

Life was good.

The people of Divinity loved and accepted me, my parents were starting to believe in me, and Mayor

Cromwell was my biggest fan. I'd finally come home. Just one more task to fulfill, and my life would be perfect. I thought of one dark and brooding and infuriating detective who still made me lose sleep at night, and thought . . .

*Game on, indeed!*

Kari Lee Townsend lives in Central New York with her very understanding husband, her three busy boys, and her oh-so-dramatic daughter, who keep her grounded and make everything she does worthwhile . . . not to mention provide her with loads of material for her books. Kari is a longtime lover of reading and writing, with a masters in English education, who spends her days trying to figure out whodunit. Funny how no one at home will confess any more than the characters in her mysteries!

Kari writes fun and exciting stories for any age set in small towns, with mystical elements and quirky characters. You can find out more about her on her website, www.karilee townsend.com, and also on the group mystery blog she cohosts, called Mysteries and Margaritas, at www.mysteries andmargaritasblogspot.com.

SAVOR THE LATEST FROM
*NEW YORK TIMES* BESTSELLING AUTHOR

# LAURA CHILDS

# SCONES & BONES

• *A Tea Shop Mystery* •

Indigo Tea Shop owner Theodosia Browning is lured into attending the Heritage Society's Pirates and Plunder party. But when a history intern is found murdered—and an antique diamond skull gets plundered in the process—Theodosia knows she'll have to whet her investigative skills to find the killer among a raft of suspects.

penguin.com